Death at the Asylum

A Rhe Brewster Mystery

(Rhe Brewster Mysteries Book 4)

by

N. A. Granger

Cover by Roy Santo

Praise for the Rhe Brewster Mystery Series

Death in a Mudflat

I recommend this story to readers of cozy novels who prefer their mysteries with a more realistic and harder edge, crossing into police-procedural terrain, and to all those who…want to immerse themselves in a charming small town with a dark (or darkish) underside. (Beware if you're on a diet, though. There's plenty of food!) – Olga Núñez Miret author of the *Escaping Psychiatry* Series and the *Angelic Business* Series

Death by Pumpkin

Death by Pumpkin was my second read in Granger's Rhe Brewster series and a pure joy ride.

The book is fast-paced and well-researched. The scene in the small plane was particularly riveting and highlighted Granger's attention to detail. Other than the villain, the characters are all beautifully three-dimensional and full of quirky personality. A perfect read for anyone who enjoys cozy mysteries with plenty of thrills. – D Wallace Peach, Author of the *Rose Shield* Series and *The Necromancer's Daughter*

Yet another cracker from the pen of Noelle Granger! Rhe Brewster is fast becoming one of my most favourite protagonists and the cases she solves get better each time. I won't give away any spoilers, but the steady paced action and plot twists are just what we have come to expect from this series. – Lucy Brazier, Author of *The Porter Girl* Series and *Who Shot Tony Blair?*

N.A. Granger
Death in a Dacron Sail

This crime mystery is well woven by fully realized characters and a
plot line that has almost as many twists and turns as the stitching on a
Dacron sail. – Boothbay Register

Death in a Red Canvas Chair

Death in a Red Canvas Chair is an enjoyable murder mystery…it was
a pleasure to read due to the well-written, vivid and flowing language.
…There are plenty of exciting moments to keep you on the edge of
your seat, in a plot which is carefully woven with plenty of twists and
turns. – Luccia Gray, Author of *The Eyre Hall* Series and *Ghost Wife*

Dedication

To my grandchildren, Eli and Alexandra, who bring me great joy and who I hope one day will read my books.

Table of Contents

Chapter 1 1

Chapter 2 7

Chapter 3 15

Chapter 4 23

Chapter 5 31

Chapter 6 41

Chapter 7 51

Chapter 8 59

Chapter 9 67

Chapter 10 75

Chapter 11 85

Chapter 12 95

Chapter 13 99

Chapter 14 109

Chapter 15 121

Chapter 16 133

Chapter 17 145

Chapter 18 153

Chapter 19 163

Chapter 20 173

Chapter 21 179

Chapter 22 191

Chapter 23 201

Chapter 24 207

Chapter 25 217

Chapter 26 231

Chapter 27 243

Chapter 28 253

Acknowledgments...263

Foreward

An author likes to think everyone would have read all the books in her series. Given that a reader might choose to begin with this book and the fact I myself tend to forget details, here is a list of the main characters.

Pequod

Aren't small towns' characters in and of themselves? Pequod is a growing town located on the coast of Maine, northeast of Portland. It is governed by a mayor and town council, and Pequod University, a private liberal arts institution, is found there. The town is experiencing all the problems of rapid growth.

Rhe (pronounced Ree) *Brewster*

Rhe is in her thirties and an emergency room nurse at Sturtevant Hospital. She is now married to Sam Brewster, the Pequod Chief of Police, following the death of her husband, Will Brewster, Sam's brother. She has a nine-year-old son named Jack, Will's son, adopted by Sam. She is also now an investigator with the Pequod Police Department.

Jack

Rhe's son, a lively child with ADHD who looks like his father. Jack is very inquisitive and has a wicked sense of humor.

N.A. Granger

Sam Brewster

Sam is a gentle bear of a policeman, who needs to wear glasses but hates to admit it. Sam wears a Stetson and a bolo tie and drives a Jeep Wrangler because he's always wanted to be a cowboy. He's loved Rhe since before she married his brother but never admitted it until after his brother died.

Paulette McGillivray

Petite and blond Paulette is Rhe's best friend. They've known each other since college and share everything. Paulette lives close by and hardly a day goes by when they're not sharing food and gossip at their kitchen tables. Paulette is married to Ted and they have two children, Tyler, who is Jack's age, and Sarah, 13, a clone of her mother.

Marsh Adams

Marsh is an Assistant Medical Examiner for the state of Maine. He works as a pathologist and coroner at Sturtevant Hospital and is an enormous help to Rhe with her cases. With his brush cut and penchant for weightlifting, he has a military bearing. His assistant is Midori Ishikawa and he is married to Bella Dunzich, who is a member of the Maine Major Crime unit.

Ruthie Hersh

Ruth is the tiny, rotund, and red-haired receptionist at the Pequod Police station and has ruled the front desk with a take-no-prisoners attitude for many years. She monitors the chief's calendar and his visitors, and her sharp opinions and knowledge of the personal lives of everyone in the department are well known. Her husband Merlin is an old biker gang member.

Phil Pearce

One of the longest-serving deputies in the department, he is now the deputy assistant chief. His computer skills are exceptional and his involvement is frequently needed in solving cases. He is warm and endearing, despite the fact he is exceptionally homely.

James Manning

Dr. Manning is the CEO of Sturdevant hospital and a forthright enemy of Rhe. One of his main objectives for the last several years is to get her removed from the hospital.

Lyle Pendergraff

An elderly and long-serving guard at the rear entrance of Sturdevant Hospital, Lyle knows everyone in the hospital by name and keeps an eye on Rhe.

I hope you enjoy these enduring characters as well as the many new ones I created for this book.

N. A. Granger
Chapel Hill, NC.
January 2023

Prologue

The sniper took a deep breath of the cool, leaf-scented autumn air and settled into his carefully hidden position. From his perch, he sighted his McMillan TAC-50 sniper rifle on the man standing at a lectern in front of a colorful crowd, 1800 yards across the Kennebec River. Governor Hatcher had been invited to officially open the shops, offices and condominiums that had originally been the Kennebec Arsenal, then the Maine State Hospital for the Insane. The governor made a great target, clearly visible on the porch of the central building.

A deep hatred burned in the sniper's core caused by both the governor and the woman he'd selected to head Health and Human Services. They had killed his little Rachel, just as sure as if they had pulled a trigger and shot her. *But that would have been more humane*, he thought with a grimace. An image of Rachel during the final days of her torment forced its way into his thoughts. Wasted to skin and bones, mostly blind, her pain relieved only by increasing amounts of morphine that took her spirit away. Those two had denied her the cancer-fighting drugs that might have given her more time, might have saved her, by their read of the fine lines of their state health insurance. His heart's joy had been condemned to death in agonizing inches by chicken-shit bureaucrats. *An eye for an eye.*

The sniper had been in the attic of the empty house across the river for nearly a day, lying on a table pushed up to a window, with his gun resting on the window sill. The view was perfect. Habit kept him there, virtually unmoving, diapered to take care of his needs, and stoked on coffee until earlier this morning.

Now he needed steady hands. Gravity, wind speed and direction, altitude, barometric pressure and humidity could all affect the bullet trajectory, and he'd taken each one of those factors into account.

Just one shot. He'd done it before with deadly accuracy in Iraq—twenty-three times. Just one more. He could do this. Maybe then the gnawing pain of his loss would lessen.

He slowed his breathing, slowed his heart rate, stilled every muscle except for those in his trigger finger, and focused on the grinning head now in the crosshairs of the telescopic lens. He heard his former spotter's voice whispering quietly, 'Now."

He gently, slowly, squeezed the trigger, felt the solid push back against his shoulder. And waited. It takes time for a bullet to get to its target from that far away.

Chapter 1

RHE

An early fall day in Maine can be perfect, I thought—trees turning color, with red and orange tops and fading green bottoms, the sound of the Kennebec River chuckling behind us, and a portent of colder temperatures in the brisk breeze. My husband, Sam, sitting beside me in the third row of this dedication ceremony for the refurbished old Maine State Hospital, fidgeted. I knew, just knew, he was thinking of hunting. I poked his ribs with my elbow.

"Sit still, Sam! I swear you're as antsy as Jack."

Jack is my son from my first marriage to Sam's brother, who died several years ago. Jack is nine and now legally Sam's son. Would we have another boy? I put one hand on my small baby bump, largely hidden by my bright red wool coat. I knew my cheeks were flushed, probably because the sun baked me in the warm coat.

Sam leaned over and asked quietly, "Are you cold? I can give you my coat."

Cold? "Honestly, Sam, I'm fine. You worry too much." *This time, I'd go the distance, I knew it.* I scrunched up my face and gave him my know-it-all smile.

I had miscarried his brother Will's second child just before he died, after slogging through a swamp in the middle of winter and nearly being killed chasing a child kidnapper. I couldn't help myself whenever I trailed a criminal, but I knew Sam feared my fearlessness. I wondered how *he* would handle this pregnancy.

Various officials mounted the concrete steps to the porch of the former asylum, taking their seats in metal folding chairs arrayed in a line and facing the audience. A lectern with its microphone had been placed in the center of the row of seats. The governor, secretary of state, and attorney general sat, along with the contractor who had converted the old building complex into condos, shops, a café, and a restaurant. The mayor of Augusta stood at the lectern and began with the usual drone.

Neither Sam nor I were quite sure why we'd been invited to this shindig, but I suspected our recent success at capturing some drug lords in the state—with the assistance of the SBI and the rest of the police department, of course—might have caught the eye of some state official. Sam loathed such ceremonies, since he was convinced they were just pompous and self-congratulatory, but I had really wanted to attend. The setting was magnificent, and Sam and I had picnicked on the sloping grounds several times, enjoying the sun and the sounds of the river, in the days before the site closed to the public during the reconstruction. Curiosity about what had been built led me to accept the invitation for both of us.

Sam's attention went everywhere but on the speakers who followed the mayor. At one point, my own eyes started to droop, and I opened them long enough to nudge Sam, whose head had dropped to his chest. When I glanced up, I saw Governor Hatcher, who had apparently chosen to speak last. He stood at the lectern, ruffling the papers of his speech, then jerked to his right side as he reached for a page the wind had lifted. His left arm exploded in a red flower of blood and bone, and he stood there looking at it, just as the report of a rifle reached us. Hatcher fell backward.

Sam stood up and shouted, "Get down, everyone! Shooter!" and pushed his way out of the row where we sat, with me right behind him. We had a clear path down the center aisle to the building, until the audience registered what they'd just seen. People began running in all directions and Sam had to clear the way for me.

When we reached the porch, the secretary of state still sat in her chair, looking at the gore that had splattered her. We leapt up the stairs, Sam yelling at the stunned officials to get down, which they finally did, flattening themselves on the concrete. I fell to my knees beside the governor, who lay unmoving in an enlarging pool of blood draining from his arm. Sam crouched behind the lectern with me and the governor.

"Belt, Sam, now!"

Sam whipped off his belt, thankfully unencumbered by the paraphernalia normally attached. I wrapped it around the end of the governor's arm, pulling it as tight as possible. The blood stopped flowing almost immediately, but from his color and non-responsiveness, he was clearly going into hypovolemic shock. If we didn't get him to an EMS truck soon, where they could start an IV, he would die.

"Sam, call the EMTs."

"I did." The secretary of state now lay flat down but held her phone in one hand. "They're just around the corner."

Just then I heard a buzz overhead, and the glass in the window behind and above us shattered.

"Tell them they need to wait," said Sam. "The shooter's still active."

I spotted two men in blue EMS uniforms at the edge of the building. Another shot rang out, and cement sprayed from the wall next to them. The EMTs ducked back, out of sight.

The scene around us was pure pandemonium, with guests pushing each other and falling down in an effort to get away. A few got down on the ground right where they were seated and pulled their seats over them. Screams, grunts, and shouting filled the afternoon air, along with quiet whimpers of fear from the people on the porch.

"We've got to get him out of here, Sam. Any ideas?"

"Well, if I'm right, those are fifty caliber bullets. There's not much that can stop them."

"How about shields? The state cops must have them."

"The shields won't be any good."

I heard sirens in the distance and thought the personnel coming would be picked off, too. "I'm going to move him."

"No, Rhe, I will." Just then another bullet banged into the wall over our heads. "Think about it—the shooter is clearly a trained sniper. If the governor hadn't moved when that guy took his shot, he'd be dead. Look at where the shots are landing. Whoever it is could pick us off easily, especially you in that red coat. We're not his target, but he wants to make sure the governor doesn't get any help."

He got on his hands and knees, placing himself between the governor and the river, then grabbed the neck of the governor's coat. Another slug embedded itself in the wall behind and over Sam's head, showering us with stone chips. I moved around on my knees to provide a barrier to the lower half of the governor's body. When a bullet hit yet another window, I flinched. Sam slowly dragged the governor toward the end of the porch, with me crawling behind him.

Fifteen feet from the edge of the porch. Ten. Five. There were no more shots.

An armored SWAT team member, surrounded by other team members, easily lifted the governor off the porch and placed him on a waiting gurney. Sam ignominiously rolled off the edge onto the ground. "Let me help you, ma'am," I heard one of the SWAT team members say to me.

Sam stood and we held each other, panting and waiting for the adrenalin to stop pumping. *His bravery and smart thinking saved us.* We ignored the EMTs until they became too annoying.

"We need to check you out, sir. And your wife."

"Relax, buddy. She's an ER nurse. She'd know if there's anything wrong."

I leaned away from him and smiled. "You were amazing today, husband, but nevertheless, I want them to give you a going over. Don't argue with me."

I let them take me away, and Sam followed.

By then, the EMT bus had left, spinning its wheels in the gravel driveway on its way out. We could still here the siren blaring as we submitted to a brief examination—heart and respiratory rate, and a cursory examination of our limbs and torsos. Freed to leave, we were pounced on by two men who showed their badges. State Major Crimes Unit.

Two hours later, after repeated questions and answers, we could finally go home. I was so proud of my husband that I let him persuade me to go to MacDonald's for a Big Mac meal. I'd deal with the calories later.

؃ ؃

At breakfast the next morning, we found our town newspaper, the *Post and Sentinel,* had blaring headlines about the event and the governor's rescue.

"What's the news about the governor?" Jack asked, as he helped himself to another piece of toast, on which he then slathered a heavy layer of peanut butter and jelly.

"According to this, EMS rushed him to the Maine General Medical Center and he went into surgery immediately," Sam replied. "His prognosis was iffy at first, but it seems he's a tough old bird. He's now predicted to make a long but slow recovery—without his left arm, of course."

"Better than without his life," I said.

"Tell me again how you and Mom rescued the governor. What kind of gun did the sniper use?"

"I told you at least twice last night, kiddo, and it's time for you to get ready for school. I'll take you this morning," Sam replied.

"In your car? Aw, Dad, I hate going to school in that thing. I'll be the butt of jokes all day. Can't Mom take me?"

From the look on Sam's face, he hadn't known this. *Being Chief of Police doesn't carry any water with nine-year-olds.*

I stood and started to clear the table. "I can take you. I'm due at the hospital at eight. Don't forget your lunch, Jack." After dropping the plates in the sink, I said, "We're off, hon. Can you put away the rest of this stuff?" I stopped and kissed the top of Sam's semi-bald head, before taking my jacket from a peg next to the garage door and grabbing my bag from the floor below. "Jack, I'm leaving."

A blur of denim and a blue sweater paused at the refrigerator, then followed me out the back door.

Chapter 2

SAM

I got up and shut the fridge door, since Jack had, as usual, failed to close it. Sighing, I started to scrape the remains of our breakfast from the plates into the compost container, wondering what the rest of the day would bring. I imagined there would be reporters hanging around and didn't relish facing them.

೮ ೮

When I entered the police station, a group of deputies and the departmental receptionist, Ruthie Hersh, greeted me with hoots and handclapping.

"Aw shucks, tweren't nothin'," I said to them, doffing my Stetson and bowing.

At that point, the anticipated reporters, who had somehow made it inside the station and were clicking away on their cameras, rushed over and stuck their microphones in my face, yelling out questions. "Why were you there yesterday?" "What led you to help the governor?" "What exactly did your wife do?" They surged forward, pushing me back on my heels. Ruthie, who had remained perched on her stool behind the tall reception desk and looked like a possum that had eaten a sweet potato, yelled, "Chief, there are a herd of reporters here to interview you." *Duh.*

"Back off!" I yelled at the reporters. Surprisingly, they did, at least a few steps. "As our receptionist probably already told you, I don't do interviews unless it concerns matters pertaining to the community of Pequod." I winked at Ruthie in the resulting short silence, followed by groans and more yelled questions.

"What did I tell you?" Ruthie told the reporters. "Positively no interviews. You might as well leave now."

After a few unmentionable swear words and questions yelled at no one in particular, they started to leave. The remaining herd parted as I headed down the corridor to my office. I looked back when I reached my office door. Two of the more daring reporters tried and failed to make an end run around Ruthie, who'd positioned herself at the entrance to the corridor, all five foot two and umpteen pounds of her. She was in her element.

Greeting me on my office desk were even more piles of paper than there'd been on Friday. "Ruthie!" I called out the door. "Get Phil to deal with some of this kindling, will you?"

""You've got an intercom, Chief Brewster. Use it."

I sat down at my desk, picked up the phone and pressed the button for the front desk.

"Yes, Chief?"

Honestly, that woman. "Can you please have Deputy Chief Pearce come and get some of this paperwork? It's about time he earned his promotion."

"Will do."

It crossed my mind that Ruthie would retire in a year, having given thirty-eight years of service to the department. I dreaded the day. Her replacement, who came in two days a week, was a complete nincompoop, and I doubted even Ruthie could whip her into shape. With that sobering thought, I heard the phone ring.

"Chief, the Secretary of State is on line one."

I hesitated, took a deep breath, and picked up the phone, for once punching the right button. "Mr. Burton, how is the governor doing this morning?" I'd only met this official at the ceremony on Sunday but knew he had risen steadily through the ranks of state government, and, as the highest-ranking Democrat and also a minority, he'd become the face of his party.

"He's a long way from recovery, but he's out of the woods, I'm pleased to say. And I wouldn't be saying that if you and your wife hadn't risked your lives to get him to the EMTs. I…we…are very grateful."

"I'm glad everything worked out. Is there something I can do for you?"

"There is. I'm going to be acting in Governor Hatcher's place until he's able to return to work. We need to investigate this shooting, and I'm creating a task force to do that. I'm aware that both you and your wife have worked very successfully on previous cases with agents from both the State Major Crimes Unit and the FBI. Would you be willing to join the task force?"

I must have taken more than a moment to think about it, because I heard, "Chief Brewster, are you still there?"

"Yes, I'm here, Mr. Burton. Just a little surprised at your request… but yes, Rhe and I are happy to help in any way we can."

"Good. There'll be a meeting here in Augusta tomorrow of the task force members. I'll have my secretary email you the details. Thank you for doing this." He hung up.

What have I gotten us into?

Ϧ   Ϩ

Sometimes my willingness to volunteer irritates Rhe. While we sat in a conference room in the capitol building the next afternoon, waiting for the others on the task force to arrive, she tapped her foot in irritation. I knew she thought our lives were already too busy. I deliberately took my time choosing a pastry from the platter on the side table, picking an irresistible one topped with chocolate frosting, something else sure to irritate Rhe. She watched my waistline like a hawk and strictly limited the sweets we had at home.

Next to the pastries were two coffee urns labelled 'regular' and 'decaf', plus packets of cream and sugar. I brought her a cardboard cup of coffee with two creamer containers and two sugars. "It's decaf. I'm sorry you can't have the full caf," I said as solicitously as possible, setting the cup down in front of her.

"Decaf coffee is like bilge water. Five more months. An eternity without the real stuff." She doused her coffee in creamer and sugar and made a face. "Yuck."

I returned to my seat with my own coffee and the frosted pastry. Rhe regarded the pastry as she might a rat turd. I took a bite and immediately said, "This isn't anywhere near as good as the ones from the Pie and Pickle," hoping maybe that would mollify her.

Before she could reply, the door to the room opened, and two men I knew entered—Agent Michael Bowers and his direct superior, Special Agent Bongiovanni of the FBI. Bowers had been assigned to work with us on several of my department's cases. The guy couldn't seem to stay out of harm's way, collecting serious injuries every time. He said it was Rhe's fault, and I almost believed him. Bowers had matured from the nervous, gawky, self-important agent we'd first met. He now projected an air of quiet confidence, but I noticed the way his eyes went immediately to my wife. I suspected he had feelings for her.

Bongiovanni still reminded me of a stork, with exceptionally long legs and a suit that draped from his shoulders like a robe from a coat hanger. He hadn't gained any weight or lost any inches from his considerable height since our last meeting, and after greeting us, sat across from us at the table, folding his legs carefully under it.

After a "Good to see you, Chief," Bowers went to the side table and brought back coffee for himself and his boss. When he sat down, I sensed from the subtle vibration of the table that one of his nervous tics, jiggling his legs, still persisted.

The door opened again, and two more people filed in—Secretary of State Burton, a compact man of medium height with golden brown skin and a bespoke suit that looked like it had been sewn on him, and a woman I recognized as the governor's choice for the head of Health and Human Services. *Interesting pick for the task force.* I wondered what she would add.

Mildred Burger, a tiny woman in her late fifties, had a face crisscrossed with wrinkles that her heavy makeup only exacerbated.

I knew she had been an officer in the Army's European Medical Command before retirement, and her appearance was what might be called 'strac' in military jargon—originally meaning skilled, tough, ready around the clock, but now neat, well-organized and well-turned out. She wore her dark blue suit like a uniform and her steel gray, curly hair was cut close to her scalp.

The representative from Maine's Major Crime Unit followed her, someone Rhe and I knew well from previous cases, Belladonna Zundich, now married to Marsh Adams, the assistant Medical Examiner for the state of Maine and a close personal friend of my wife's. Bella had an imposing presence, over six feet tall and built like a rock wall, but a rock wall with designer suits. Today's was bright red. No one would call Bella a shrinking violet.

After everyone had taken a seat and we'd done a round of introductions, Burton, sitting at the head of the table, said, "I think our only aim here is to find the shooter. To that end, I've already asked Agent Zundich if she could determine who might have a grudge against our governor. Agent Zundich, do you any information for us?"

"I do indeed, Mr. Burton. The MCU decided to start with any hate mail the governor may have received over the last few months and also questioned his personal assistant, a Mr. Cornwell. He told us no one had made any threats against the governor in person, but he recalled the governor receiving some hate mail.

"Not email, but actual letters. He believed the sender knew email could be traced. Unfortunately for us, Cornwell didn't save the letters and hadn't shown them to the governor, considering them to be written by cranks. He did recall some wording that made him think the sender was a present or former member of the Armed Forces. Assuming that the sender had a military background with sniper training, we began a search for such persons in the state." Bella paused to consult a printed sheet she had in front of her. "We have over 114,000 veterans in Maine, plus one hundred or so active service members, but we managed to reduce that number by limiting it to veterans under the age of sixty plus those on active duty. That left around fifty-six thousand, so we asked the US Department of Veterans Affairs to cull these down by sorting for those with sniper training. Hopefully, this will result in a manageable number."

"When do you think you'll have that information?" asked Burton.

"I'm not sure. The people I spoke with said they might have to co-ordinate with the Department of Defense to get what we need. I've already talked to Agent Bongiovanni about having the FBI help us with interviewing anyone on the final list, but I suspect we're going to be short on manpower." She looked at Bongiovanni, who nodded in agreement.

"So, Chief Brewster, would you mind interviewing some of the people on that list?"

"No problem," I responded and immediately regretted it because Rhe kicked me under the table. I knew who'd be doing a lot of the interviewing—Rhe. She looked at me sideways and grimaced. I had a chronically short-handed department, Pequod having been 'discovered' as a nice place to spend the summer by folks from New York, New Jersey, and Pennsylvania. The prices of rentals had skyrocketed and, because some of our visitors decided to stay, the real estate market was hot. Unfortunately, along with them and the welcome influx of money, came crime.

Burton broke into my thoughts. "Thank you, Chief. The floor is now open for ideas and comments."

It seemed none of our professional colleagues had anything to add, but Ms. Burger spoke up. Her voice was startling for her petite size—deep and husky. "I should mention that I've also received some threatening letters lately, concerning the medical treatment that members of the writers' families had received, or rather not received, under the aegis of the state medical plan." Her tone, impassive and business-like, made me wonder if she harbored any empathy for the patients on that plan, and I knew Rhe would be thinking that, too. I was certain this information was the reason Ms. Burger had landed on the task force.

"Do you still have the letters?" asked Bella.

"No, I threw them out. And anyone who tries to see me in person without an appointment and who acts belligerently is stopped by the guard at the entrance to our office building. Perhaps you could check with the guard. He may have taken names. "

Bella made a note on the paper in front of her.

"Well, it seems we have a plan moving forward. I'll make sure you receive the names of all the possible shooters and those you will be assigned to check out. Are there any questions?"

Rhe raised her hand. *Of course she would.*

"Is there a time frame for these interviews?"

"As soon as possible would be optimal, but I understand some of you have other jobs." He chuckled. "So as soon as you can." Burton stood, and we all followed him out the door like good little soldiers.

Chapter 3

We hiked back to Sam's Jeep, which he had parked in an open space on the far side of the parking lot so it wouldn't get dinged. That Jeep, with all its gear, was his baby. As we approached it, I noticed a sheet of paper, folded in half, under the driver's side windshield wiper. *Probably an ad.* But looking around, I didn't see anything on the other cars. Sam grabbed it just before unlocking the door and gave it to me when I got in, while he started the car. I froze when I opened it, just staring at what had been pasted on the paper.

"What's the matter?" Sam asked.

The note was comprised of large, cut-out letters from a magazine:

THE GOVERNOR MUST DIE. HE IS GUILTY OF MURDER. DON'T GET IN MY WAY AGAIN OR YOU WILL PAY TOO.

I held it up for him to see, a frisson of fear running down my spine. "The sniper is threatening us, Sam." I moved my fingers to the corner of the note. "You need to put on a pair of gloves before I give this back to you."

Sam had a box of latex gloves in the middle console of the Jeep and put some on before taking the note from me and reading it again. I rummaged for an evidence bag in my purse and then the console.

"What does he mean by 'get in my way again.' How could *we* get in his way now?" I asked. "The governor has his own security detail."

"I don't know, honey, but we're going to have to be careful. The media coverage told him who we are and about the meeting today. It wouldn't take much of a guess to figure this is my vehicle."

Duh. Pequod Police Department was printed on both its doors.

"So what do we do now?" I asked, once he'd secured the note in a bag I'd found under the box of gloves.

"We don't have a choice. Threatening a police officer falls under federal jurisdiction. We have to notify the FBI."

"I'll call Bongiovanni and maybe Bella." I fumbled with my phone, scrolling through my contacts with a shaking hand.

"I'd have thought you'd have both of them on speed dial by now," Sam said, trying to lighten the moment. But I noticed he scanned the parking lot before heading to the exit.

On the way home, I told both Bella and Agent Bongiovanni about the note. Neither of them had received one but agreed we needed to proceed with caution in interviewing the people whose names we would be given.

We made a stop at Hannaford's so I could buy some fresh grouper for dinner. After that pastry, Sam needed something healthy. When he didn't display the proper enthusiasm for fish, I put some Brussels sprouts in our cart. I knew he would eat them, but unwillingly. Jack, on the other hand, usually covered them with sour cream and pronounced them delicious.

As Sam and I unpacked the food, Jack ran in and dumped his backpack on the floor. "Hiya, Mom, Hiya, Dad." He grabbed an apple from the basket on the counter and ran out again, yelling over his shoulder, "Heading over to Tyler's. He has a wicked new game," just before the door slammed. Tyler had been Jack's best friend forever and lived diagonally down the street. His mother, Paulette, was my BFF and our two families had become entwined over the years.

Sam and I sat at the kitchen table having a late afternoon cup of coffee, high test for him and bilge water for me. Sam decided to look at the mail we'd brought in from the mailbox. I could see two letters addressed to me from banks I didn't recognize. I ripped open the first one, expecting the usual credit card offer. For the second time that day, I was stunned. I handed the enclosure to Sam. He scanned it and whistled. "I take it you didn't open a Visa card from City Bank in Portsmouth?"

"No!" I shook my head vigorously.

"The statement here says we owe six thousand dollars on this account, and it's in your name."

"I never opened a credit line with them. What are the charges for? I only looked at the bottom line."

"A Bosch French door refrigerator for $2500 and a Samsung washer and dryer for about $3500. Someone has stolen your personal information. All the information on this is correct."

I opened the second letter, from Pequod Savings and Loan and whistled. "Another credit card bill, one with…" I scoured the top page "…no limit. I owe $77,000. Apparently I bought a new Mercedes GLS." I fell back in my chair. "Well, I don't see any new appliances in the house…and why would I buy a Mercedes? This has to be a joke."

Sam took the second statement, scanning it. "No joke, Rhe. Someone is using your personal information and credit rating to buy things."

"So I'm in real trouble? What do we do?"

"First thing, we've got to talk to those banks, ASAP, to put a stop to this. It's not closing time yet and I see there are 800 numbers on the statements. Why don't you alert them about what's going on and ask them to put stops on the cards. They'll want your personal identification to prove that you're you. The Mercedes dealership should be open late. Can you get more details on the car when you inform them they've been scammed? Then I'll put a BOLO on it. How about I get dinner started?"

As always, Sam kept his cool—one of the reasons why I loved him. 'Okay, you can begin by slicing cucumbers, carrots and bell peppers for a salad. Then get the grouper fillets from the fridge and sear them on both sides. I'll take it from there when I'm done," I called over my shoulder, taking the bills with me as I headed down the hall to Sam's 'office.' The room used to be my late husband's, but Sam had made it into a man cave by redecorating it with a large comfortable couch, a big flat screen TV, a minifridge, and lots of team paraphernalia from the Patriots, the Celtics, and the Mariners, a professional hockey team based in Portland. And a desk for any work he brought home. The room drew Jack like a magnet, and they'd started watching football games together, arguing over popcorn about the players and the referee calls. Before I made the calls, I sat for a few minutes, trying to get my anxiety under control.

By the time I'd finished, Sam had made good progress on the recipes that Paulette, my personal Julia Child, had given me and he now sat at the kitchen table, awaiting further instructions. "Let's get dinner made first," I told him in response to his questioning look. The grouper filets went in the oven after I doused them in some white wine. With a little grumbling, Sam cut the Brussels sprouts for steaming and made sure a container of sour cream sat on the table.

Just then, Jack came in and I noticed clots of mud dropping on the floor from his jeans. "What smells so good?"

"You'll get to eat it if you take your jeans off right there and roll them up so no more mud gets on the kitchen floor."

"Aw, Mom, in front of you and Sam?"

"Well, it isn't as if I haven't seen you naked before." Seeing his frown, I added, "Okay, we'll turn away."

I heard a plop and then footsteps on the stairs to his bedroom. Sighing, I picked up the offending pants and tossed them in the washroom. After thoroughly washing my hands—*who knows what's growing on those jeans?*—I stirred up a lovely lime and butter sauce for the fish, which was just about done, and a soy dressing for the salad.

Jack magically reappeared.

After we were seated and the meal on our plates, I told Sam, "The banks have been notified, I have enough information for you to send out a BOLO, and I told the Mercedes place you'd stop by on the way into work tomorrow. I'm not sure the manager believed what I told him, but your badge and Jeep might impress him."

"A Mercedes?" asked Jack, whose ears were like antennae. "Are we getting one?"

"And the Easter bunny is coming next week. You eat your dinner, and I'll tell you about it," I replied.

Sam and Jack proclaimed dinner a success, but only Jack got dessert.

α   β

The following day, I had a shift in the Sturdevant Hospital ER. Being an ER nurse was my passion. Each patient had a story to tell behind the injury, disease, or pain they presented, and my work never bored me and often challenged me in treating them. Over the past twelve years, the heart attacks, strokes, broken bones, and overdoses, along with the fevers, sniffles and sneezes had immersed me in patient care, and those experiences had built my skills and confidence.

Toward the end of my shift, I heard a loud "Just who is in charge here?" coming from the reception area of the ER. I stood in a cubicle where I'd just finished putting an IV line into the dorsal venous arch of the foot of an emaciated young man with a heroin overdose. All of his other veins had collapsed from frequent injections.

When I emerged from the cubicle, I saw the CEO of our hospital looming over Nancy Ellis, our petite charge nurse. James Manning looked like a vulture ready to pounce. He had a temper to go with his red hair and, in my opinion, was nothing more than an empty, puffed-up white lab coat. He had earned his nickname, the Woodpecker, because of his hair, but most of us privately called him by the last part of that name. I'd had a number of run-ins with this man over the years, and he had done his best to get me fired. Thus far, I'd won every time, which only served to exacerbate our fractious relationship.

I hung back and listened, not eager to be seen by Manning, especially in his current state.

"Nurse…er…Ellis," he said in a penetrating voice, after scanning her name tag, "I need you to explain why morphine, fentanyl, Dilaudid, and ketamine are missing from the drug cabinet on this floor. Someone from the ER, I forget who, notified me at the end of the last shift that the accounting of each of these drugs had come up short."

Nancy's face became almost as red as Manning's dyed hair. "I don't know, Dr. Manning. We obviously had a thief on the floor last night, one with access to the cabinet." She stared up at him, unfazed. "I heard from the night shift that you visited the floor. Did you see anything out of the ordinary?"

Manning sputtered. "Of course not. I just did a quick walk-through on my way home." Everyone knew of his dislike of the ER, plus he never liked being challenged.

Before he could say more, Nancy continued, "My repeated requests for a cabinet with a keyless lock have been ignored for some reason. If you could approve it, hopefully that will solve the problem. I've also called Chief Brewster to report the theft."

"Chief Brewster? That man is useless. I'll see to your request. Carry on."

As he turned to go, he spotted me and smirked.

I joined Nancy with the other nurses who had been drawn by the sound of Manning's voice. "What do you expect from the Pecker?" one of them said.

Nancy's face gradually paled to its normal color, and I placed one arm around her shoulders to comfort her. I knew exactly how it felt to be in Manning's crosshairs, and she still shook a bit from the encounter. "We'll get to the bottom of this, Nancy, I promise. Just get that keyless lock as soon as possible. Manning can't deny your request now."

"We've got your back, Nancy," someone said, and others chimed in.

"We'll keep a watch on that cabinet."

"Don't let the bastard get you down."

These comments got a small smile from my friend.

; ;

By five o'clock I was exhausted, my usual state at day's end, but I stopped on the way out to see Marsh Adams, Bella's husband and a medical examiner. His office and the autopsy suites came off the corridor leading to the back entrance of the hospital. I took his open door as an invitation, so I knocked on the frame and entered.

"Hi, Rhe! You look like hell." Marsh was nothing if not honest. "How about a ginger ale?" Diet ginger ale had now become Marsh's drink of choice. The days of sugar-laden sodas had ended because his wife now governed his diet, much like I did for Sam. He winked at me. "But I have a lemon doughnut for an infusion of sugar."

"Marsh, if Bella ever caught you, there'd be hell to pay. But I happily accept." Our assistant state medical examiner worked out almost every day at a local gym. Just across the street stood a doughnut shop, from which he bought lemon-filled doughnuts, his favorite food on earth. "You'd better hope your wife doesn't come in here for a spot inspection. The powdered sugar is a dead give-away."

He looked alarmed and inspected surface of his desk, then offered me a waxed paper bag he took from his bottom drawer. I pulled out the last doughnut, immediately taking a bite and letting the lemony sweetness fill my mouth. I smiled. *Heaven.*

"So why am I honored by your presence?" he asked, smiling back.

Donut filled my mouth. Marsh retrieved a can of ginger ale from his minifridge, opened it and slid it across his desk to me. After taking a sip, I replied, "Did you know there are drugs missing from the ER drug cabinet?" He nodded. Marsh never missed anything going on in the hospital, although his sources remained unnamed. "Well, our beloved CEO came to the floor this morning to harangue Nancy Ellis. She's pretty smart, though. She got him to agree to a new cabinet with a keyless lock. I'm figuring it's an inside job. Any new hires you know of?"

He shook his head. "Maybe you could check with HR. You do have an in there."

"I do," I said, thinking of the woman who headed that department and whom Manning had tried to fire because she was a lesbian. Another one of my wins.

I stood up, brushing the powdered sugar from my lap. "I enjoyed seeing Bella the other day. We need to get together for a meal. I hear she's teaching you to cook."

"What I'm making is not food – quinoa, sprouts, kale, and other unappetizing vegetables." He pronounced quinoa, "kin-an-oah," and made a face.

"Then I won't tell you what we're having for dinner tonight. Gotta go." As I left his office, I heard, "That Sam is just plain lucky."

Or maybe not. We were having vegetarian burgers. No cheese.

Chapter 4

SAM

I stopped at the Mercedes dealership on the way into work, parking my Jeep carefully in a slot next to a brand new G class SUV. Just for fun, I looked at the price tag. $130,900.

Shaking my head, I entered one of the doors in the glass front wall of the building and stood for a moment looking around.

"Ah, Chief, I've been expecting you. Raymond Fidder." A small, nattily dressed man with a comb-over of sparse black hair and lips tightened to a thin line approached me and held out his hand. "I don't know what happened."

I shook his hand briefly. It felt oily. "So let's talk about what you do know."

He looked around, as if worried someone might overhear our exchange. "Shall we discuss this in my office?"

We wandered through the show models on the dealership floor and went into a glass-walled office at the rear of the building. After we'd sat down, Fidder picked up his phone and punched a button. "Judy, could you find Ryan and send him to my office?" Replacing the phone, he said by way of explanation, "Ryan is one of our younger associates and is the one who sold the car to your wife…"

I glared at him.

"I mean to the person posing as your wife."

Just then a young man wearing an ill-fitting bright green jacket appeared at the office door. He had the ultra-thin build of a marathoner, almost emaciated, with stringy muscles.

"Come in, Ryan, and take a seat." After he dropped into the chair next to mine, Mr. Fidder added, "Please tell Chief Brewster about the sale of the GLS."

Ryan twisted in his chair to face me, grasping the armrests so tightly his knuckles turned white. "I'm sorry, Chief Brewster. The man had a driver's license with the name Rhe Brewster—I didn't know that was a woman's name, but he told me it meant old French for river. I checked out his credit rating, proof of car insurance in that name, and I checked out his—your wife's—credit rating, all the things we usually do. He asked to finance through Pequod Savings and Loan. I checked with the bank, who had approved a loan, and the man wrote me a check for two thousand dollars down. Here's the check. You can see it's from Pequod Savings and Loan." By this time a sheen of sweat had gathered on his forehead and upper lip.

I looked at Fidder, "You realize I have to take this check as evidence in a case of fraud." I pulled a plastic evidence bag from my pocket, and holding the check by its edge, I deposited it inside.

"Do you have any of the paperwork he handled?"

"We do, but he wore gloves, even when he signed the check. I thought it was pretty strange. "

Damn. This perp thought of everything.

"Nevertheless, I'll need the paperwork. And I'll need you to come to the station and be fingerprinted, so we can eliminate your prints on this check and the loan papers."

"I have a break at noon. Is that okay, Mr. Fidder?"

Fidder nodded.

"Noon is fine with me, too. Just tell Ruthie at the front desk what you've come for. She'll get you sorted out. Mr. Fidder, do you have CCTV inside the dealership?"

"Unfortunately we don't, only outside to deal with anyone trying to steal a car from our lot."

"Do you have the outside video from the day this person bought the car?"

Mr. Fidder grimaced. "We did, but it's overwritten every 48 hours."

Damn again. Turning back to Ryan, I took a pad and pencil from my breast pocket and asked, "Can you describe the man posing as my wife?"

"Sure thing. Young, in his twenties…"

"How about his voice? Distinctive?"

"He did have a rather broad Maine accent. And he wore really thick glasses—you know, the ones that look like bottle bottoms."

"Did the birthdate on the driver's license jibe with his apparent age?" I asked.

Ah…no, I just looked at the picture…sorry." He cleared his throat and continued, "He was about my height, but more heavily built, light brown hair, brown eyes I think. Dressed in a blue sport coat and chinos."

"Is there anything else you can remember? Right-handed or left-handed? Any tattoos or scars?"

He was right, no, left-handed, but I didn't see any tattoos. He had really short hair, which made me think he was military or ex-military, and a fuzzy beard. When I asked if he had ever served, he said no."

"After you get fingerprinted. I'd like you to describe this man to our sketch artist. See if we can get a likeness."

Ryan looked at his boss, who replied, "Yes, if necessary, he can have the afternoon off. I want this resolved as much as you do, Chief."

"I do appreciate your cooperation, sir. I realize that this all comes out of your dealership's pocket. I have a BOLO out on the car, and you can rest assured if we find it, we'll return it as soon as it's been processed."

Both men seemed to have been straight with me. I collected the loan papers, thanked them, then I drove to Pequod Savings and Loan. The story there was much the same. Although this was not our personal bank, the manager knew me. However, he didn't know Rhe by sight, and our unknown had opened his account with one of the several new hires made to accommodate our growing number of residents.

The man asking for the loan had all of Rhe's personal information, and the loan officer had approved the loan and processed the paperwork in less than an hour. When I asked the loan officer what the man looked like, I got a description completely unlike the one Ryan had given me. Our perp had also avoided the bank's cameras, which told me he had scoped out the bank before coming in for the loan. When I asked for the loan papers for fingerprints, the loan officer told me the man had worn gloves, which he thought odd but didn't question. Before I left I asked him to come in to be fingerprinted and to visit our sketch artist.

Grinding my teeth in frustration while I drove to the station, I wondered if the long drive to City Bank in Portsmouth would be necessary. I decided to call first, got the bank manager, and told her what had happened. Her very nasally voice, dripping with disbelief at my story, informed me Rhe would have to appear there in person to challenge the charges. We'd go together—perhaps my uniform would lend some gravitas to the meeting. I told her we'd call back to arrange the visit.

I had just ended the call when line one buzzed. "Yes, Ruthie?"

"Today is one of Feather's days at the front desk. I just wanted to let you know I'm leaving for the rest of the day."

I wondered again about the parents who would name their child Feather. *I hope she's not featherbrained.* I groaned into the phone.

"Chief, be nice. She's still learning." Ruthie hung up before I could make an inappropriate comment.

I decided to take the bull by the horns and proceed as I would if Ruthie were there. I pushed the first button on the phone. "Feather?" Silence. "Feather, are you there?"

Giggles, then, "Yes, Chief."

"I have two things for you. First, two young men are coming in to be fingerprinted around lunch time, as rule-outs in an ongoing case. Have them see Deputy Birch, and ask Deputy Birch if, after they're fingerprinted, she could sketch a likeness of the man they each saw. Have her work with them separately, then compare the sketches." I could hear a pen scratching. "Second, can you ask Assistant Chief Pearce to come to my office and bring any information he has on the BOLO I issued last night?"

"Chief Brewster, what's a BOLO?"

"It means 'be on the lookout.' Thank you for asking."

Phil Pearce arrived a few minutes later, saying, "I've got some news for you. The car's been found. But you're not going to like its condition."

"Why?"

"It's been crushed flat at a junkyard in Augusta. The only way we found out about it is that the owner of the yard couldn't imagine why anyone would want to destroy what appeared to be a brand-new car. He wrote down the VIN number and also the engine number—did you know all the Mercedes engines are numbered and signed by the employees who put them together?—so it didn't take him long to find out where the car came from.

"I'll get the car hauled to our impound lot and call Midori. Maybe one of the techs can pull some prints from it," he added.

Midori Ishikawa was Marsh Adam's assistant and had become a crack forensic technologist. Currently she ran our forensics lab, which we had just established to save us the time, expense, and frustration of sending samples to the Maine State Police Crime Laboratory. The lab occupied the first floor of a house down the street from the station and was thus inconvenient to both the station and the hospital. Since Midori was still assisting Marsh, she had her hands full with training and overseeing the two technicians who worked there. We were currently interviewing for someone to take over as head of the lab, to take this extra responsibility off her shoulders. Slumping in my chair, I thought of the next interview scheduled for that afternoon.

"Something wrong, Sam?" asked Phil.

"Not really. I have another interview for Midori's position this afternoon after he—I think it's a he—meets with Midori and Marsh. Oh, wait, you get to meet him, too."

"I've already looked over his qualifications and he looks pretty solid."

"Good to know." I immediately felt guilty for not having prepared for the interview. "Better than the last two?" Phil nodded and we both smiled.

"Let me get that car hauled," Phil said, as he rose and left.

Our first candidate had been a tiny, shy, bird-like woman with a quiet voice in the upper octave range. She had minimal qualifications and, in my opinion, could never command a lab with two men, both of them young and eager and still learning. The second one reminded me of Mr. T., complete with gold chains. He would definitely have taken charge of the lab but lacked the background we needed. His fingers had reminded me of sausages, and I'd wondered if he could manage any of the more delicate lab work. The references for both candidates were tepid, to say the least.

Lunch—I'd read the file during lunch.

෬   ෬

The next applicant's name was Kitpoo Moncton, based on which I assumed he was a member of the Mi'kmaq tribe. His credentials were excellent—a double major in forensic science and biology and a certificate in cyber forensics from the University of Maine, plus three years' experience with the state police crime lab. His letters of recommendation left no room for doubt as to his abilities. The only question was why he would want to move to Pequod.

Just as I swiped my desk of the crumbs of a tuna salad sandwich made by Rhe, the phone rang.

"Chief, those two men you mentioned are with Deputy Birch. And there is a Mr. Moncton here to see you. Shall I send him down?" Feather sounded surprisingly professional.

"Sure thing." *Maybe she'll work out after all.* Ruthie said she'd had a good feeling about her, and she was seldom wrong.

I stood as Mr. Moncton entered my office and leaned over my desk to shake his hand. "Have a seat." I gestured toward the only chair in the room besides mine and realized it had a stack of files on it. "Just put them on the floor."

Mr. Moncton was a wiry, compact young man, neither short nor tall, with neatly trimmed dark brown hair and dressed in an inexpensive, but well-fitted, tan sports coat and black pants. He sat ramrod straight in the chair without crossing his legs, which I interpreted as nervousness. "Nice to meet you, Chief Brewster."

I gave him a smile. "This meeting is just pro forma. Dr. Adams and Miss Ishikawa are the decision-makers in this process, but I'm impressed with your credentials. My only real question is why do you want to leave the state lab and move here to Pequod?"

Moncton took a deep breath and visibly relaxed into the chair. "Two reasons. First, I want to move into a supervisory role and do some teaching. The other reason is that my father is a fisherman. He and my family live in Machias. I've grown up on the coast and love fishing myself, and this position gets me right to where I want to be—on the coast." He paused for a minute, took a deep breath and then said, "Just so you know, Chief Brewster, and because people in Maine tend to wonder, I'm gay and I'm partnered. My partner's name is Christopher Wright. He's a talented baker, and we hope he can find work here in Pequod."

"Your personal or marital status makes me no never mind, son. Pequod is growing exponentially and a lot of people from out of state are moving here. I think both of you will fit in just fine, and your partner shouldn't have any problem finding a job. You probably already know we have only one bakery, and it's part of a café. Maybe he'd want to open his own place?"

Moncton smiled. "That's the plan."

"You have an unusual first name."

"Yes, Kitpoo means 'eagle' in Mi'kmaq. My friends call me Kit."

I stood. "Well, Mr. Moncton, if you get the position, I look forward to working with you and I'll certainly call you Kit. I'm going to send you back to the front desk. Feather will take you to Deputy Chief Pearce, your last stop. Pleasure to meet you."

"Interesting name, Feather." He smiled again. "It was nice to meet you as well."

❧   ❧

I called Marsh about an hour later, after a brief conversation with Phil, who was also impressed. "What did you think of our latest candidate, Marsh?"

"What's not to like? Midori is over the moon. As far as we're concerned, he's hired. Do you agree?"

"Absolutely. I'll email him the offer. Do you know when he could start?"

"He said as soon as possible, depending on their finding a place to live. Hell, I'd offer him my own house if it would speed things up!"

"Bella might have a few things to say about that."

I heard a chuckle from Marsh. After I hung up. I asked Feather to send Deputy Birch to my office when she'd finished the composite sketches.

Deputy Birch had worked hard to make a place for herself within the department. Rhe told me many times that women had to do twice the work in half the time to be accepted, and Birch had done that. She had a real future with us. I heard a knock on the door frame—I hardly ever shut my door—and Birch came in with a frown on her face.

"I think the perp used disguises, Chief," she said, laying her two sketches on my desk. She'd drawn an older man with a mustache and graying hair at the temples, and a younger man with a military style haircut and thick glasses, distorting his eyes. One had blue eyes, the other brown. "The shape of the face is similar, as is the jaw line, width of nose, and shape of mouth. But since these are just sketches, I can't go any further in the comparison," she told me. "Is there any way the department could get some facial recognition software?"

I snorted. "With our budget? I've read that software isn't all that accurate, but I can look into it, if you think it would be helpful. Can you give me a sketch of the older guy without the beard and the glasses? I'd like to circulate it to banks in this part of the state."

"Sure thing," she said, taking the sketches.

Wait until Rhe hears this. Someone is definitely out to get her. But who? I need to remind her to be careful.

Chapter 5

RHE

That evening, Sam and I sat at the kitchen table. Sam sipped a before-dinner glass of wine, which I envied, playing with his glass, twirling it by the stem. "This is a planned attack on you, Rhe, digital or not. The perp wore different disguises when he applied for the credit card and the bank loan. Take a look at this composite sketch Deputy Birch made from the descriptions by the car salesman and the loan officer. Do you recognize him?"

I stared at the piece of paper Sam had placed on the table. *Who is this?* "No, I don't know him, but there's something about the eyes…" I kept looking at the sketch—a young man with an ordinary, fairly symmetrical face—but no one came to mind. "What can we do?"

"We've circulated the sketch to banks in the eastern part of the state and warned them to flag anyone applying for a loan or a credit card with the name Rhe Brewster."

"I guess that's a start." I sighed. "Maybe it's time we paid for one of those personal information protection programs."

"I was just thinking that. I'll look into it tonight. That way we'll know if he tries it again when the program blocks him."

"Did you find the Mercedes?"

Sam then told me about the crushed car. It had been towed to the parking lot next to the station, and the two forensic techs were, in his words, crawling all over it. When he'd finished, I said with a grin, "That Mercedes manager is going to be sooo pleased to get his car back…I assume they have insurance. By the way, did Nancy Ennis call you today about the second drug robbery?"

He nodded. "Why didn't Manning, or Woody, or Pecker, or whatever you call him contact me himself? He *is* the CEO after all."

"Would you be surprised if I told you he doesn't think much of you?"

"That somehow pleases me." Sam smiled, and I got up to start dinner.

È È

The following day both Sam and I received an email with the names of three men who fit the profile of the sniper who'd shot the governor, along with the news that the governor would be going home to recuperate. I didn't know him personally but knew the physical transition to having only one arm could be difficult. I suspected he would have PTSD-related issues as well.

Our candidates were all former Army snipers or Navy SEALs. I have a soft spot in my heart for veterans, Sam being one of them, so I was loathe to approach these men, knowing they would feel accused. We decided to visit the first one on our list, Chief Petty Officer First Class Elias Morgan, a former Navy SEAL—except I knew that SEALs were never former. He lived in Machias about 135 miles north from Pequod, in the heart of wild blueberry country.

While Sam would be in uniform, I would wear civvies, even though as a part-time detective with the police department, I had a uniform. The waistband on the pants had become too tight for my growing belly. Although Jack begged to go with us—*road trip, Mom!*—we sent him over to Paulette's to play with Taylor.

We hopped onto US 1 and, avoiding the traffic around Bar Harbor, meandered through small towns paralleling the coast. While Sam concentrated on the road, I went over Morgan's file one more time. His was a success story. He joined the Navy out of high school, with the intent of becoming a SEAL, aced the Armed Services Vocational Aptitude Battery and the SEAL physical training test on the first try, then earned a spot at the SEAL Prep School in Great Lakes, Illinois. There he excelled in all phases of his training and finished with advanced education as a sniper. He'd spent twenty years with the SEALS, retiring as a Petty Officer First Class after what appeared to be a stellar career.

"A wild blueberry farm," I said, after seeing the rows of plants on either side of the paved road leading to Morgan's farmhouse. The small wild Maine blueberry is a highly sought commodity because of its tangy sweetness, and also because it contains a high concentration of antioxidants. Jack would eat them like candy, very expensive candy, if I let him. "I've never seen a blueberry farm. Very seasonal work. I wonder if he can make a living. And quite a transition, Navy SEAL to blueberry farmer."

Sam harrumphed. "You can ask him when we find him." His sour mood came from the fact he was hungry, and I had refused to stop at a pancake house on the way north.

We had called ahead, so Mr. Morgan expected us. A tall man with short, fuzzy, gray hair and a formidable physique came out of the barn on the right, and an equally tall woman emerged from the house onto the porch. When he reached us, Morgan held out his hand and a broad smile broke his ebony face into wrinkles. "Elias Morgan, Chief Brewster. And this is my wife, Ella," he added as the woman came up.

"Pleased to meet you both," she replied. Then observing me with curiosity, she asked in a soft tone, "And when is your baby due?"

"Not for another five months."

"Well, then, come inside and have a sit. I have a pie and some coffee waiting. Don't mind the grandkids. We have them for the weekend and they can be a handful."

Once we were all seated in their large country kitchen, Mrs. Morgan poured us coffee and put sugar and cream on the table before cutting us substantial slices of pie, blueberry of course. We had just started to tuck in when a small face appeared from under the table. I must have startled, because Ella said, smiling, "That's our youngest grandchild, James. One of five. He's never far from food. Come here, rascal!" She dragged him out from under the table, plopped him in a highchair and gave him milk in a sippy cup along with a tiny piece of pie, which he ate with his fingers. As I took a bite of mine, I watched in fascination as he ate, smearing purple goo on his chin and cheeks. I noticed Sam smiling at him.

"So what can I tell you, Chief?" Morgan asked, when we were all seated and eating.

"Well," Sam stopped to swallow a mouthful, "we're looking into the shooting of Governor Hatcher last weekend. Please don't take what I'm going to tell you as an accusation, but the shooter had to be a well-trained sniper with an axe to grind. He only missed killing the man by a few inches— with a shot taken from about eighteen hundred yards away. He may have missed, but the shot blew off the governor's arm."

"I'm right sorry to hear that. You must have my name on your list of possible suspects because of my background." Morgan said this in an even tone, with no hint of rancor.

"Yes. So I have to ask you where you were last Sunday, and if you have any problem with the governor."

"The answer to the first question is easy," replied Mrs. Morgan. "The whole family saw Elias here that day. We had a cookout. So lots of people can confirm his whereabouts." She reached over and grasped her husband's hand.

Morgan then added, "With regard to the second question, no, I don't have any problem with the governor. Hell, I voted for him in the last election."

"Do you know offhand anyone who might fit the profile?" Sam scraped his plate.

Morgan shook his head. "Nope. I'm the only former sniper I know." He smiled. "But always a SEAL."

"Then you've made our trip an easy one," I replied, "as well as delicious. This is the best blueberry pie I've ever had, Mrs. Morgan."

"Made with our own blueberries. I'll give you a jar of blueberry jam before you leave."

"Thank you! That's very kind." *I can imagine how long that jam will last.* "So tell me, is blueberry farming profitable? It's such a seasonal thing."

Morgan responded in his mellow voice, "Between the berry business and my pension, we do quite well. This farm belonged to my parents, and I always figured I'd come home to it when my Navy days were over. We also run an online business out of the barn, selling fresh berries in season, along with jams and jellies and blueberry honey." When my eyebrows went up with that, he chuckled. "We have beehives out back. They do a good job pollinating the blueberry plants."

We chatted for another half hour over a second cup of coffee and another slice of pie. After offering our sincere thanks for their hospitality, we left with full stomachs and the jar of jam.

"He is definitely not the sniper," I said to Sam as we drove out the driveway. *Moot point.*

⚃ ⚂

We relaxed for the rest of the weekend. Sam took a last swim in the pool before we closed it, and I napped. I seemed to be more tired with this pregnancy than the last. On Monday, I headed back into the ER.

I could feel tension in the air the minute I stepped into the unit. None of the nurses were chatting but mostly keeping to their work with their heads down. Spotting Nancy Ellis, I asked, "Was there another robbery?"

"Yes, and Woody's already been here to chew me out again. You could hear him out in the parking lot. And he called me a bitch to my face, then threatened my job if I told HR. The new keyless drug cabinet isn't here yet, and we don't have the personnel to watch the old one twenty four seven. Woody seems to think we can."

"We should talk to Lyle." Lyle Pendergrass was the ancient guard who monitored people and deliveries coming in via the loading dock. He'd been there from when the hospital was constructed and knew everyone and everything. Last year he'd become a celebrity for shooting a Russian thug who had attempted to kill Agent Bowers and then tried to escape via the loading dock. He'd run into Lyle.

"I hadn't thought of that," replied Nancy.

"I wonder if anyone else has. I can do it when I leave today." I smiled at the memory of Lyle with his concealed carry revolver. "What about mounting a hidden camera? We couldn't stop a theft, but we could find out who's doing it."

"Hah! Do you think Woody would pay for that?"

"No, but I can probably get one on loan from the police department."

"Let's do it. Maybe that will get Woody off my back."

⅋ ℛ

On my way home that afternoon, I stopped to see Lyle. He lived behind a counter with a Plexiglas shield and gave a wrinkled, lop-sided grin to people he knew. You couldn't help but smile back.

"Hi, Lyle. I need to test your memory." He grinned even wider, because his memory was close to eidetic.

"Last night and last Friday, some drugs were stolen from the ER. Do you recall anyone new coming into or out of the hospital on those days?"

"Yup. Dr. Manning came down here and asked the same thing. I shoulda known when I heard about them thefts and said something. I remember one woman. Wore blue scrubs, so I thought she might be new to the ER. She signed herself in as…," and here he paused to consult his computer, something he still struggled with but an improvement from the notebook he previously used. "…Ah, there it is. A Mary T. Smith, ER."

"Mary Smith, huh? We've had no new personnel in the ER by that name or any other that I know of. She's credentialed?"

Lyle fumbled with some more keys. "Yep. Her record is right here."

"May I look at it?"

Lyle frowned. "You know I can't do that, Nurse Brewster. Private information, and it would get me in a lotta trouble."

I knew I wasn't entitled to see it. "And Dr. Manning didn't ask about her?"

"No, he said he knew her and asked if I'd seen anyone else. I hadn't."

"Can you at least tell me what she looked like?"

"Tiny little blonde, thin. She had on a ton more make-up than you other nurses wear. Rather pretty…someone on the top floor would find her appealing," he replied with a wink. Lyle stood up, looked around, and said, "It's about time for my coffee break. See you on Wednesday?"

I nodded as he sauntered down the hallway, having left his computer screen up. I tucked around behind his counter, took out my phone and took a snap of the screen, scrolled down and took another, then shut down the screen.

ᘓ   ᘓ

Over dinner that night—store-bought chicken pot pies for everyone—we chatted about Jack's soccer team and his coach.

"I like Coach Tony a lot," Jack said with a mouthful of chicken and vegetables. "Hey, this is good, Mom. You should make it more often."

I grimaced. *When does he think I'd have time to make pies?* "Why do you like him?"

"Well, he's patient with us, doesn't yell when we make mistakes, and takes time to explain what we should be doing in our positions."

"Are you still playing center mid?" asked Sam.

"Yeah, I'm perfect for it because Coach Tony says I have field smarts!"

"And now you need to apply your smarts to your homework," I replied. While Jack went to his room with some ice cream to do just that, Sam and I—or rather Sam—had coffee. I decided on tea. "Sam, did Nancy Ellis call you about another drug theft?"

"She did. That drug cabinet must be cleaned out by now."

"It's interesting. Whoever is taking the meds leaves enough to cover maybe two days in the ER, which is about the time it takes to restock. Almost as if the thief knows how we work."

"Is there anyone new working with you?"

"Funny you should ask." I then told him what Lyle had revealed and how I'd gotten the information about Nurse Mary T. Smith.

"That Lyle is a wily character. Let's see your phone screen."

I brought up the two photos I'd taken and enlarged them on the screen. "Not too shabby a resume," I said with a sigh. "But Mary T. Smith? Come on."

"And you've never seen this woman in the ER?"

"Nope."

"Hmm…Rhe, check out one of the people recommending her."

Wow! None other than Woody! "I hate to say it, but with his record on women, I wonder if he's sneaking her into the hospital to visit him."

Sam gave me an odd look.

"I mean that pejoratively."

Another strange look.

"Sam, think!"

"Oh…I get it. You think she might be servicing him."

I rolled my eyes. "That's the idea. Look, I can't see us catching him en flagrante, but I can check with my buddy in HR to find out more about her and check on her school credentials."

Sam and I had discovered Manning, aka Woody, at the edges of various dirty businesses for the past several years—the illegal acquisition of human body parts for transplant, patronizing a high-end brothel employing college students as escorts, threatening the head of HR with losing her job because she was gay, and providing free breast implants and expensive jewelry to a woman who later turned up dead. He'd always wiggled away, worm that he was, because of friends in high places. I wondered if they were getting tired of saving his butt. In retaliation, he'd set up a situation where a drunk beat me into unconsciousness in the ER, during a time when security personnel were mysteriously unavailable. Could we ever rid the hospital of him?

I took a desultory sip of my tea and immediately put it down. "In the meantime, do you think the department could loan me a camera to monitor the drug cabinet?"

"Sure. Since you're off tomorrow, come by the department and I'll ask Phil to show you how it operates."

"Sounds like a plan."

"One other thing, my dear wife." Sam paused to drain the last of the coffee from his mug. "I had an interesting phone call today."

I raised one eyebrow.

"From Elias Morgan, our blueberry farmer and former SEAL. He told me after thinking about it, he did recall another sniper in the area, one John Patterson."

"And he's next on our list."

Chapter 6

SAM

When I arrived at the station on Monday morning, the usual chaos of a shift change and the beginning of a week greeted me. Ruthie and Feather were at the front desk, Ruthie pointing at something on the computer screen in front of them. Feather looked like, well, like Feather, wearing some loose, patterned dress and flowers stuck in her braids. *Shades of the hippie years.* They both looked up as I entered. "Chief..." they said in unison.

I had to smile. "Which one of you wants to tell me something?"

"I will," replied Ruthie. "I'm going to take the two weeks' vacation I've accrued and I'm confident Feather can run things."

I tried hard not to roll my eyes, but they sort of did it anyway. Ruthie harrumphed.

"Chief Brewster, both Deputy Chief Pearce and Deputy Birch want to see you first thing," said Feather.

I had to admit she maintained her poise in the face of my eye rolling. "Going there right now." I headed down the hallway to Phil's office where I found him and Deputy Birch peering at some fuzzy closed circuit TV footage. "What have you got?" I asked, pulling up a third chair.

"Well, not much," replied Phil. "This is from the Mercedes dealership. It seems they did have footage of the perp's visit. And this video is from the bank. Both of the men posing as Rhe appear substantially as our witnesses described them. We've managed to get a more exact height, based on a comparison Birch did with the descriptions from both the salesman and the bank rep. Our fraudster is about five foot seven, so a bit shorter than we thought."

"That's it?"

"Sorry, Sam. That's all we could get."

Just then my phone rang with my chosen tune, *I'm Back in the Saddle Again*. I opened my messages and found a new one from SecureLife, the company I'd just paid a bunch of money to, so they would oversee any new purchases or credit card openings in Rhe's name. They'd caught something. *So soon?*

The message read:

Someone just took out a large loan in the name of Rhe Brewster at Bangor Savings and Loan.

Is this you?

I immediately got up and stepped out into the hallway and called the SecureLife number. After identifying myself to someone named Rashid, I gave him my account password and I said, "It's definitely not my wife who got that loan. Please notify the bank. Can you provide me with footage from the bank of the person taking out the loan?"

"Normally, sir, we don't ask for the footage. We're only authorized to block or cancel fraudulent accounts."

I heard some keys clicking in the background. "Well, thank you for notifying me. I assume the loan will be terminated today?"

"Doing that as we speak, sir."

"Thanks, Mr.…Rashid."

I went back into Phil's office. "Well, the guy tried to take out another loan in Rhe's name, this time at Bangor Savings and Loan. It's been blocked, but he'll know we're on to him now. Birch, can you get on the horn and see if the bank can send us any footage of the transaction? I want to see what the perp looked like this time."

"Yessir."

I went back to my office, stopping on the way at the alcove where every morning Ruthie made the swill some of us called coffee. I was so irritated that I took a doughnut, too. Rhe be damned. *I'm so friggin' mad.*

My day only got worse when Rhe stopped by to borrow the camera for the ER and I had to tell her of the latest assault on her identity. She wasn't pleased and when she spied the sugar from the doughnut on my desk, we got into a staring contest. I lost.

ۈ ۈ

I spent the next two days feeling like another shoe would drop, and it did.

My office phone buzzed. "Chief, there are two FBI agents here with your wife. They need to see you urgently. Can I send them back?" Feather asked in a very professional tone.

"Of course. And Feather, if it's my wife and/or the FBI you don't need to call me ahead. Just send them directly." *What in hell is it now?*

Agent Bongiovanni stuck his burr-cut head in the door. "We'll need the conference room for this, Chief."

I followed him and my for-once silent wife, along with another agent I didn't know, down the hall. As we sat down around the conference table. I noticed Rhe's face had become a mask of worry. "What's all this about, Agent Bongiovanni?"

"I'll let Lin tell you. She's CIA."

Oh, crap. What now?

Agent Monica Lin was a young woman with her hair tightly bound in a bun at the nape of her neck and dressed in a tailored navy blue suit. "Nice to meet you, Chief Brewster. Wish it were different circumstances, but I'll get to the chase. Your wife is wanted for murder."

"What?" I shot out of my chair. "That is *not* possible." I could feel my pulse pound in my forehead.

"Calm down, Chief," Bongiovanni said in an even tone. "We know that."

"Wanted for murder? How exactly?" Still loud, I sat down again and glared at Lin.

"There was an assassination in Syria, one of President Bashar Al-Assad's deputies. A woman with your wife's passport was one of the assassins. We only heard about it because the Syrian government contacted us about this Rhe Brewster, the woman they had in custody. They sent a copy of the passport and a photo of the assassin, and the woman definitely was not Mrs. Brewster. Plus there are no travel records for your wife from the US to Europe or the Middle East. However, your wife's personal information has been severely compromised because the forger had everything they needed to create the fake passport. Do you have any information that might help us? Any idea who might have done this?"

I loosened my bolo tie and leaned across the table towards Lin. "As a matter of fact, I do.

Someone here in Maine has been taking out loans and credit cards in my wife's name, piling up thousands of dollars in debt for us. We've filed reports with this department."

"Don't you have a company that handles personal security for you?" she asked.

"I do now, and they called me two days ago to tell me someone was in the process of taking out another loan in Rhe's name, this time at the Bangor Savings and Loan."

"What? Not again!" Rhe interrupted. "Why didn't you tell me?"

"You've got a lot on your plate right now, hon, and besides, SecureLife assured me the loan was cancelled." Directing my attention back to Agent Lin, I continued, "We have CCTV footage of the person doing this on two previous occasions. He wears different disguises each time he uses her identity.

"The bank footage from the Bangor bank finally arrived this morning, and I was about to look at it when you arrived. Do you think the perp made the fake passport himself and sold it?" I asked Lin.

"I doubt it," she replied. "More likely he sold Mrs. Brewster's personal information on the Dark Web."

"What exactly is the Dark Web?" I asked. "I've heard of it but certainly never used it."

"The Dark Web is a hidden part of the world wide web accessible with a web browser known as Tor. It allows users and website operators to remain anonymous or untraceable while visiting illegal marketplaces. This poses a new challenge for us in law enforcement because its users can browse without anyone, such as the CIA and FBI, knowing what they're doing. People go to the Dark Web to sell or buy illegal pictures of child pornography, sell children, stir up revolutions and anarchy, sell black market drugs, and buy personal information. And that's just a few examples."

"Can't you access it and find out who sold Rhe's information?"

"We can, but users of the Dark Web have masked IP addresses. However, we have some of the best computer geeks in the world. We'll find him."

"What if another passport shows up with Rhe's info?"

"Then we'll intensify our search. I would advise not using your passport any time soon, Mrs. Brewster. We have it flagged. Could I see the footage you have?"

We all got up and I led the way down the hall to Phil Pearce's office, knocking on the door before entering. Phil looked up in surprise at the number of people crowding in after me. After introducing Agent Lin, I explained the reason for the visit, and Phil first pulled up the footage from the Mercedes dealership and then Pequod Savings and Loan.

Agent Lin sat down beside him and stared intently at the screen. "Can't tell much except height with those disguises. Did you get a description from Mercedes and the bank?"

"We did." Phil fumbled in a pile of papers on his desk and pulled out a yellow folder. "Here is our in-house artist's rendition of each disguise, along with a composite she made from both. She's not yet sure if this person is a man or a woman disguised as a man."

"Hmm. Not bad. She's talented. Can we see the latest footage from the bank in Bangor?'

"Got it right here." Phil tapped his computer and everyone leaned in to see what the person looked like this time. To my surprise, we saw a woman, mincing along in four inch stiletto heels. I couldn't help but notice her ample curves. With dark shoulder-length hair, a wide-brimmed hat, and Hollywood-style sunglasses that covered half her face, she might be mistaken for my wife. The woman shifted her chair so her back was to the camera and, although she took off her glasses, she kept her hat on so we couldn't see her face at all. Clearly she'd scoped out the bank in a previous visit.

"That is *not* me!" I heard from behind me. "First of all, she's too short, even if you take into account those ridiculous heels. Second, my pregnancy would show in a dress like that, and third, I wish I had breasts like those."

Agent Lin turned around and stared at Rhe, then nodded. Turning to me, she asked, "Have you estimated how tall this person is?"

Rhe answered. "Five-seven. And I'm five-ten. I'd be well over six feet tall in those heels."

"Are you absolutely sure this is the same person we saw on the previous videos? Is this man masquerading as a woman? Or are the others a woman who masqueraded as a man?" Lin asked the right questions and her answer was silence.

"Phil, can you get Deputy Birch in here. Maybe she can tell us something. She's our artist, Agent Lin." When Birch squeezed into the already crowded office and had been introduced to Lin, I said, "Have you seen this footage, Birch? It's from the second bank."

"No, I forwarded it to Deputy Chief Pearce as soon as it arrived, so he could clean it up." We made an opening so Birch could get to the computer screen, and she sat in Lin's vacated seat. "It's a woman this time! Well, what do you know?"

"I know we've been assuming this is a man," I said, "but do you think it could be a woman?"

Birch's lovely face scrunched itself into a picture of deep thought. After a moment, she replied, "I don't think so. There's a couple of things both from the descriptions and the footage that make me think this person is more likely male." She looked off at the wall as she organized her thoughts. "First of all, although it's hard to see them, the woman's hands—what we can see of them here—are large. Also, females tend to have more hair on top of their heads, which brings their eye line a little below the center of the head. Males tend to have less hair on top of their heads, and more on their chin. This makes the eye line higher than the center of the head, which is the case in my two sketches. Another thing that can determine a male from a female is the size ratio of shoulder to head. Male shoulder width can be almost two and a half heads wide, while female shoulder width is generally less than two heads wide. When I look at this person, even from the back, the shoulder width reads as male."

"Are you positive?" asked Lin.

"Look at this last of the footage, where this woman is standing, about to leave, with her back to us. Can you bring that up and freeze it, Deputy Chief? There, look at the shoulders of the dress. They don't look padded and the shoulders are wide. So I'm ninety-nine percent sure that this 'woman' is a man."

"Then I think we can proceed as if we're dealing with a man, thanks to the deputy's assessment," Lin concluded, and everyone nodded in agreement.

"Chief, can I ask that loan officer to come in so I can get a description of his face?" Birch asked.

"No problem, do it." I was surprised Rhe hadn't tried to insert herself further into the discussion, but I figured being escorted from the ER in the middle of her shift by both FBI and CIA agents had stunned her.

಍   ಍

Later that afternoon, I walked down the street to the forensics lab to see if any fingerprints or material had been gathered from the crushed Mercedes, which sat in the department parking lot looking a lot like a silver platter. The techs were there, but Midori had just left, and they weren't going to go around her and share their findings with me. *I should have called.* I took my time on the way back to the office, inhaling the fine aroma coming from the pizza restaurant just down the street. Then I called Marsh's office. "Is Midori there, Marsh? I need the report on the Mercedes."

"Hello to you, too, and she just came in."

"Yes, Chief?" Midori's high, soft voice betrayed nothing.

"Where's the report on the Mercedes? I walked down to the lab to find you and those boys of yours wouldn't tell me a thing."

"I've trained them well. And I was just going to type up our report, which will provide no new information. The person driving the car must have worn gloves and had it detailed before it went to the junkyard. We found absolutely nothing. Not a hair, a fiber, a scrap of dirt. If I didn't know better, I would think he wore one of our personal protective suits."

I gritted my teeth.

"But I heard you think this guy is about five foot six or seven, and that would fit with the position of the seat compared to the steering wheel. Is it true Rhe got hauled out of the ER by the FBI and CIA today? The gossip flying around is that she was charged with murder…which of course is complete nonsense. I can't imagine how upset you both are."

"Upset doesn't begin to describe it." I explained what had happened. "The little prick who's doing this is pretty clever. We need to find him, because Rhe's hunting for bear. You know what that means." I heard a chuckle. "Midori, has our new head of the Forensics Lab arrived?"

"I understand Dr. Moncton dropped everything and will be here by the end of the week."

"Well, that's one good thing. I'll bet you're looking forward to his help."

"Yes and no. The trips back and forth to the lab have been keeping my weight down but also giving me blisters." Another chuckle, rare from Midori.

I smiled to myself as I hung up, since Midori resembled a small beach ball, and I hadn't noticed any shrinkage.

ڃ ڃ

As I'd anticipated, I got the cold shoulder and then the third degree that night.

"How could you not tell me about the latest attempt to ruin my credit rating by that…that…evil piece of chicken shit?"

"Rhe! Jack can hear you!"

"What? He's in the family room and I didn't swear."

We were both in the kitchen, each chopping a different vegetable for a salad to go with the chicken roasting in the oven. The aroma of that bird made my mouth water.

"I have more, even less salubrious words for that man, along with what I'd personally like to do to him." She sliced the cucumber as if she were chopping off his head. "So why didn't you tell me?" She gave me the evil eye, so I could tell how serious she was.

"Because of this—you're upset and I don't think it's good for the baby."

"Piffle. The baby's just fine. Kicking right now if you want to know."

"See? He's upset."

"No, it's a she." Rhe dumped the sliced cucumbers in a bowl. "Seriously, Sam, when is this going to stop? Do you think the CIA can find him?"

I put down my paring knife and wrapped her in my arms. "They'll find him, you know they will. This faked passport is such a stretch, it has to be his last go at you."

"But if he can do that, he can come after you or Jack or the department." Her voice climbed an octave. "I want this to be over with."

I hugged her tighter and kissed her neck. That usually relaxed her, and it worked.

"Okay, let's drop it. Except…Lin and Bongiovanni walked me right out of the ER this afternoon. I can just imagine what the Pecker's going to do when he hears about that."

"And we'll deal with that tomorrow. Let's eat!"

Chapter 7

RHE

Our CEO proved as predictable as ever. When I walked into the ER the following morning, Nancy Ellis handed me a note:

See Dr. Manning immediately. Do not begin your shift.

I rolled my eyes when I read it. Nancy sniggered.

"I assume what happened yesterday was a giant mistake?" she asked.

"Yeah. That person who stole my personal information sold it on the Dark Web. A woman arrested in an assassination attempt in Syria, of all places, had a passport in my name."

Nancy's eyes opened wide. "Really? This person who stole your info isn't fooling around, is he? Oh, Rhe, I'm so sorry." She put one arm around me. "Well, you'd better go see the man. Give him hell, girlfriend."

Manning's office occupied most of the top floor of the building, the suite expensively furnished with thick, dark blue carpet, color-coordinated wallpaper, and high-end teak desks. Nothing but the best for our CEO. I checked in with his secretary, the third since Delores Richmond—his partner in crime as far as I was concerned—had been fired. It seems the series of nubile young women he hired to replace Delores couldn't fill her size 12 LL Bean gumboots. I didn't know this young woman, but she must have known me because she just waved her hand in the general direction of his office door. I entered without knocking.

Dr. Manning didn't look up from his desk. "Don't bother sitting, Mrs. Brewster. I'll make this short and sweet—you're fired."

"On what grounds, might I ask?"

He raised his head and snorted. "What grounds? What grounds? You've been arrested for murder!"

"Then why am I here this morning and not in a jail cell?"

"I don't know and I don't care. Finally, I get to say, 'You're fired'!"

I gave him the nastiest smile I could muster. "Guess you didn't read the *Post and Sentinel* this morning, did you? Turns out the woman who committed the murder in Syria used a forged passport in my name. I'd be happy to provide the names of the CIA agents in charge of the case."

I could see just the slightest twitch at the corner of his eye. I had to give him credit—he recovered well. "Then get back to work before I dock your pay." He nodded towards the door.

As I closed the door behind me, I swore I could hear his fist pounding on the top of his boat-sized desk.

I returned to the ER with a shit-eating grin on my face, which earned a round of clapping from the other nurses. I couldn't help myself—I took a bow. Just as I asked Nancy for a patient assignment, a pair of EMTs came through the double doors, pushing a gurney before them, and stopped in front of us.

"Female, approximately twenty years of age, no name, found wandering in the local Hannaford parking lot, blouse torn, only underwear below, no shoes, and clammy to the touch. No obvious wounds or trauma. Pulse ox is eighty-five percent, heart rate one-ten, respiratory rate nineteen and shallow, BP one hundred over sixty," reported Micah Stern, one of my favorite young EMTs. "She was confused and combative when we tried to help her and her speech is slurred."

"Put her in two," Nancy told him. "Rhe, she's all yours."

The young woman was clearly in shock, and my first thought was hypoglycemia. While the two EMTs transferred her from the gurney to the bed, I rustled up a blood test kit, a glucagon nasal spray, and a rapid glucose test kit from the storage unit. Then I grabbed some peanut butter crackers and an orange juice packet from the snack cart.

When I returned, the EMTs were still with her and had tucked the blanket she'd come in with around her. "I've got this, guys, and thanks. You've both done well."

The two men left. I put on gloves and attached a nasal cannula to her nose to deliver oxygen, then uncapped the tube containing the nasal spray and removed the device from the tube. As I did so, I thought I heard the woman say something and leaned down to see if I could catch her words. I heard, "Dia…" and considering all her symptoms, I knew she was slipping into a diabetic coma. Just then, my patient's arms and legs started to twitch uncontrollably. *She's seizing!*

Holding the spray between my fingers and thumb, I quickly placed the tip in one of her nostrils and pushed the plunger all the way in, then turned her on her left side. Within a few moments, her twitching ceased. The glucagon had worked, raising her blood glucose level. After attaching the bedside monitor, I checked her heart and respiration rates and blood pressure and was relieved to see they were approaching normal. Shortly thereafter, she rolled onto her back, focused on me, and asked, "Am I in the hospital?"

I smiled. "You are. EMTs found you wandering in a parking lot this morning. Can you tell me your name?"

"Naomi Parkins. I'm a student at Pequod U."

Pequod University had been a fixture in our town for several decades. My deceased first husband had been on the faculty of the previously named Pequod College. It had grown, along with the town.

"Naomi, I'm going to sit you up. Here's some orange juice and peanut butter crackers for you. I'm sure you know the drill."

She sat up, unwrapped the food, gulped down the orange juice and began to nibble on the crackers.

"I know this is a difficult question, but do you recall what happened to you?"

Her face crumpled and she looked away.

"It's okay, dear. I'm here to help you. Let's just get your sugar levels stabilized, then we'll talk more about how you ended up here. When was the last time you took your insulin?" She looked puzzled and said she didn't remember. As a nurse, I knew that when the glucose levels in the blood become too low, brain function is seriously affected, so she'd been teetering on the edge of coma and death when she came in.

"Who's your physician?"

"Dr. Rutledge."

Luke Rutledge was a hospitalist—an internist practicing solely in this hospital, so I left Naomi long enough to ask Nancy to call him and ask him to come to the ER as soon as possible. "Your physician is on his way down," I told her when I returned.

I opened the glucose test kit, removed a strip and slid it into the glucose meter. After opening the package with the sterile lancet, I told her, "This is going to hurt a bit."

She chuckled. "I'm used to it."

I jabbed her finger, pressed it to get a drop of blood, and held the test strip to the drip. After a few moments, the glucose level appeared on the meter. *Normal range.*

After wrapping the tourniquet from the blood draw kit tightly around her arm, I told her, "We need to confirm your blood sugar level and test for a few other things." She looked away as I inserted the needle into the vein at her elbow. When I finished, I sat down by her bed. "Do you know why you were wandering around in that parking lot? If you can remember anything at all, I can help you."

Tears filled her eyes. In a whisper, she replied, "I think I was raped. And I don't remember much. I went out with some girlfriends to the Dirty Gull. There were some guys there who bought us drinks, and one of them paid a lot of attention to me. After that it's just a big blank."

I placed one hand on hers. "It's okay. The blood sample will tell us if you were drugged. After Dr. Rutledge checks you over, I want to do a rape kit."

Naomi pulled her hand away. "Do I have to?"

"It's your choice, but I think you might want to find the guy who did this to you."

"I already know who he is."

"Another student?"

"No, but I've seen him around, I think at that bar. I don't remember his name, if he even gave it to me."

"But you can provide the police with physical data to identify him—scars, tattoos, hair color—that sort of thing. The blood work and the rape kit will back up your claim. The rape kit's going to take time, but I'll talk you through it. We'll do this together, and I'll be as gentle as possible." I took her hand.

Just then Dr. Rutledge bustled in, and I stepped out to send the blood sample to the police forensics lab with a note to test for drugs, then collected a rape kit. When I came back into the cubicle, he had finished examining Naomi and was sitting down, having what sounded like a sympathetic chat. He patted her on the shoulder before he left and said to me, "You did a great job managing her, thanks. I'll leave instructions for her care at the desk."

"I'm soooo hungry," Naomi said to me then, pleading with her lovely brown eyes. "Can I get some real food now?"

Diabetics were usually really hungry after a shock. "Not quite yet. Finish those crackers first. Then after we finish the rape kit, I'll get you something from the cafeteria." I wrinkled my nose. "It's not cordon bleu, but the food is USDA edible."

Naomi managed a smile.

"Who can we call for you? Roommate? Parents?"

"My brother, I guess. We share an off-campus house." She gave me his number and I had one of the nurses at the main desk make the call.

Since I was an official investigator with the Pequod PD, it fell to me to perform the sexual assault forensic exam on any victim of alleged rape who came to the ER during my shift. Several other nurses and I had been specifically trained for this duty, so all shifts would be covered. On a side table I laid out the contents of the rape kit: bags for the victim's clothes, head hair, and pubic hair; sheets of butcher's paper; swabs; sterile sample containers; a comb; clear glass slides; a nail pick and documentation forms.

Placing one of the paper sheets on the floor, I explained, "First, you need to get out of your clothes so I can collect them for testing. After that, I have to take some pictures of any bruising and do a vaginal exam." I helped Naomi to stand on the paper and disrobe, then bagged her clothing and the paper. The worst part had to be the picture-taking. I hated the embarrassment it caused the victims. By the time I'd finished, she was shaking, so I had her lie down again and called Nancy in to hold her hand while I swabbed her genitals, rectum, mouth and the inside of her thighs, and combed her pubic hair. There were no bruises apparent, but they might take more time to develop. Nancy had just brought in a warm blanket for Naomi when we heard a commotion outside the curtains of the cubicle, and Nancy stepped out.

A man's voice demanded, "Why can't I see my sister? I want to see her now!"

Nancy replied in a soothing voice, "She's undergoing a procedure right now, and you have to wait. Please have a seat over there and I'll call you when it's over." Nancy is very persuasive and extremely attractive—I figured the combination of the two had won the day since there were no more demands.

"This is almost over, I promise, and then you can see your brother," I told Naomi. "I'm going to comb your hair onto a sheet of paper and then clean under your nails, and that's the end of it."

A few minutes passed before I said, "We're done! Put this blanket around you while I get you a warmed hospital gown and robe. And now I can get you some food. Would you like a hamburger?" She nodded. "And let me check your insulin schedule." At that point she wrapped herself in the blanket and lay back, tension draining from her face to be replaced by the sagging of exhaustion. The hospital gown and robe arrived and I helped her don them and then re-covered her with a freshly warmed blanket. Beginning the chain of custody, I packaged the rape kit and, on the outside, wrote my name, Naomi's name and the date and time. A courier would sign for it and take it to the forensics lab that afternoon.

"Your brother's outside. Can I send him in?" She nodded slowly, but said, "Please don't tell him about how this happened. I'm not really supposed to be drinking or visiting places like the Dirty Gull. Last night I told him I was going out for burgers with my friends. I'll figure out how to handle it."

"I can't share details with him anyway, Naomi. Your health record is protected by federal regulations called HIPAA, unless you've specified he can be told."

"I haven't."

"And since what happened to you was a crime, your brother can't be told about it unless the authorities decide they need him to be." I opened the curtain and motioned at a young man who looked enough like Naomi to be her twin. When I left them, she had sat up and he held her to his chest while she sobbed.

Ϙ   ʘ

Later that day I asked Nancy if she had found a place for the TV camera I had brought from the police department. She had and directed me to the ER cart for fresh linens, which she had moved to a spot in full view of the drug cabinet. I nestled the camera in the clean blankets. "Now we just have to hope no one moves the cart."

"I'll tell everyone the cart is now in a new location and will pass that info along to the next shift. You know that new ER nurse you told me about? I'm wondering where she is. She certainly hasn't shown up here."

"Let me check her arrival and departure times with Lyle. The CIA and FBI had me a bit distracted this week." I winked at her. "And perhaps it's time I check out her credentials."

"What? How did you get them?" Nancy's eyes lit up.

"Let's just say Lyle left his desk unattended after I asked him about her, and I couldn't help but sneak a look. I've already noticed the Pecker himself recommended her, so I plan to ask my friend in HR to check out her creds. I can at least tell you who to look for..." I paused, teasing her.

"And?"

"Her name is the very ubiquitous Mary T. Smith. She's a tiny blonde, wears a lot of make-up."

"Got it. Now let's hope we capture her on that camera."

 C3   C3

On my way out after my shift ended, I stopped to talk to Lyle again.

"You here about that ER nurse you never seen?" He squinted up at me from his seat and smiled, wrinkling his already wrinkled face even further.

"You read my mind. Can you tell me the dates and times she's been here and for how long?"

"Thought you'd ask, got it right here. I wrote it all down for you. This here back door gets locked when I leave for the night, so she might sneak in another way. Have them nurses in the ER been seeing her?"

"Not that I'm aware of. I may have to make the rounds and question everyone. Thanks, Lyle, this is a big help. You might even make detective."

His chest swelled with pride and his grin cracked his face in two.

Chapter 8

SAM

We had cheeseburgers for dinner, which I thought were pretty good. But there was something about them…then I spotted the package in the trash. They were vegetable protein burgers! My wife had put one over on me, but I had to admit they actually did taste like meat. *Not something this cowboy's gonna eat on a regular basis.*

When Jack went off to do homework and we were having our after dinner brew, I asked, "So veggie burgers? Really?"

Rhe gave me a know-it-all smile, then told me about her meeting with Woody. I took a sip of my coffee, trying not to look too satisfied with the caffeine. "He's gunning for you, hon, and this proves it. Not that he hasn't done this before, but now you *really* need to watch your step. He's looking for any excuse to get rid of you, even one he creates."

"Yup, that lawsuit I won after my beating hasn't slowed him down one bit. By the way, are you planning for us to interview the next sniper on our list this weekend?" I asked.

"Sniper? Are you going to meet a real sniper?" Jack called from the family room.

"Yes, Big Ears. But you're not invited to go along. Could be dangerous."

"Why are you always leaving me out? Isn't it dangerous for you, too?" He walked into the kitchen, glaring at us both.

"Yes, you might say that. But we're trained to deal with it. How about I give you money to see a movie with Tyler? What's that latest superhero one you've been dying to see?"

Jack's face lit up. "The new Avengers. Everyone's seen it but me."

"Okay," said Rhe. "You and Tyler are booked for a movie."

⚅ ⚃

Very early Saturday morning, Rhe and I hit the road again. We anticipated about a four hour drive, heading north toward Presque Isle into potato country. As we drove north on I-95, Rhe read me the information about the man we would visit that day, former Army lieutenant John Patterson.

"He graduated from the Army ROTC program at the University of Maine, trained at Fort Benning and finished the Ranger program there, specializing as a sniper. He then deployed to Afghanistan, where he spent almost a year at a forward operating base in the mountains and then spent two, one-year stints in Iraq. This guy survived two IEDs but left the Army after the second one because of post-traumatic stress disorder. I don't see any mention of a wife."

The woods on either side of the highway gradually turned to mostly conifers, with a smattering of white birch, whose bright trunks and golden leaves glowed in the sun against the green. "Betcha don't know all those trees out there," I teased Rhe.

"And you do? Really?"

"Ahem. Cedar, balsam, hemlock, juniper, larch, eastern white pine, and black, red and white spruce to name a few."

"How do you remember that?"

"Science fair project in middle school," I replied with a big grin. *Gotcha.*

"Smarty pants." She punched me lightly on the arm.

The highlight of the drive was a stop for coffee, where I also had a banana nut muffin to quell my rumbling stomach. Rhe had brought muffins, but she hadn't followed Paulette's recipe, making some substitutions for ingredients she didn't have on hand. The result reminded me of hockey pucks. Rhe made a brave try at eating them, but even she gave up.

Just before Houlton, we exited 95 and continued north on US 1. Finally the clipped, female British voice I'd chosen for the GPS—because it reminded me of British spy movies—told us to turn at the next right and we found ourselves on a narrow two-lane road. "Look at all the potato fields," said Rhe, always the tour guide. "Did you know Aroostook County is the center of potato agriculture in the state and seventh largest producer in the country?"

I could see she was reading from her phone.

"Potato sales bring in more than two hundred and thirty-three billion dollars to the state economy."

"Okay, teach, can you tell me what kind of potatoes are growing in those fields?"

She placed her hand on her forehead and closed her eyes as if willing the answer to come forth. "Kennebec, no wait, maybe Red Norland or Yukon Gold."

"You're cheating!"

Just then, the GPS warned us of a right turn in one mile. As we made the turn, the Jeep skidded onto a gravel road. "Damn! I'm going to have dings on the Jeep." I slowed us to a glacial pace.

A double wide trailer finally appeared at the end of the road, and I sighed in relief when we finally parked. The engine ticked with heat as we got out. Then I saw it. "Gun!" Throwing myself over the Jeep's hood, I crouched next to Rhe on the passenger side.

"Where?" she asked.

"There's a rifle barrel pointing out the front door…Patterson? John Patterson?" I raised my voice. "I'm Chief of Police Sam Brewster from Pequod. Remember? I called you. I'm here with just my wife. We aren't here to arrest you or anything. We only want to talk. Can you put the rifle down?"

"*Just* your wife?" she hissed.

"I thought maybe he'd stand down if he knew I had a family member with me."

A long moment later, I peeked out and saw the barrel withdraw. Then a thin, balding man in his mid-thirties emerged, opening his hands to show he was unarmed. Rhe and I stood up and walked around the car. I didn't know about Rhe, but my heart rate hadn't returned to normal yet.

Patterson apparently noticed my wife's pregnancy. "I'm so sorry, ma'am. I hope I didn't frighten you. I don't get many visitors out here and sometimes they haven't been so friendly. Chief Brewster is it?" He held out his hand, which I took, if only to calm its shaking.

"That's okay, Mr. Patterson. I understand. Is there somewhere we can talk?"

"Sure, is it all right with you if we sit outside? The inside of my trailer is pretty messy, and I like being outdoors." He led us around to the back of the doublewide where a poured concrete patio sported a teak table and chairs, somewhat worse for wear. Long flower boxes filled with colorful chrysanthemums sat on two sides of the patio. When Rhe commented on them, he explained, "My wife liked flowers and I've tried to keep some in the planters each season."

"Liked?" asked Rhe.

"Yes, Ma'am. She died last year." His angular face drooped with those words.

"I'm so sorry to hear that. It must have been a very difficult time for you and your family," she replied.

"Just me and my brother now."

He pulled out a chair for her so she could sit down. I was already sitting, and she raised an eyebrow at me. *I know, I forget these polite gestures.*

I pulled out my little notebook and a stubby pencil from my pocket—Rhe has been threatening to get me a small recorder, but I'd rather use the notebook. She calls me a Luddite.

"I know you must have heard about the governor being shot," I said, using a deliberately low and calm voice.

"Yeah, I figured it had to be a trained sniper. Is that why you wanted to talk to me?" Patterson frowned.

"Yes, and please don't assume you're under suspicion. We're interviewing many vets in Maine with sniper training, just hoping something will shake lose. Can you tell me where you were on the Sunday the governor got shot?"

"Probably in the fields, helping my brother. He's a potato farmer. All those fields you passed by on the road are his. But I can't be sure. One day is just like the next."

"Can you give me your brother's contact information? Just so I can get him to confirm where you were. Don't take this the wrong way— we just have to cross the t's and dot the i's."

As Patterson gave me the information, I noticed that his leg had started to jiggle up and down. It reminded me of Agent Bowers when we first met him—he'd been a bundle of nervous tics.

"Do you mind if I smoke?" he asked.

"No, go right ahead."

Patterson looked at Rhe, and she nodded. He took a pack of cigarettes from the breast pocket of his work shirt, along with a battered metal lighter with an engraving on it, probably his Army unit. He shook out a cigarette with one hand, grabbed it in his lips and lit it, then closed the lid on the lighter with a flick of his hand. After placing the lighter and cigarettes on the table, he drew in a deep breath and blew the smoke out slowly, aiming it away from us. Then he leaned back, and the leg jerking subsided.

"How are you managing your PTSD?" asked Rhe, leaning over to place her hand on Patterson's arm.

"Sure, that would be in my record, wouldn't it? It can get pretty bad, especially at night. I have nightmares and the sweats. I work myself to exhaustion in the fields because it helps me sleep. And I use a little weed. Hope that's not a problem."

"No, of course not," replied Rhe. "Are you seeing a psychologist or are you part of any support group?"

"I am. We meet once a week, and I can always call one of my brothers if things get bad."

I knew what 'brothers' meant and asked, "Is it helping?"

In response, he tried to smile but it morphed into a grimace. "Yeah, I think, a little. I've only been goin' for a few months."

"Would you mind giving us the name of the group sponsor? It might be a lead."

Patterson thought for a moment. "Okay, I guess, but I won't tell you who else is in the group. That's private."

"No problem," I replied. "Have you remarried?"

That question got another grimace. "No, sir. I had a girlfriend after my wife died." He paused and looked up at the sky, finished his cigarette and lit another one. "Let's just say I didn't make good roommate material. She moved out after a few months."

We didn't stay much longer since it was evident our visit had clearly disturbed Patterson's fragile composure. I gave him my card and told him to call me if he thought of anything.

We were quiet driving away, listening to the dings of the gravel on the underbody of the Jeep. When we reached the main road, I asked Rhe, "See if you can get a signal on your phone and call Patterson's brother. I need confirmation on his whereabouts. So far he looks like a possible shooter."

Several tries later, Rhe finally connected with Patterson's brother, who confirmed they were together in the fields that Sunday. When she finished the call, she said, "I thought he might be our sniper, too. But I wondered what would have triggered him…sorry for the pun… to shoot the governor. He's suffering from PTSD, but why would he blame Hatcher?"

"Who knows? A mind warped by PTSD can make some strange associations. Well, we're onto number three. I'll call the leader of Patterson's support group and see if he has any ideas."

∛ ∛

When we finally arrived home, Rhe and I walked over to the McGillivray's house to get Jack. They lived across the street and just down from our house, and when we came in through the kitchen door, the rich smell of stewing beef filled our noses. I could hear Tyler and Jack whooping it up in the family room.

"What's cooking, Paulette?" I asked, giving her a hug.

"Beef bourguignon. I haven't made it in ages and it just sounded good. You look bushed. So stay and have dinner with us. I made enough for an army." She laughed and then stood away, giving a critical look at Rhe's figure. "Starting to show, kiddo. How do you feel?"

"So-so. Sitting for hours wasn't great. Depending on how far away our next trip will be, I might have to send Sam by himself."

"I hope you're hungry...Sarah?" she called. "Is the table set?"

"Yes, Mom." Sarah, the McGillivray's teen-age daughter, came into the kitchen. Not for the first time, I noticed she'd become an attractive young woman—blonde curls like her mother, but tall and with a teenager's impossibly thin and gangly limbs.

Ted, her father, then appeared. "Long time no see, Sam." He winked.

"What, last night when you borrowed my trimmer?"

Ted was a good friend and an even better father, who had been through the fire of having Sarah kidnapped. Rhe had saved her.

The beef bourguignon, noodles, and vegetables quickly disappeared, while Jack and Tyler regaled us with a recap of the Avenger movie, complete with sound effects. Over pumpkin pie with whipped cream, they started in on their puns, something Jack excelled at.

"Did you hear about the cross-eyed teacher who lost her job because she couldn't control her pupils?" asked Tyler.

"This girl said she recognized me from the vegetarian club, but I'd never met herbivore."

Silence. "Get it?" asked Jack.

Finally some groans from the adults, and Rhe said, "I think that's enough for tonight, boys. If you're finished, take your plates to the kitchen."

They left noisily, followed by a clank of dishes in the sink and the sound of a video game beginning in the family room. In response to a question from Ted, Rhe recounted our trip and the lasting effects of the war in the Middle East on Lieutenant Patterson. "It's such a shame he has PTSD," she said at the end.

"Will he recover?" asked Sarah.

"Sadly, no. His nervousness and nightmares may ease, but I suspect he'll always struggle," replied Rhe.

Paulette, who had become enthralled with sleuthing during some of Rhe's past adventures, asked me, "Sam, what if I go with you next time? If the ride is too long for Rhe…"

"Other than the fact you're a civilian and have no training in firearms, plus I have no idea what to expect from these men, sure. What do you think, Ted?" I asked.

"Knowing my wife, she'd find trouble. I think you'll be safer with Rhe."

Paulette pouted, then smiled.

She'll insert herself into this somehow.

Chapter 9

RHE

The following morning at breakfast I had an idea. "Sam, we're looking for a sniper. What is the one thing a sniper needs to do to keep his talent honed?"

"I dunno—hunt?" He was busily slurping down the milk in the bottom of his cereal bowl while checking his text messages—totally distracted.

"But hunting doesn't guarantee you a long-range target and you have limited hunting seasons. Think!"

He looked up from his phone. "Practice at a range?"

"Exactly."

"But I can't think of any places in this area where he could practice on a one thousand or two thousand foot range, Rhe. There can't be many of those."

"How about I do a little research on that today?"

"Fine with me," Sam replied, pushing back his chair and standing up with his legs on either side of the chair.

Cowboy move.

"A thousand yards, that's a long way, right Dad?" asked Jack, mimicking Sam as he got up and following him to the sink with his cereal bowl.

"A little over half a mile, kiddo. Brushed your teeth?"

"Going right now."

"Got your stuff ready for school?"

"Yes, sir. Are you or Mom taking me?"

"It's Tuesday, remember? As soon as you've brushed your teeth, head on over to Tyler's," Sam replied.

I had no shift on Tuesdays and Thursdays, and Paulette had volunteered to take Jack with Tyler and Sarah to school those days. We took Tyler and Sarah on the others.

Sam kissed the top of my head and then leaned over and gently rubbed my stomach with one large hand. "Have a good day and take care of the Bump."

"She'll have a name soon!"

"It's a he."

"You wish!"

Smiling, he headed out to his Jeep. A few moments later, Jack tore through the kitchen, grabbed his backpack and went for the door.

"Jacket, bud. It's chilly today!"

"Aw. Mom." But he took his lined windbreaker from the peg by the door before he left. Good-bye kisses had gone the way of the dinosaurs.

I leaned back and sighed. Three things I needed to do—research the shooting ranges, read over the info on our next sniper candidate, and plot our Saturday safari. Then I absolutely had to view the video from the hidden camera from the past few days. Oh, and clean up the kitchen, which looked like entropy had taken over.

☙   ☙

An hour later, I knew checking out long range practice sites would not be a problem. Most shooting ranges in Maine were listed at twenty to thirty yards, including the one right outside of Pequod where I'd learned to shoot. The only one with the distance we'd been talking about was on Mount Katadhin. I made a note of its address and its operating hours, then pulled out the file on the next sniper, our last on the list.

Kenneth Craig had been a Special Forces operator, trained at Fort Bragg. In his early forties now, he'd done the full twenty before mustering out and lived the closest to us, distance-wise, of all the men we'd been assigned—in Lewiston, only about fifty miles away. He was married, had no kids, and worked as a salesman at a local Jeep dealership. This should please Sam.

I made myself a tuna sandwich for lunch and took some lamb chops out of the freezer to thaw for dinner, then called Nancy Ennis to see if any further drug thefts had occurred.

"Funny you should ask that," she replied. "We had another one, last night."

"How much is missing?"

"The usual. Same amount as the last two and not enough to affect ER operations until we can re-order."

"Interesting. The thief is considerate. Okay, I'll check the video now. Can you give me an approximate time, so I don't go blind trying to find something?" I chuckled.

"After our shift yesterday, for sure."

"One other thing. Has anyone from hospital security come around investigating this?"

"Yesterday the head of security finally showed up and asked a ton of questions. He seemed clueless but was impressed we'd placed a camera. He wants to see the footage."

"I'll bet he's happy. We're doing his job for him. I'll let you know what I find."

Sam had asked Phil, the police department's computer guru, to install an Android 5 lollipop program on my computer so I could download the video from the cloud. This technology was so far beyond me that he had to walk me through how to do it, and I pulled out my notes from his instructions. I spent ten minutes bumbling around before finally retrieving the footage from the previous night. After a half hour of watching nurses and patients walk by, with brief stops by nurses and MDs to take out drugs and note their sign-outs on the computer, my eyes were drooping. I sped it up until it appeared like an old time movie with people flashing in and out. However, no one stopped at the cabinet for anything longer than what I thought would be a normal amount of time nor did anyone walk away with a bag or loaded pockets. I didn't think scrubs had much pocket room for more than a few small bottles or vials of drugs, anyway. I yawned. Maybe I needed to time myself taking drugs out of that cabinet. And when would the cabinet with the programmable lock finally arrive?

I needed to make a trip to the ER.

ଔ   ଔ

Lyle grinned at me when I came through the loading dock door. "You're not supposed ta be working today."

"You know my schedule?"

"Yeah, and just about everyone's 'cept for that ER nurse who comes and goes at all hours."

"How about I give you my cell phone number and you call me the next time she comes in. Maybe I can track her down."

Lyle wrote the information down carefully with a serious look. I thought he secretly liked being included in an investigation.

In the ER, I greeted the nurses at the main station. "Don't pay any attention to me, I'm just checking the drug cabinet contents for the CEO." There were no blank stares, so they clearly knew we were investigating the drug thefts. I hoped they didn't know about the camera.

I'd worn my scrubs so I could figure out how many vials and pill bottles could be hidden in my pockets. Signing out the keys from the main desk, I asked the charge nurse to time me on her watch starting as I opened the cabinet with the key. I stuffed as many vials and bottles as possible in my pockets, then closed and locked the cabinet.

"How long?" I asked.

"Twenty-five seconds," she replied.

Not long at all. Returning everything I'd removed from the cabinet, I saw that I'd taken quite a lot, but not as much as our thief.

Then I asked the charge nurse if I could time her removing one item from the cabinet, by way of comparison.

"What drug do you want me to take? I'll have to search for it," she asked.

Of course! I didn't think of that. Not everyone would be as familiar with the layout of the cabinet as I. "How about oxycodone?" I gave her the key and timed her as she had timed me. Our average time was ten seconds, including unlocking and locking the cabinet. We then timed each other again, removing two different drugs this time: fifteen seconds.

After ensuring that we'd replaced all the drugs and giving back the key, I left the ER thinking it might be hard to pick out someone spending more than the normal time at the drug cabinet, even if I timed it. If a nurse didn't know where the drug could be found, the search could take more than fifteen seconds. Maybe I needed to note how many times the same person visited the cabinet and the times they did so. The thief might have made several visits. I really dreaded having to watch all that footage again.

CB   CB

On my way home, I got a call from the forensics lab about Naomi Parkin's rape kit, since as a part-time investigator with the police department, this was my case. So I drove to the PD's parking lot and walked down the street. Looking around, I thought it was way past time for a new, larger building to house the police and the lab. Sam planned to present a proposal to the city council and the mayor at the next meeting, and I hoped he could persuade them.

The forensics lab had been created in an old warehouse, Pequod having originally been a fishing port. At that time, warehouses were needed to store, process and sell the catches fishermen brought in. I imagined I smelled herring when I stepped inside. The receptionist at the front desk asked how she could direct me. Having a receptionist was new and told me Kit Moncton had already made changes. "I'm Rhe Brewster. I need to see Dr. Moncton, please," and I flashed my police badge.

Her face furrowed in confusion seeing me in scrubs, but she picked up the phone and dialed, announcing my name when she got through. A moment later, Moncton emerged from a door behind her. He looked just as Sam had described him, compactly built and neat with soft brown eyes.

"Mrs. Brewster, so nice to meet you. I didn't have the pleasure when I came to Pequod for my interviews. And please call me Kit."

I shook his proffered hand and smiled back. "And I'm Rhe. I've heard a lot about you…all of it good. And just look at this place! You've made it very professional."

"Thank you," he replied quietly. "Why don't you come back to my office and I'll tell you what we found from the Parkins rape kit."

We went through the same door he'd used, into a short corridor with an office on each side, leading back to the lab. His office opened on the right, just before the glass doors to the lab.

Once we sat, he opened a file on his desk. "I'll get right to the point. Unfortunately, we found no semen on the swabs from her vaginal canal, just evidence the man used a condom."

My face must have given away my disappointment.

"All is not lost. We identified powered particulates, lubricant and spermicide, all of which can be linked to a certain type of condom. Examining past rape cases for this evidence may give us a link to the perpetrator. If an identified rapist has used this type of condom before, he can be brought in for a victim ID. Did Ms. Parkins describe him?"

"She did, and I've asked her to come in and work with our artist. I'll see if there's any information about the type of condom used in previous rape cases.

"By the way, I do hope you're planning on being at the town council meeting where Sam's going to ask for a new building for the police station and lab. He could use your support and maybe you could say something to the council?"

Kit laughed. "The department's building is straight out of the 1960s and this one dates to 1906. Who could possibly deny his request? Tell Sam I'll be there, and I'll have facts and figures to back up the need for a new lab."

"Wonderful, Kit. And how is your partner's bakery coming along? I noticed renovations to one of the empty commercial spaces on Water Street. Is that him?"

Kit beamed. "It is! He hopes to open next month and I can guarantee he'll have people coming from all over for what he creates."

I put my hand on my stomach and smiled. "Just what I need—a few more pounds."

ᚖ   ᚖ

I stopped in at the station to see if Naomi Parkins had come in to work with Deputy Birch on a sketch of her rapist. Birch told me she would be in the next day. Before I could finally head home, I got a call from Lyle.

"She's here," he whispered conspiratorially. "I follered her to the elevator. She went to the fifth floor."

Another one of Dr. Manning's dalliances? No time like the present. "I'm driving back to the hospital right now, Lyle. Let me know if she leaves before I get there."

ᚖ   ᚖ

I spoiled my boys with dinner that night with grilled lamb chops, one of their favorite dishes, along with garlicky green beans and a salad. Both Jack and Sam would eat salad as long as it had ranch dressing all over it. While we ate, I baked some apples stuffed with dried cranberries, sugar and cinnamon for dessert.

After we had finished eating and clearing the table, I sent Jack to the family room to finish his homework, then whispered to Sam, "Have I got news for you! Can you make us some decaf coffee?"

He wrinkled his nose but brewed a pot. By the time we had our mugs on the kitchen table, Jack had completed his assignments and was now engrossed in a video game, so we could talk, but quietly.

"Well, what's this exciting news? Did you identify the rapist?"

"No, but in terms of salacious value, this is much better." I paused to glance into the family room, making sure Jack's antennae were in OFF mode. "You know that new ER nurse that no one's seen?"

"Yeah, the one whose credentials you looked up."

"Well, I told Lyle to call me when she came in because her visits are irregular. He called me right after I met with Kit about the Parkins rape—no DNA in case you're wondering—so I went back to the hospital and up to the fifth floor, you know, where the Pecker has his office. His secretary had gone home, so I pretended to write a note at her desk in case someone popped in. When everything stayed quiet, I went to the Pecker's door and listened, thinking I needed a glass…" I smiled.

"And?" He leaned across the table in anticipation.

"Turns out I didn't need the glass," I whispered. "That was no massage I heard. It sounded like the track from a porn movie."

"You sure it wasn't?" he asked with a grin.

"Not unless the Pecker starred! I waited in the shadows down the hall from Manning's suite until the 'nurse'"…I used quotation marks…"left the office, stuffing a wad of something into her bra. Then I followed her out to the parking lot."

"Did you find out where she went from there?"

"Nah, I had what I needed, and besides, you guys were waiting on dinner. She drives a white Beemer, though, a late model sedan."

"Did you get a license plate number?"

I shook my head. "She parked in an unlighted spot way in the back."

Sam thought for a moment. "She must make good money to have a car like that, so probably an elite escort. What are you planning to do with this?"

"Nothing for the time being. It's just an ace in my pocket. Maybe I can follow her home the next time, so I can find out who she really is. Lyle says he'll call me when she comes for her next 'visit'."

Just then, Jack came into the kitchen. "Who's visiting?"

"Nothing, Big Ears," we said at the same time.

Chapter 10

SAM

We scheduled our last interview with a potential sniper for Saturday, and Rhe and I left early for Lewiston to meet with Kenneth Craig, the Special Forces operator. We'd called ahead to let him know we were coming. I wore my dress uniform and I have to admit my wife looked maternal and blooming in a blue wool coat, which fastened over the baby bump and brought out the blue in her eyes.

Somewhat to our surprise, Craig lived in a new, glass-walled, high-rise apartment building on a bank of the Androscoggin River, with a view of the Great Falls. The building projected dollar signs. We parked down the street and stopped to admire the river, with brilliant foliage on either side now at its peak.

At the door to the apartment building, we had to buzz in. In response to my rather insistent button-pushing, a deep, artificially cultured voice came from the speaker mounted over the door. "May I help you?"

"I'm Chief of Police Sam Brewster of the Pequod Police Department. I'm here to meet Mr. Craig. He's been informed we were coming this morning," I answered in an equally deep voice. Rhe raised her eyebrows at me in surprise. I whispered, "I can be cultured, too."

"Mr. Craig said nothing to me of an appointment, but in any event, he's not here this morning. I believe he's at work. You can find him there."

Dismissed. I turned to Rhe. "Do we have his work address?"

"Yup, we can just plug it into our GPS. No problem."

Fifteen minutes later, after following directions that seemed to take us on a tour of Lewiston, we arrived at a Jeep dealership. I parked mine in a spot at the front of the lot, where acres of various Jeep models sat shining in the sunlight. I wondered if they had employees tasked with polishing those cars every day. I'd love to have one polish mine. Maybe my Jeep could chat with its neighbors about being a police car…

We entered the big glass double doors, stepping onto a plush red carpet. "I can imagine the poor cleaning crew having to scrub this rug everyday of mud and dirt from the parking lot," whispered Rhe, looking down.

I looked behind me to see if I had tracked anything in on my boots. When I turned back, a young man in a loud, brown-checked sports coat approached with his hand extended.

"Welcome to Craig Jeeps. What are you in the mind for today? A new car? Used?"

Before he got any further and without shaking his hand, I showed him my badge. "I'm here to see Mr. Craig. Where can I find him?"

"Oh…well, let me see if he's free right now."

"We're not here to wait. We had an appointment with him at his residence this morning, which he seems to have forgotten."

He turned on his heel and trotted off toward a desk staffed by a person I presumed to be the receptionist. Rhe wandered off to look at some of the Jeeps on the showroom. It was way past time for her to trade in her ancient Jeep, affectionately called Miss Daisy. As the old gal slowly fell apart, we had her in for repairs more often than not. I held out hope a new Jeep would eventually catch Rhe's eye, just not today.

The salesman came back. "Right this way."

Rhe broke off from admiring a shiny, bright red Jeep Wrangler and followed me toward the back of the showroom, where we were met by the receptionist. A tall blond, who towered even higher in five inch stiletto heels, said, without introduction, "Follow me."

Which I assuredly did, admiring her shapely bottom in a skintight, short blue dress. A cloud of her perfume drifted back and surrounded us. Rhe poked me in the ribs and flapped her hand in front of her face to dispel the fumes. The receptionist teetered down a long, carpeted hallway which had glass-doored offices on each side and terminated at a huge double wooden door. She opened it and waved us in, like an assistant on a game show.

A muscular, barrel-chested man rose from behind his enormous desk. He looked every inch the salesman, nicely tanned and with wavy hair bleached by the sun or something else. He came around the desk and held out his hand. "Kenny Craig. Nice to meet you, Chief Brewster. And this is…?"

"My wife, Rhe. She's an investigator with my department."

His eyebrows rose, but he recovered quickly enough. "What can I do you for?"

I was a little surprised at his question, since we'd already talked about what he 'could do me for.' "Well, it would have been nice if we hadn't had to chase you down at your business. I understood we were to meet at your home, today being Saturday." Rhe gave me another poke in my already poked ribs.

"About that, I'm sorry. Something came up this morning and I had to be here. I should have called you or left a message. In any event, let's sit down." He smiled and gestured toward an area on one side of the large room, defined by what appeared to be a Persian rug, where two white leather sofas faced each other. A coffee table separated them. "Do you want some coffee?"

"That would be very nice, but decaf for me," replied Rhe, trying to alleviate any tension.

"That's easily arranged." Before he joined us, Craig pushed a button on his desk. "Christina, two coffees, one decaf, and some of those muffins I like."

When we had removed our coats and settled on one of the couches, with Craig sitting opposite us, I got to the point. "Mr. Craig…"

"Call me Kenny, please."

"Kenny, then. You must know about the sniper attack on the governor three weeks ago. A shot from that distance could only have been made by someone highly trained. We know you're a qualified sniper…" He started to say something, but I held up my hand to stop him. "We have absolutely no reason to believe you're the assailant, but we're here at the behest of the lieutenant governor to see if you might know someone who has a grudge serious enough to warrant killing Mr. Hatcher."

At that moment, the gorgeous woman in the tight dress strutted in, balancing a tray with cream, sugar, a plate of muffins, and three mugs with steaming contents. She set the tray down carefully on the coffee table, bending over so I could appreciate her assets. I began salivating. For the muffins. She indicated the cup of decaf and then left, closing the door behind her silently but leaving her perfume behind. Kenny took a muffin and leaned back, spreading his legs in a posture of utter relaxation.

"I can tell you truthfully I had nothing to do with that attack," he said after a bite that took half the muffin. "I only used my sniper training in the Army, and I haven't pulled the trigger on a rifle or any other firearm since. Please help yourself." He gestured toward the tray, and Rhe took her coffee, adding cream and sugar.

I extended a hand to the muffins, but after a glare from Rhe, redirected it to pick up my cup. My eyes stayed on the muffins, however, in the hope I could snag one as we were leaving. "Do you know of any men or women who are sniper-trained and who might bear the governor a grudge?"

"No, I don't, but as you can imagine, a lot of my customers own guns and hunt, so I can ask around. May I ask how you became involved in trying to find the shooter?"

"We're the ones who dragged the governor to safety. Perhaps you've read about it," Rhe answered.

"That was you? Really? Then you have more composure under fire than I would have had. I recall that more shots followed the one that hit him." He leaned forward, now clearly interested in what we had to say. "How many shots were fired? Where did the sniper fire from?"

"I can't tell you more than what's been publicly reported," I said. "Ongoing investigation. But the sniper made a pretty spectacular shot from across the Kennebec River, from the second floor of a house on the bank."

"So that would be…?"

"Two thousand yards, more or less."

Craig whistled. "Well, whoever it was, he would need something like a .338 Xtreme Tactical to make that distance these days. I'll definitely ask around for you."

"A .338 Xtreme Tactical? I haven't heard of that model."

"It was introduced in 2008."

I took my notebook and pencil stub from the breast pocket of my uniform and wrote the information down. "If I can give you a word of advice, Kenny, you should be careful asking questions. I'm sure this person doesn't want to be identified and you might put yourself in danger if you get too close."

"I'll take that advice, Chief. Have you visited the shooting range at Mount Katahdin? I know from a customer that they have the only long range course for target shooting in the state."

"That's our next stop."

"Well, if there's nothing else…" Craig rose from the sofa. "I'd love to chat, but I do have some work to do. Saturday is usually our busiest day."

"Of course," replied Rhe, putting down her coffee cup and standing. I stood and shook Craig's hand, and when Rhe had turned toward the door, winked at him and took a muffin, covering it with a napkin.

ڃ   ړ

When we were back in my Jeep, I saw Rhe glance at the napkin I had placed on the floor next to the console. Before she could comment, I asked, "Could you check on something for me on your phone? I need to know when Craig left the service."

Rhe checked the file she'd brought. "2007."

"So if the model was new in 2008, he either has a passionate interest in everything sniper rifle, or he's lying to us about not picking up a gun since he left the service."

"Pretty thin evidence, Holmes."

"Agreed. Where to now?" I eyed the napkin next to my right foot.

"Well, that shooting range is about two hundred miles away. Do you really want to spend all day on the road? And what's in that napkin?"

"Nah, let's head home. We can make a day of it when we go there, bring our guns and do some target shooting."

Rhe reached over the console and grabbed the napkin, revealing the muffin. "Oh, goodie. I'm starved." She peeled the paper off and took a bite which nearly consumed the whole thing. At least she offered me the rest.

؃   ؒ

We had the shock of our lives when we turned onto our street. "Is that a 'For Sale' sign?" Rhe asked. "I didn't know our neighbors were selling."

We got closer. "No, that sign is on our property. What the hell?" We turned into our driveway, got out of the Jeep and approached the sign. "Looks real to me. I've gotta check with that realtor." I had a sinking feeling in the pit of my stomach and Rhe's face had blanched.

"He's at it again, isn't he, Sam?"

I nodded. "Why don't we pick up Jack at Paulette's and see if she saw anything?"

Paulette already stood at her back door, holding it open for us by the time we got to her porch. "What's going on?" she asked, ushering us in. "I know you're not selling your house."

"I wish I knew, hon," replied Rhe. "Did you see anybody outside our house today?"

"Oh, I definitely did." She waved us toward her large kitchen table and we sat down, putting our coats over the backs of the chairs. "Had lunch?"

"Only if you count less than half a muffin," I replied.

"I've got some ham, leek and potato soup I made this morning.

Let me dish you up." She got out some large soup bowls, ladled in the soup and brought them to the table.

"So what did you see?" Rhe clearly wouldn't eat a spoonful until she heard more.

I dug in without waiting for Paulette to answer, but not before inhaling the soup's hearty aroma.

The cook paused for dramatic effect, and Rhe flapped her hand — get on with it. "Okay, a little after ten this car pulls up and two people get out, a woman dressed in a business suit and totally unsuitable heels, and a guy with a camera. They walked all around your house, including the back yard, taking pictures. While they were doing that, another car drove up, a green Lexus that looked new. The man who got out was medium height and wore a light weight tan jacket, black pants, tan baseball cap with the brim pulled down over his face, and dark glasses. He scanned the neighborhood and then approached the woman. I couldn't get a look at his face because he faced away from me, and he turned too quickly while looking around. I think his hair might have been blond."

"You're better than a camera, Paulette," I said.

Paulette beamed, continuing, "This man and the woman I presumed to be a real estate agent had a fairly vigorous conversation, with her pointing to the house and him shaking his head. I'm betting he was the seller, and she asked to get inside to take pictures. He must have put her off for the time being because they shook hands and he drove off. Then the agent took a 'For Sale' sign out of her trunk and drove it into your lawn yard with a mallet, before leaving with the photographer. This is your stalker, isn't it?"

Rhe started eating, and I answered. "I'm sure of it. You wouldn't have gotten that guy's license plate, by any chance?"

Paulette got up and retrieved her phone from the counter. "Sending you a picture of it right now, along with one of the man driving it. You can't really see him, though."

Rhe paused, spoon halfway to her mouth, and smiled. "Paulette, the super sleuth."

ڃ   ڃ

When we got home, I called the realtor. We had an unpleasant conversation, made even more so by the raspy tone of her voice.

"Is this Betty Williams?"

"Yes, how can I help you?"

"This is Sam Brewster, Chief of Police for Pequod. You put a 'For Sale' sign on my front lawn this morning."

"I'm sorry, Chief Brewster, did you say *your* front lawn?"

"Yes, *my* front lawn."

"You must be mistaken. That house is owned by a Mr. Jackson Spratt. I met him there this morning."

"But he didn't let you photograph the inside of the house, did he?"

"No, he said he didn't bring his key."

"He didn't bring the key because he doesn't have one. It's *not his house*. My wife and I have lived there for two years and she lived there with my deceased brother for ten years before that."

"Well, I'm sorry to tell you I have the title to the property and a deed of ownership with Mr. Spratt's name on both, right in front of me."

"Then I believe you are in for a lot of trouble. This Jackson Spratt is obviously an alias —Jack Spratt, get it?—and he's undoubtedly the man who's been stalking me and my wife for the past several months. Somehow he's managed to steal our house. In my official capacity as Chief of Police, I am asking you to delay putting the house on the market until I can get this straightened out. Legally."

Silence stretched out for a long moment. Then, "How do I know you're the Chief of Police?"

"I'll call on you at your office this afternoon and bring my credentials and the whole damned police department if I have to."

"You don't need to get testy, sir. I'll wait here for you. But make it snappy."

I hung up the house phone and slammed it on the counter. Then picked it up again and called Phil Pearce. Without even greeting him, I asked, "How can someone steal a house?"

"Chief? Whose house? Yours?"

"Yes, dammit. That creep who's been making trouble for us has apparently done it again. There is a frigging 'For Sale' sign in our front yard."

I heard some computer keys clicking. 'Well, he's already stolen Rhe's identity so all he needs to do is record a forged deed giving him ownership of her property. Is the deed to the house in Rhe's name only?"

"Yes, it became hers when my brother died."

"Okay, then it should be easy. You've probably forgotten that deeds are public records, so anyone can go online and print the recorded deed to your house, then forge a deed and signature showing her sale of the house to him. Do you have title insurance? You should have been alerted by the insurance company."

"I got a message from an insurance company on my phone today but I ignored it. I thought they were trying to sell me something."

"That would have been the alert."

I groaned. "Now what happens?"

"Now that this guy owns the house, at least on paper, he can sell or borrow against the property. He's clearly trying to sell it and this real estate agent is so eager to make a sale that she hasn't bothered to check the credit reports, employment and income verifications, back tax returns, appraisals, and title insurance, which are all in Rhe's name."

I pounded the kitchen counter a few times but didn't feel any better. "I'm going to need a lawyer."

Phil replied, "I think you do. I can recommend one if you like."

I took out my pad and pencil and wrote down the information. "Two more things, Phil. I need you to run a license plate." I gave him the number Paulette had provided. "It may be a rental car, but maybe we can nail him when he turns it in, so issue a BOLO.

And then, if you would do me another favor, I need you to come with me in dress uniform to the real estate agent's office. When I called, she questioned if I was really the Chief of Police."

Chapter 11

RHE

The stalker's latest gambit stunned me. Clearly he had now upped the ante.

Sam returned from the Realtor's office confident he'd convinced her he *was* the chief of police, and, as result, she'd agreed to pull the listing. After letting me know, he went back to the front yard and pulled up the 'For Sale' sign. Then he tried, without luck, to break the post over his knee, resulting in a large bruise. Meanwhile, the gastric reflux I'd experienced with my previous two pregnancies returned with a vengeance, and I ate TUMS like popcorn. We were still on edge Monday morning, when Sam left for an appointment with the lawyer Phil had recommended. I headed to the hospital after carpooling Tyler and Jack.

When I arrived in the ER, the Pecker was once again on the floor, and many of the nurses and other personnel had found work out of his line of sight. Something was definitely up.

"There you are!" he shouted, his face almost as red as his hair. "You're late."

In fact, I'd come early, but the truth never mattered to our CEO when he was angry. I arranged my face into the most sincere, fake smile I could manage. I'd had lots of practice. "What seems to be the problem? I'm not the charge nurse." I looked at Nancy Ennis, who stared at the floor, apparently in the hope it might swallow her.

"Don't you think I know that? I would never put you in charge of a shift. You can't be trusted." He raged on. "Have you figured out yet how drugs are being stolen from the ER? I think not because another theft occurred last night. Even after the installation of the keyless cabinet. Care to explain how that happened?"

I continued smiling at him, a real smile because I knew it punched his buttons. "No, sir, I don't know how that happened, since I wasn't there. But I would be happy to enlighten you on what I *am* doing to find the thief. I just think it should be done in a less public place."

"Why would you think that?"

I tilted my head at everyone looking at us.

He seemed on the verge of yelling again, when half a dozen beats later, he finally got it. "Okay, let's go to my office."

After a grimly silent ride upstairs in the elevator, he marched in front of me to his office and opened the door, which he didn't bother to hold open after he walked through. "Well? What do you have to say?"

I had relaxed my aching smile muscles in the elevator but forced them into use again. "I have installed a camera from the police department with a view of the cabinet. I haven't had time to review the video footage since Friday. When did the theft occur?"

"Last night some time. A camera from the police department? Are we paying for it?"

"No, sir, it's a loaner. Also Deputy Chief Pearce will help me review the tapes."

"Obviously you haven't been productive with this line of investigation so far."

"Not yet, but we're working on a theory." I relaxed my face. I can only hold a fake smile for so long with him.

"And what exactly would that be?"

"The one thing we do know is the thief is not an outsider. It's an employee who signs in. Or perhaps it's the nurse who visits you here regularly, according to the logs I've reviewed."

Manning had the decency to flush, an ugly purple-red. "I can vouch for her. She's, ah, a consultant with my department."

Yeah, right, and my mother's a horse.

"So," he said, "it's definitely an inside job…I suspected as much. What are you doing going forward?" He squinted at me, making his pig-like eyes even smaller.

"If necessary, Deputy Chief Pearce can use facial recognition to identify who takes drugs from the cabinet and at what times."

Silence. Then, "Fine. You can return to the ER, but I am the first one you notify when you've identified the thief. Understood?"

൰ ൰

When I returned to the ER, Nancy stood at the triage desk, waiting for me. I think the Pecker invasions had taken a toll on her. I could see bruise-like bags under her eyes.

"I'm so sorry, Rhe. I tried to call you when he first showed up, but my hands shook so badly I couldn't punch in your number. These thefts have had a terrible effect on my nerves, and this morning it was almost the last straw. I've got a terrible migraine and need to go home. Can you run this shift?"

I laughed. "Right after our beloved CEO said he wouldn't trust me to do it? I'm in." When I put an arm around her shoulders, their feel reminded me of how frail and thin she'd become in the last month. Not many people can withstand Manning's overbearing personality, and she'd borne the brunt of it longer than most. "Go get some rest, and don't worry about the ER. I'll review the video tonight and hopefully we'll have an answer soon. Take your migraine meds and sleep." Nancy had had migraines since I'd first known her, but they'd become more frequent lately and I cursed Manning for his effect on her.

Toward the end of a more or less uneventful shift, someone appeared whom I hadn't expected to see—Naomi Parkins. She'd apparently waited patiently with the other people who'd walked through our doors for their health care, and when her turn came, she asked specifically for me. When she came in, I saw a girl vastly changed from the last time I'd seen her in the ER: thin, haggard, and looking around nervously.

"Naomi, what's wrong? What can I do for you?"

She started shaking and tears filled her eyes. "I just need to talk with you. I think I need help."

I took her to a cubicle, drew the curtain and we both sat on the bed, facing each other. "Tell me what's going on, Naomi."

She took a deep breath. "I can't sleep, I have nightmares about the…you know… the rape. Sometimes the memories come when I'm doing ordinary things, liking walking on campus, and I can't catch my breath. Those memories also give me headaches. I can't seem to focus on anything, and I'm so frightened that I made my brother change all the locks on our doors. The worst is I can't tell my father because he'd blame me."

I took her hands in mine. "What you're experiencing can be normal for someone who's been raped. You're having your own version of PTSD—you know what that is?"

"Yes."

"Did you call the Rape Crisis Center on campus? I gave you their number."

"My brother didn't think I would need it. I think he doesn't want anyone knowing what happened. So I sort of lost the number."

My hackles went up. *What would her brother know about being raped?* "Your brother is not a physician and shouldn't be giving you advice in this situation. You need to contact the people who run the center. They'll set you up with a professional who can help you and everything you say to this professional will be confidential. You need to do this for yourself, Naomi. Understand?"

Tears overflowed her beautiful dark eyes, and she nodded.

"Here's the number for the Rape Crisis Center." I wrote it on a scrap of paper I found in my pocket. "You need to call and go there today. Can you do it?"

She nodded again, then took a deep, shaky breath. "Thank you, Mrs. Brewster. I can and I will. Were you able to identify the rapist from the drawing Deputy Birch made?"

I'd forgotten all about it. "Not yet. You'll be the first to know when we do."

Naomi stood, smoothed down her coat, and finally gave me a wan smile. "Thanks again. I'm going to call the Rape Crisis Center as soon as I get home."

I squeezed her shoulder and, as I watched her leave, I felt guilty that I'd forgotten about the sketch.

☃   ☃

I thought about both Nancy and Naomi as I drove to the police department after my shift. Both suffering from harassment, both showing signs of PTSD. I wondered what I could do about Nancy. *Find the thief!*

Entering through the front door, I called a hello to Feather, who occupied Ruthie's chair that day. Her dress—some sort of kaften in tie-dyed turquoise and yellow—made her hard to miss. Then I walked down the hall to check in on Sam, wondering if he'd calmed down. From the increased height of folders and papers on his desk, he had plenty to distract him. "Hi, sweetie." I carefully picked up the stuff sitting on the chair next to his desk, deposited it on the floor without dumping it, and sat down, examining his face for clues. He appeared calm on the outside, yet I saw some anger in the lines around his eyes.

But he did smile. "To what do I owe the honor of your visit?"

"I need to look at the sketch of Naomi Parkins' rapist, the one Deputy Birch drew. Naomi came into the ER today to see me. She's not doing well, Sam. In my professional opinion, she's suffering from PTSD, and her brother told her *not* to call or visit the Rape Crisis Counseling Center. He's afraid it will shame the family or their community."

"So what did you tell her?" His forehead wrinkled in concern.

"To visit the center, to not wait and to *not* consult with her brother."

"Why don't I get Birch to come here with the sketch and we can both look at it." He picked up the phone, consulted the list taped down next to it, punched in a number and asked the deputy to come to his office.

My husband, the Luddite, found a number and called it? Must be Feather. She probably didn't baby him, like Ruthie did.

Deputy Birch arrived, breathless, three sketches in hand. "Here it is, Chief. I brought two other sketches along for comparison." She carefully lay them side by side on the top of Sam's desk, trying not to dislodge anything under them. Then she stood back. "Do you see what I see?"

Sam and I both stood and hovered over his desk, looking from one sketch to the other. "Sam, the sketches all look like the same person."

"Which is the sketch of the rapist?" Sam asked.

"There on the left. The other two are of your stalker."

"You're right, Rhe, they could all be the same person."

"Let's have Paulette take a look," I said. Taking out my phone, I snapped a picture of the rapist sketch and sent it to Paulette with the subject: Do you recognize this man?

We had our answer in a moment: *I think it's the guy who tried to sell your house.*

Sam shook his head and sat down. "Good get, Deputy Birch. Thank you."

Birch beamed her lovely smile and left.

"You made her day, Sam."

"Yeah, and this just made our case infinitely more convoluted."

I sat. "I don't see how these two crimes are connected. Do you?"

Sam shook his head. "Only that this is one very nasty and very smart guy. Do you mind if we wait to discuss this until after dinner? I have a pile of work to catch up on." He waved his hand over the papers on his desk, maybe hoping he could make it disappear.

"No problem. I need to talk to Phil. I had another run-in with Manning today. He was in the ER when I arrived and beating on Nancy verbally because of another drug theft last night. I have to review the video from last night and another pair of eyes could help.

What if Phil joins us for dinner? Then we can both view the video afterward."

"Sure. What's on the menu, chef?"

"Let me surprise you."

"Then, please, *no* fish."

෨ ෮

After bringing Phil up to date on the latest theft and inviting him for dinner, I was rewarded by a luminous beam on his homely face. Then I headed to the Hannaford store for something quick but tasty. Having recently purchased one of those 'instant' electric pots that cooks meat quickly, I decided to make turkey meatballs marinara with spiralized zucchini. *Not pasta but good enough.*

The meatballs had just finished cooking, the marinara sauce bubbled on the stove and the spiral zucchini was al dente when Sam came in the door from the garage. After taking off his coat, he wrapped his arms around me from the back, kissed my neck, and asked, "What smells so good?"

"Meatballs marinara." I'd ask him later if he could tell they were turkey. Jack sat at the kitchen table, scowling at his math homework. A look of relief came over his face when the doorbell rang.

"I'll get it, Mom."

"No, you clear your stuff off the table. Sam, could you get that? It's Phil."

Jack started to put his math pages in his backpack.

"Not so fast, kiddo, you still have to finish it after dinner."

"Aw, Mom, don't chirp at me."

"What? What is chirp?"

Jack's cheeks turned pink. "Ah, you know, don't hassle me."

I smiled. "And where did you learn that?"

"Sarah says that all the time to her mother."

"And Paulette is okay with that?"

"Not exactly…"

Sam came back from the front door with Phil in tow, announcing, "The gang's all here!"

"Hi, Phil, help yourself to some wine." I pointed to the glasses and wine bottle on the counter. "And Jack, help your dad set the table. I'm chirping at you."

⅋ ⅋

After dinner—where the only complaint was the spiralized zucchini instead of noodles—Jack returned to the table with his homework while Sam cleaned up the kitchen. He said he'd try to help with the math. Phil, who'd had two servings of the meatballs and probably would've eaten more if we'd had it, sat on the sofa in the family room with me, coffee in hand. Phil preferred decaf, thank heavens. He called up the previous night's video, beginning twenty minutes before the four pm to midnight shift. The last person to go to the drug cabinet before the shift began was Nancy. We watched, in sped-up time, the usual back and forth of the various nurses to the cabinet, from the beginning of the video to the end. Nothing unusual.

I leaned back in my chair. "Damn, Phil, what the heck is going on? No one took more than a normal amount of drugs."

Phil sat up straight, his eyes widened at some recognition. "I'm not so sure. Go back to the start of the video, at the end of the day shift."

I backed it up until we again saw Nancy at the drug cabinet.

"She's taking a longer time to remove the drugs than the other nurses," Phil commented. "What did you tell me from your experiment? Twenty-five seconds to remove a good load? Let's time it."

Twenty-four seconds. *Damn.*

"Notice she's trying to keep her back to the camera. And why, if it's the very end of the shift, would she be getting drugs? Wouldn't she leave that for the nurses coming on, with an explanation of what was needed and why?"

Phil sure had a lot of reasonable questions. But still…"No, it can't be Nancy. I've known her for years. She's not using drugs. She can't be."

"Let's go back and check the footage for each night when drugs were taken. Hopefully we'll catch the end of the day shifts."

I slumped lower on the sofa with each view—on the nights in question, Nancy worked the previous shifts and we saw her at the drug cabinet at the end of her shift. She always kept her back to the camera. I shook my head in disbelief. "I know she's been under a lot of stress and has lost weight, but who wouldn't be with Manning on her case each time? Her mood's been fairly even, and she's as sharp as ever in triage and diagnoses. Plus she works straight through her shifts, often with no breaks. I can't believe she's using." But Nancy's pallor, along with her apparent sleeplessness and occasional shakiness nagged at me. *Is it possible?*

Chapter 12

SAM

I don't believe I'd ever been as angry as when I saw that 'For Sale' sign in front of our house. After convincing that friggin' real estate agent that I *was* the Chief of Police, I took my rage out on the sign. I impressed Rhe when I yanked the post out of the ground and ripped the sign off, but not so much when I tried to break the post across my knee. Two days later I still limped, and I ignored her advice to see an orthopedist. Feather repeated the suggestion when I walked through the police department reception area on Monday. A cartoon artist would have drawn a black cloud over my head. *And where the hell is Ruthie?*

I spent the day banging together a first draft for my upcoming speech to the City Council about the need for a new police station. I came out of that fog to have a lunch of a cheeseburger and fries, which Feather had popped out to get for me. Luckily, she didn't know Rhe had me on a short leash, calorie-wise. Ruthie did know, so I would pay the piper eventually.

Phil stuck his head in my door just as I crunched up the fry box and cheeseburger wrapper and dropped it in the wastebasket under my desk. "Something smells good. You get that from Monster Burger?" He came the rest of the way in and deposited himself on the top on the folders stacked on my visitor's chair.

"Yes, and you'd better not mention this to Rhe," I said with a wink.

"My lips are sealed. Did you talk with Rhe about what we saw on the video last night?"

I frowned, remembering. "Not an easy conversation. She's known Nancy as long as she's been at Sturdevant, and they've seen each other through some rough patches. No matter how we handle this, Nancy will lose her job and her nursing license…and probably do time."

"So how are we going to handle it?"

"With kid gloves. Nancy's arrest will be bad publicity for the hospital if it gets out. That would enrage Manning, who will then attack Rhe as the messenger. And Manning's going to be out for blood when he hears the thief was his second favorite ER nurse. We just might be able to muzzle Manning if we promise to keep this under the radar. Rhe will talk to Nancy today about her motive for stealing the drugs and hopefully get Nancy to turn herself in. She's already called a lawyer to represent Nancy—you remember Sawyer Smith, Ruthie's nephew?"

Phil looked pensive for a moment. "Ah, right. The guy Rhe hired when that man Donnelly attacked her in the ER and then sued her and the hospital."

"One and the same. There are times when I wonder whether our family and friends constitute his entire practice."

Phil smiled and got up to leave. "Well, let me know how it turns out. If anyone can get Ms. Ennis to come in, it's Rhe."

I went back to writing my speech, giving in to procrastination after an hour's struggle by getting coffee and a stale doughnut from the department's kitchen. *I wish I'd known making speeches was such a big part of this job.* I was delighted for the interruption when Feather called mid-afternoon to tell me the Secretary of State, Robert Burton, was on line one.

"Good afternoon, Mr. Burton. How's the governor doing?"

"So well that he might be back in his office in a couple of weeks. And please call me Robert, Sam."

First name basis? Hmmm. Does he want something? "What can I do for you?"

"I read over your report on the three snipers you interviewed. You did a very thorough job, and did I read this right? One of them gave you a hint he might be prevaricating?"

Government-speak for lying. "Yes, Kenneth Craig."

"How do you plan to follow up on that?"

"Well, you can thank my wife for the report. She wrote it. And we do have something in mind with regard to Mr. Craig. But first, did anyone else find a possible candidate in their investigations?"

"No, I'm sorry to say. While the other reports weren't as detailed as yours—and your wife's—there's nothing to suggest anyone else on our list could be the shooter. So what's your plan?"

"A visit to the only shooting range with long-range targets this weekend, where we'll nose around. We'll go as a civilian couple. Rhe needs some practice with her Sig Sauer, which is not exactly a lie."

I could hear him speaking to someone, then he returned to our conversation, saying, "I've got to go. Another meeting I totally forgot. Keep in touch." The line went dead.

Guess he just wanted to know where we were with the investigation. But his call reminded me I needed to contact Agent Bongiovanni at the FBI. I hoped some of the FBI's software might help us identify the man in Deputy Birch's sketches. Feather had to search through Ruthie's little black book for Bongiovanni's number, since he wasn't on my speed dial.

"To what do I owe the pleasure of this call, Chief?"

"Not so much a pleasure, sir. I've been thinking it would help if someone at the FBI could run a facial recognition on a sketch we have of a perp."

"This wouldn't have anything to do with that stolen identity case involving Rhe, would it?"

"One and the same. And he's upped the ante. The creep somehow managed to get the deed to our house made over to him and put our house up for sale. The kicker in our investigation is that the sketch we have of our stalker matches the sketch and description of a local rapist." I heard a deep intake of breath.

"Okaaay, but it's hard to identify someone from a sketch. It's worth trying, but I can't be encouraging. We have two programs we can use, the Next Generation Identification system or NGI, and the Facial Analysis, Comparison, and Evaluation Services Unit, called FACE."

"What's the difference?"

"Any authorized law enforcement agency can submit a photo of the person to be searched by NGI against the mugshot repository. The system then returns photos of two to fifty likely matches, which have to be reviewed manually. These results are just leads and are not considered to be a means of positive identification."

"And the other?"

"FACE accepts photos which are part of an FBI investigation, but in this case I'll authorize it for use with a sketch. The program does a search against databases authorized for use by the FBI to create a photo gallery of potential candidates—again, just an investigative lead. And, truthfully, I have no idea whether a sketch will work in either case."

I sighed, which he must have heard.

"Chief, the best lead would be if this guy contacts you directly. He sounds pretty smart, but we have smarter people here who can pin him down."

I sighed again. "Do you really think he might try to contact me directly?"

"He's upping the ante, so why not?"

"It's something to think about. I'll send you the sketch right now, sir. And thanks."

Ϩ   ʘ

I struggled on with my speech, fortified with more coffee and another doughnut, until nearly five. I was about to give it up when I noticed I had a new email. I opened it and stared at the screen. *Now this might just be our lead.*

Chapter 13

RHE

The morning after the video review with Phil, I drove to Sturdevant Hospital in a fog of despair. *How can the thief be Nancy?* But I couldn't deny the video evidence. Lyle Pendergraff's greeting barely registered as I came in through the loading dock door, and I passed Marsh's office door without looking in.

A beehive would describe the ER that day, with nurses and doctors bustling here and there. We were in for a busy day, it seemed, and I found myself looking forward to it. Checking the computer for the names of those who had been admitted, I shook my head in disbelief when I saw Naomi Parkins on the list, assigned to me. I went to her cubicle and drew back the curtain, a greeting on my lips. Instead I swallowed a gasp. *What the…?* The young woman sitting on the bed had a half-closed, swollen eye, a cut lip still bleeding, and a bright red spot on her cheek.

"Naomi, what happened to you?" She just hung her head, tears and snot dripping onto her lap. "Let's get you to lie down." I gently swung her feet up on the bed and she sank back on her own, limp as a cloth doll.

Whoever had triaged Naomi would have done a rapid physical assessment and recognized that she didn't have a life-threatening condition. I repeated that initial assessment by checking her breathing, listening to her heart, taking her blood pressure, and attaching a pulse oximeter to her index finger. Except for an elevated blood pressure, her vitals were normal.

I then used a simple mnemonic—'AVPU'—as a prompt for the standard ER exam: determine if the patient is alert (A), which in this case, I doubted; if the patient responds to the examiner's voice (V)— and Naomi did not when I asked her again what had happened; and if the patient responded to pain (P). For this I pinched her shoulder, and she grimaced and leaned her head toward that shoulder. The U stood for unresponsive. Since Nancy fit three of the four categories, I considered she might be in shock or have a brain injury.

I took out my pen light and flashed it in both eyes, carefully opening the eye that was swollen nearly shut. The size and shape of her pupils, their equality to each other and responsiveness to light were normal, so I doubted she had a brain injury. Or, if there were, it was developing very slowly. I'd request a CT scan of her head anyway. She remained unresponsive as I removed her blouse, shoes, socks and pants in order to do a physical exam, then I ran my hands over her head, neck, limbs and torso. Bright red areas on her arms, chest and back showed she'd been grabbed and hit or kicked. She'd have large, purpling bruises within twenty-four hours. So whatever the cause of her injuries, it'd been recent. When I felt her ribs, she cried out. I detected some crepitus or grating on ribs eight and nine on her left side and decided those ribs were broken. Since her breathing sounded normal so far, I doubted a broken end had pierced her thoracic cavity, but she would need chest X-rays as well.

After fetching two warmed blankets to wrap her with, I called in Dr. Morrell, a brand-new resident. I reviewed my findings and Morell checked her eyes and ribs. He'd quickly learned ER nurses knew what they were doing, because he immediately called Radiology before popping out of the cubicle and on to his next patient.

I sat down beside Naomi and took her hand. She stared at the ceiling. "Naomi, you know me. I'm only here to help you. Can you tell me what happened?" A long moment passed, then she slowly turned her head towards me, fixing her one open eye on my face. *Thank heavens, she's more responsive.*

Tears continued to seep from the corners of her eyes. "Why would he do this? Why would my father do this?"

"Your father?"

She nodded.

"What about your mother? Did she try to help you?"

"She died two years ago." She closed her eyes when she said it.

This poor girl. "What happened right before he beat you?"

"I did what the counselor at the Rape Crisis Center recommended. I told him about the rape."

Dear God, I never anticipated this.

☘   ☙

The ER calmed down as the morning wore on, and by eleven, I needed a coffee pick-me-up, even if just decaf. Plus my baby bump signaled I needed to eat something. I found Nancy free for the moment, so after signing off to another nurse, we headed to the cafeteria. I didn't say anything on the way down in the elevator, and Nancy squinted at me.

"You're awfully quiet, Rhe. Something up? The baby OK?"

"We need to talk. Let's get coffee first. And maybe some oatmeal for me, if they're still serving it. Someone needs to be fed," I said, placing one hand on my belly bump and giving her a wink. With no oatmeal available, I countered with French fries and made a silent mea culpa to Sam. We were mostly silent as we sipped our coffee and I ate half my fries, sharing only a word or two about the situation with Manning. Tension hung in the air like a bad smell. Then it was time. I reached over and took one of Nancy's hands in both of mine. "I reviewed the latest video of the drug cabinet last night with Deputy Chief Pearce."

Nancy pulled her hand away. "So you know." She wouldn't look at me.

"Why, Nancy? Why would you do it when you knew what it would cost you?"

She swung her head to and fro as if trying to shake an explanation loose. Finally, she looked me in the eyes. "It's my son, Rhe. I did it for my son."

"But why? Is Ryan into drugs? This must be something recent."

Nancy settled back in her chair and took another sip of coffee, placing the cup carefully back on the table and letting out a deep sigh. "You know we thought we'd lucked out with Ryan. Always a happy-go-lucky kid, lots of friends, good grades, a good athlete."

I nodded. I remember hoping my Jack would be like Ryan.

"Until last year, when he became friends with some rough characters at the high school. He did the Goth thing, listening to terrible music, staying out late, tanking his grades, and so angry! He screamed at both Art and me when we tried to set limits. He completely ignored anything we said to him and eventually took out his anger at us by destroying things around the house. Abbie suffered a lot. Ryan taunted and bullied her, ripped up her homework, trashed her room. We had to put a lock on her door. I wanted to call the police and have Ryan committed to the hospital for observation, but Art wouldn't hear of it. "

"Why not?"

"He thought we could fix it. I secretly think he was ashamed and didn't want anyone to know. The perfect family…"

"Why didn't you tell me about this? Maybe we could have worked together on a solution."

"Art insisted that no one know. The excuses he made to Ryan's advisor at school were ridiculous. He blamed Ryan's friends, the pressure of high school. His lies didn't fool her, and she suggested professional counseling. Art finally agreed, but Ryan refused to go. So Art and I went, along with Abbie. The counselor told us Ryan undoubtedly had a drug problem, something I knew in my heart, and advised us to see what we could find in the house. Art wouldn't accept that his son was into drugs.

"And although we did a thorough search everywhere in the house, Ryan had been really careful. We never found a thing. Then Ryan got into heroin, something hard not to recognize. He quit school, stole money from us to pay for his drugs, and threatened us physically if we didn't give him the money he needed. I wanted to call Sam, but Art said we had to handle this ourselves. He followed Ryan to see if he could identify his heroin supplier, but he couldn't watch him twenty-four hours a day, and Ryan was very elusive. Art couldn't handle the idea of his son going to jail, but when he tried to persuade Ryan to go to an affordable rehab center, Ryan flat out refused. Well, more than that. He hit his father."

Tears started to course down Nancy's cheeks, and I pulled my chair around to sit beside her. *How had she managed to keep all this stress secret and still maintain her professional work ethic? She's been a good friend for so long. Why hadn't I noticed her suffering?*

"At that point, giving him money for drugs had all but bankrupted us and when we had no more to give, he took an axe to the back door and told me to get the drugs from the hospital or he would take the axe to Abby. He was out of control, Rhe!"

"You should have called Sam. Why didn't you?" I wrapped one arm around her shoulders.

"Art, again. I pleaded and pleaded with him. Then I told him I would go to Sam myself. He became so angry, Rhe…" she took a deep shuddering breath, "… he threatened me physically, if I didn't steal the drugs for Ryan. I honestly thought either my husband or my son would harm me if I didn't do as they demanded. I didn't know how to get out of this nightmare. And what would happen to Abbie if I reported them?"

I knew Art as an overbearing and demanding husband but hadn't expected his behavior to escalate to this point. The stress of the situation had brought out the worst in him. I squeezed her hand. "How *is* Abbie handling all this?"

"We try to keep her isolated from the anger and the tension, but she sees it. She hides in her room with the door locked most of the time. I can't imagine how this has damaged her. The only good thing is that Ryan has calmed down, probably because his heroin supply is guaranteed by the money from selling the drugs. And so Art has calmed down, too.

"I'm not stupid, Rhe. I knew this couldn't go on. Not only does Ryan look like a drug-addicted zombie—how can Art hide *that?*—but I knew I'd be caught. I did what I could to help you do just that, and now it's finished. The nightmare is over."

But it wasn't over. Her life would only get worse now. I squeezed her shoulders. No wonder she'd become so thin. *Damn men.* "Okay, kiddo, here's what we are going to do. We're going to get through this shift together and then I'm going to drive you to the police station. When you get there, you can call Art. I've lined up a lawyer for you who will meet us there. But Nancy, there is no way out of this. You *will* be charged, and you can expect Ryan is also going to be arrested for the possession and sale of illegal drugs. I hope he can be sent to a prison where there's a good addiction recovery program that can get him clean."

Nancy began to sob. I hugged her more tightly.

"What's going to happen when Manning finds out?" she asked me after a moment. "I'll be gone, of course, but he'll come after you. Weren't you supposed to inform him the minute you identified the thief? I can just see his face when he finds out." At that thought, Nancy started to laugh hysterically. Suddenly she stopped, aware of the curious gazes of the people around us.

"I'm pretty sure Manning won't do anything to me. I've got something on him, something so serious, I doubt he'll dare."

Nancy started to cry again, hiccupping, so wrapped up in her situation, she didn't even ask me what that something was.

While I waited for Nancy to use the restroom to soak her swollen eyes with cold water, I called Sam and told him that Nancy and I would come in after our shift. When I described Ryan's involvement, he reassured me Ryan would be arrested, too. I also mentioned that Naomi had appeared in the ER after a beating by her father. I knew he'd talk to her about pressing charges, but I doubted she would.

When we returned to the floor, Nancy seemed lighter, almost happy, as if her confession had provided a needed release. But she also seemed unfocussed on the work in the ER, so I had her lie down in an unoccupied bed and covered her with a blanket. She was asleep in minutes.

Dr. Morell came by to tell me that Naomi's trip to Radiology revealed she had two broken ribs but nothing else. He had admitted her for observation overnight, just in case of a slow brain bleed.

̓̓ ̓̓

I drove Nancy to the police station, arriving just after five. Feather called Sam when we came in, and he directed us to an interview room. "Phil will handle the interview, and he'll wait until both Art and Sawyer arrive," Sam told me, once Nancy had taken a seat. He turned to Nancy. "Would you like some coffee or water or a soda?"

"Just water, please, I'm really thirsty."

"I'll have Feather bring some and sit with you until everyone is here."

"Feather?" Nancy asked, actually breaking into a half-smile. "Is that a real name?"

"Yup. Can you believe it?" he replied. "Just relax. She'll be here in a minute."

I followed Sam down the corridor to Feather's desk and waited while he told her what he needed. "And stay with her, will you?" he asked. "She's had a rough day and could use someone with her."

He turned to me and said, "I've already sent a deputy to arrest Ryan, so he should be here soon to join his mother. You've had a tough day, too, from the looks of you. Come here." He wrapped his arms around me and I willingly sank into his chest, breathing in the comforting scent of him—the laundered shirt, the faint aftershave, the Sam smell. One of the reasons I'd married him was his ability to ease my stress. He kissed my forehead. "There's some good news, too, Rhe. Come with me. You've gotta see the email I just got."

I followed him to his office, where he sat and brought up his messages on his computer screen. He clicked on the last one, entitled "Surprise!"

It read:

Dear Sam and Rhe,

By now you have fully experienced my ability to destroy your lives. And I will most certainly do that, unless you pay me $1 million. Aren't your safety, security and happiness worth that amount? Think it over. I will let you know where you can deposit the money.

"And how is this good news? The guy is certifiably insane," I said after reading it. "This isn't a berserk stalker. It's about money! But why us? We're not rich. And what is that email address? Is Bongiovanni going to trace it?" My stress level began to rise again and darned if I could do anything about it.

Sam stood and took me by the shoulders. "Listen to me, Rhe, this guy's still our berserk stalker. He knows we don't have that kind of money. Think! He stole all our personal information and knows what's in our bank accounts. He's just playing with us. But now we have something tangible besides the sketch. I just talked to Agent Bongiovanni, and he said if the stalker contacted us, the FBI should be able to locate him."

"So do it! Send him this email now." Sam might have thought this was a good development, but I saw it only as another load of crap added to the pile sitting on our shoulders.

Ϙ   ʘ

Sam and I waited outside the interview room and spoke quietly with Sawyer and Phil after they came out. Nancy would be arraigned the next morning, then released on bond. Her son proved to be elusive, but Nancy had named some places where he might be found.

"Art is a piece of work," said Sawyer, "belligerent, loud, and he kept interrupting me with various sorts of threats. Deputy Pearce finally threatened to arrest him as an accomplice. That shut him up."

I gave Nancy a hug when she emerged from the conference room, which I knew she would have reciprocated if she hadn't been handcuffed. "Does she really have to wear the cuffs?" I asked Sam.

"Yup. It's departmental policy and applies to everyone, even those we know won't try to escape."

Art, tall, ascetic, and beak-nosed, tried to follow her to the cell block at the rear of the station, loudly demanding to talk to her in private. The deputy escorting her blocked his way. "Why can't I talk with her?" he asked Sam.

"Because we have regular visiting hours for our prisoners, and right now I think you should be concerned about raising the bond for her release," Sam replied.

"Yes, of course, yes, I need to do that." Art finally seemed to focus as Sawyer and Phil led him down the hall.

"He should be arrested for aiding and abetting Nancy and his son," Sam said to me. "But I'm not going to pursue that now. That family is wrecked, and someone has to hold it together. I only hope Art can be there for Abbie. I'm not so sure. "

"What do you think he'll do when Ryan's arrested?"

"He'll try to bail him out, too, if they can afford it. I hope the judge decides Ryan is better left in jail."

೮ ೮

I felt a huge sense of relief when we all got home that night. Our home had always been my sanctuary from the array of disturbing things I'd witnessed or experienced each day. Jack seemed to know I'd had a rough one and, after giving me a big hug, went into the family room to do the remainder of his homework. Paulette told us when she picked the boys up after school, she'd laid down the law about getting their homework done. We weren't surprised to hear there'd been a lot of horseplay and giggling if she didn't sit on them.

While Sam peeled vegetables for a salad, and I seasoned some chicken breasts and dumped them in our instant hot pot, I told him about Naomi. "You should talk to her before she's discharged tomorrow. I doubt she'll consider pressing charges against her father, she's too afraid of him. And maybe of her brother, too. But this would give you an excuse to have a chat with the father."

"I'll do it first thing tomorrow morning. I don't like getting into the middle of a family's private affairs…"

"I know you don't, hon, and I always worry you're going to run into a hothead with a trigger finger. What if you met him in town? Maybe in some public place? Do you think he'd agree?"

"Worth a try. But I'll talk to Naomi first. What's for dessert?"

"Jell-O with fruit."

"And whipped cream?" Jack yelled from the family room. I think the word 'dessert' had registered.

"Okay, but not a lot." That caveat was like spitting into the wind with both of them. I sighed. *Time to confess.* "I had some French fries for lunch today, Sam. The baby got hungry and they were out of oatmeal. What did you have?" Silence. I knew he'd eaten something with lots of fat. "Well?"

"Um, a cheeseburger from Monster Burger with fries."

"Okay, we're even," I said with a smile. "But no whipped cream for either of us." *As if that will make up for the calories.*

Chapter 14

RHE

The next morning, Sam and I drove together to the hospital after dropping Jack, Tyler and Sarah at their respective schools. I didn't have a shift that day and wanted to be there when Sam spoke with Naomi. Then we would both report to my favorite CEO about solving the drug thefts.

Naomi had a bed in the surgery ward, as a precaution in case of a cerebral hematoma, but we found her sitting on her bed, alert and dressed to go home. When I entered the room, she smiled at me. Then she saw Sam in the doorway.

"Good morning, Naomi. How are you feeling?" I checked her digital chart while waiting for her answer.

"Umm, fine I guess. I'll be discharged as soon as they give me a prescription for some pain meds." She clenched her hands in her lap as she glanced nervously at Sam.

"I'm sorry there's not much else recommended for broken ribs *except* controlling the pain. Did the doctor tell you not to use a wrap around your chest? I know you might think it will make you feel better having the support for your ribs, but the wrap prevents you from taking deep breaths. And that makes you susceptible to pneumonia."

"Yeah, I think he already told me that. Will it really be six weeks until they heal?" She finally turned toward me.

"Yes, but the pain will gradually lessen. Just remember to be careful—no lifting or sports."

"Mmm." She frowned.

"I'm serious, Naomi. If you displace the end of one of the broken ribs, things could become very serious, even fatal. Who's coming to pick you up today?"

"My brother."

"I'll need to talk to him," said Sam, coming fully into the room and then sitting in the chair next to Naomi's bed. "Hello, Naomi. I'm Sam Brewster, Pequod Chief of Police." He held out his hand, and Naomi responded by giving him her fingers.

"Are you two related?" she asked, looking at me.

"Chief Brewster is my husband."

"Oh."

"I need to talk to your brother," Sam told her, "but first I'd like to hear the details of what happened to you, straight from the horse's mouth."

She stiffened. "There's nothing to tell. I had an accident. I fell down some stairs."

"That's not what you told Rhe."

"Well, she misheard."

"Okay, I get it. You don't want to press charges against your father. But you must realize if he hits you again in your ribs, you could die."

"He won't," she said without thinking.

Sam and I looked at each other.

"So he did hit you?" I asked.

"No, I fell down some stairs." She looked down, hiding her eyes.

Just then, I heard someone enter the room and turned to see her brother.

"Ready to leave, Naomi? Get your things. I have the car outside."

Sam stood and approached the young man, hand out. "Hi, I'm Sam Brewster, Chief of the Pequod Police. And you are?"

"Luke Parkins, Naomi's brother." In contrast to Naomi, he gave Sam's hand a vigorous shake. "May I ask why you're here?"

I sensed an underlying nervousness despite the confidence in his voice.

"I believe your sister has been beaten, and that means a crime has been committed. If so, I need to investigate," Sam replied.

"There's been no crime, Chief Brewster. My sister just fell down some stairs." His voice now wavered a bit.

Obviously they've contrived to get their lies straight. "That's not what Naomi told me when I treated her in the ER, Luke."

"She had to be in shock from the fall. I'm sure she didn't know what she was saying."

"Did you see her after she fell, Luke?" I asked.

"Yes, I drove her to the hospital."

"Then why didn't you come in with her?" Sam asked.

"I…er…had some things that had to be done at home. I couldn't stay and I could see she would be okay."

"Really?" I asked. "With two broken ribs, an eye swollen shut and bruises all over her body?"

"Well, she's all right, isn't she?" He gave me a stony stare.

"Where did this fall occur, Luke?" asked Sam.

Clearly he hadn't anticipated this question because he didn't answer for a moment. I could almost see the gears turning.

"Uh, uh, in the place we're renting off campus."

"Is that where you're taking her now?"

"Yes, sir."

Sam had been taking notes in his little notebook. He folded it up and returned it to his breast pocket. "Well, I guess we're done here. Luke, I'd like you to assure me that your sister won't take any more falls. Can you do that?"

"Yessir."

After giving Naomi a long look, I followed Sam out of the room. "They're both lying, Sam," I hissed when we'd barely gone ten steps. "There's no way those injuries were caused by a fall."

"Parkins…Parkins, where have I heard that name?" Sam stopped by the elevators. 'Give me a minute. Are we off to see the Woodpecker now?"

I nodded. We reluctantly headed to the fifth floor.

α   α

Manning's secretary, yet a different one from the last time I'd been there, apparently expected us. She pushed a button on the intercom on her desk and announced, "Chief Brewstah and his wife ah he-ah to see you." *A real down Mainer.*

The door to Manning's office opened almost immediately. Manning stood there and beckoned us in, his face alight with anticipation, since he undoubtedly guessed the reason for our visit. "Do you have news for me about the drug thefts? Have you identified the thief?" He returned to his chair on the other side of his huge desk, motioning us to the chairs in front of it.

"Yes, we have, thanks to some long hours put in by my wife and our deputy chief." Sam sat down with a thump, never taking his eyes off Manning.

Manning clasped his hands, anticipatory to rubbing them in delight, I assumed. I sat down on the edge of the other chair.

"Yes, yes, I'm sure it took time. So who is it?" he asked me.

"Nancy Ennis," I replied.

The surprised look on Manning's face was priceless. "You're sure?"

"Yes, she turned herself in late yesterday afternoon. She has a lawyer and there's a bond hearing today," I told him.

His face immediately morphed into its usual imperious look. "Well, well, a thieving nurse. I shouldn't trust any of you. In any event, she's fired as of yesterday. I'll have the Emergency Medicine Department install a new charge nurse for her shifts. As for you, Nurse Brewster, you were supposed to report to me immediately. And yet, here you are, the day *after* the arrest."

Why am I surprised that Manning's not interested to know why Nancy stole the drugs.

"I told her not to call you," said Sam.

"And just why would you do that, Chief?"

"Because I wanted to figure out a way to avoid bad publicity for the hospital, as I'm sure you do. Wouldn't the hospital board like to know everything has been taken care of when you tell them?"

"Ah…yes, of course. Thank you. Do you think it will be reported in that local rag of a newspaper, maybe get picked up by state news?"

"If you mean the *Post and Sentinel*," I replied, "I pulled in a favor with Rutherford Harrington, the editor. He agreed not to report on it."

'Well, it seems I owe you both a debt of gratitude," Manning said.

I could bet he had his fingers crossed under the desk when he said that. He waved his right hand in a royal dismissal and didn't get up, now suddenly interested in some papers on his desk top. Frankly, I couldn't wait to get away from the miasma of his hypocrisy and brain-penetrating cologne. Sam and I skedaddled, saying our good-byes as we left.

As we walked back to Sam's Jeep, he snapped his fingers. "Parkins, I knew I recognized that name. Abel Parkins is a religious fundamentalist who heads up a sort of commune up the coast, just beyond the row of seaside McMansions. Their owners have been trying to get rid of him for years."

"Perhaps Parkins' religion is why he beat Naomi when she told him she'd been raped?"

"And the brother is trying to intercede." Sam unlocked the Jeep's doors and he got in.

"I only hope he doesn't bring Naomi back home," I replied. "Where do we go from here? I struggled to get into my seat, which was too high for me to do it gracefully in my condition.

"I'm sorry, babe, I forgot getting into my Jeep challenges you these days." He looked down, muscles around his mouth pursing. "I'll help you next time."

By that time I had managed to get into the seat, panting a little. "I forgive you for forgetting your manners this time. So, Sherlock?"

"I think it might be time to pay Mr. Parkins a visit."

"But Naomi isn't talking."

"It'll be just a word to the wise, so he knows I know and that I'll be watching."

☙　❧

We stopped back at the police department so Sam could check his emails and messages and find out whether Ryan Ennis had been picked up. He had, and he sat in an interview room with his father, as he was only sixteen. Sawyer had been persuaded to represent him as well, and sat across the table from father and son, with Phil alongside. Sam and I stood in the room next door, where we could watch through the mirrored, one-way glass.

I could tell things were not going well. Art stared at his son, who leaned back in his chair, arms across his chest, a surly frown on his face. I hadn't seen Ryan for several years, and I almost didn't recognize this wreck of a boy. Looking more closely, I saw he'd grown into a meld of his father and mother: Art's height and beak-nose and his mother's eyes. But he now resembled so many of the meth addicts that had passed through the doors of the ER: sweat sheening his face, a stick-thin body, and twitching that appeared uncontrollable. His face and neck had the scabs of a chronic meth user, places he'd picked raw imagining bugs crawling under his skin.

How could Art have let this go on and bullied his wife into providing his son with more drugs? "Sam, I think Ryan is spiraling—he needs a fix. You should call the paramedics."

"Sure thing, hon, but Phil's gotta finish the interview first." He flipped a switch so we could hear what was being said.

"Ryan," said Phil, "you're in deep trouble. We found enough pills in your possession to prove you're dealing, along with a good amount of meth. You *are* going to be charged."

Art banged on the table. "This is not his fault. His friends made him do it. My wife gave him the drugs. You can't charge him with anything."

"Art, be reasonable. Of course we can charge him, and we will. Ryan's best chance to get a sentence reduction is to tell us who else is involved."

"You know who," Art said in a defiant tone. "His mother."

"I meant the friends you said made him deal."

"I'm not saying nuthin." Ryan leaned forward, arms showing visible needle marks on the inside of his elbows. "I'm not a rat."

He sounded just like his father.

We could hear Phil sigh. "Stand up, Ryan. I'm arresting you for possession of illegal drugs with the intent of distribution."

Ryan remained sitting. Phil went to the door and called out. Two of our most muscular deputies came into the room, pulled Ryan to his feet and cuffed him.

"You can't do this! It's not his fault!" yelled Art.

Sawyer, who had been quiet during the interchange, leaned over and grasped Art's arm, telling him something we couldn't hear. Art sat back, deflated.

"That's it," Sam said and we left the room, heading off the deputies and Phil in the hall. "Phil, you can book him and put him in a cell, but you need to call the paramedics first. Rhe says Ryan is in withdrawal."

"Will do, Sam. I thought the same thing myself."

At this point, Ryan stubbornly refused to move, sitting down on the floor.

"Okay, bud, we'll do this the hard way." One of the deputies picked Ryan up, flung him over his shoulder like a sack of potatoes and walked down the hall to the cell area.

Sawyer and Art came out, and I couldn't help staring at Art, thinking how his bullheadedness had wrecked his entire family. He glared back at me. "This is your fault, too, Rhe."

Right. Blame everyone but yourself, Art, I thought, watching him retreat down the hallway.

Sam and I went to his office, where he found an email message from Agent Bongiovanni in response to our sharing the one our stalker had sent. I read it over his shoulder.

Chief Brewster: We have, with your permission, accessed the email message sent to you by your stalker. Our best digital trackers are on it. I will get back to you when and if we find him.

"Well, that's encouraging, Sam. Let's hope his trust in the FBI's digital wunderkinder is merited. What say we have an early lunch, and then I can go with you to that commune?"

Sam looked hopeful. "Where should we go for lunch?"

"How about the *Pie and Pickle*? You like their sandwiches and soups."

Sam's face fell. I think he wanted some place with fat and beef. Then he brightened. "They have good Reubens."

෨ ෨

After lunch, which did not include a Reuben sandwich, we drove north from Pequod on the local route that ran directly behind the McMansions, a lovely road lined with trees dressed in fading shades of orange, red and russet. Then we hit a stretch where the fields to our right had been farmland but now grew weeds, bushes, and baby pine trees. "This is it," said Sam. "Abel bought all this from a farmer for a ridiculously low price about fifteen years ago. Now he's sitting on a gold mine in terms of property value but has no interest in selling."

"How can he afford the taxes? Wouldn't the town assess the property on what it would be worth in the current market?"

"That's a good question. I remember checking the town's tax records for him a few years ago, can't remember why. He's taxed on farmland and he pays every year."

"He hasn't claimed a tax exemption for having a church?"

"Nope."

"So how does he make his money?"

"Another good question. Maybe we can find out."

At that point, Sam turned onto a gravel road leading east, toward the ocean. Overgrown trees lined the drive, some branches so low that they scraped the top of the Jeep. Sam swore and went slower, turning this way and that to avoid the branches. At the end of the drive stood a typical New England farmhouse, white, with a front porch that ran its width, a chimney at each end of the pitched roof, with a gable in the middle and a dormer on each side. Its bright white paint, green trim, and the new roof dispelled my preconceived notion that the house would be a rundown old wreck. Large, dazzling red bushes fronted the porch. These so-called burning bushes made a spectacular contrast with the house and were much brighter than the worse-for-wear red barn, which stood off to the right side.

The acreage on either side of the house had been mowed and tilled for winter. A large fallow garden could be seen peeking out from behind the house.

Sam pulled the Jeep to a stop in the graveled area between the house and barn and got out. He came around and opened the door for me. Just as he did, I heard the screen on the front door open with a metallic squeal, and a squat man emerged carrying a rifle.

Why do all the men in this state feel they need to brandish their rifles when they see Sam? The guy had an unshaven face and a comb-over of thinning hair and wore stained bib overalls. *This is a charismatic religious leader?*

"Whaddaya want?" the man yelled at us.

"Reverend Parkins, can we speak with you for a minute?" Sam approached the porch with his hands at his side, palms up, saying, "There's no need for a gun."

I emerged from the far side of the Jeep. When Parkins saw me, he turned and rested the rifle against the door. *I guess he sees a woman as non-threatening.* As I walked up behind Sam, I noticed two young women wearing plain blue dresses and white aprons peeking around the corner of the house. The curtains in the windows twitched.

"Stay where you are, Deputy. We don't invite visitors."

"It's Chief, Reverend Parkins. Chief Sam Brewster, Pequod Police." Sam stopped at the bottom of the steps to the porch and pointed to his badge with a thumb.

"Again, Chief…" Parkins sneered the word "…what do you want?"

"As you undoubtedly know, your daughter spent last night in Sturdevant Hospital for observation following what appeared to be a serious beating. I'm just here following up."

"Well, you can follow up with her. Clumsy girl, she fell down a flight of stairs."

"Here?" I asked.

"And just who are you?" he asked, looking directly at me for the first time.

"The nurse who treated her when she came to the emergency room, since she'd been traumatized as well as injured," I replied.

"So you just decided to come along with the chief here?"

"No, I'm also an investigator with the police department."

"Well, there's nothing to investigate here, missy, and she didn't fall down any stairs in this house," Parkins replied. "You can leave now."

More twitching of the curtains. I noticed from the corner of my eye a youngish man wearing bib overalls and a white, long-sleeved tee emerge from the barn, also carrying a rifle. Parkins waved him off and he went back into the barn.

"Good day, sir," Sam said pleasantly, and he motioned me back to the Jeep.

"Well, that was productive," I said with a release of breath, as Sam turned the Jeep and we headed back up the driveway.

"Yep."

"Is that all you're going to say?"

"Yep. But maybe I'll check their gun permits when I get back to the department."

I had a thought. "Can we drive by the place Naomi gave as her residence? I copied down the address and I want to take a look."

Where Naomi lived turned out to be a street of single story, older homes, which I sensed were rentals occupied by students, based on the number of bicycles parked in the dirt yards. "There, that one." The single story house blended in with its neighbors, gray from peeling paint, but with chairs on the front porch with seats that sagged almost to the deck. Two steps led to the porch. "And just where are the stairs Naomi fell down?" I asked.

"Dunno. Maybe the place has a basement?"

"I don't think so. I think these houses date from when workers at the old fish processing plants needed places to live. They wouldn't have bothered with basements, just flung them up cheaply. Besides, I don't see anything that would make me think there's a basement here—there's no windows or grates at ground level. They've most certainly decided to lie. What can we do?"

"Nothing." Sam's voice sounded flat and dispirited. "But my experience tells me it won't stop here."

Chapter 15

SAM

The weekend rolled around and Rhe and I took her old Jeep, Miss Daisy, and, dressed in mufti, headed for the firing range near Mount Katahdin. I brought along my customized M4 rifle and Rhe brought her Glock. The Maine Firearms Unit has to certify law enforcement officers on rifle and pistol twice a year, so we both had to train to keep up our skills in order to qualify. With the time involved in investigating the drug thefts, Rhe hadn't had much opportunity to train. It's hard to come down on your pregnant wife, even if you are the Chief of Police.

The overcast day dulled the remaining leaf color and made for a dingy trip, but occasional pops of scenery seemed to energize Rhe. Since no one else knew how to drive Miss Daisy, I sat contentedly in the passenger seat. The old Jeep had too many quirks and unknown rattles to count, plus it had a sticky stick shift.

We left at the crack of dawn for the four-hour-plus drive, stopping for coffee when we hit US 95. And a doughnut. Driving with Rhe was never boring. She never had a problem keeping up a steady chatter about Jack, Paulette and family, the hospital, and all sorts of things that seem to pop out of her head. At least until I leaned back and pulled my hat down over my eyes. Today was no different.

"Sam, do you know what's happening with Nancy?"

"She and her son are out on bond, but I understand Art had to take out a second mortgage on the house."

"I'll bet that pleased him. When do their cases come to court?"

"Nancy pled guilty, so only her sentencing remains. Ryan, with Art's encouragement, pled not guilty, so there will be an adjudicatory hearing in Juvenile Court."

"You want to remind me what that court does?"

"It's where a judge hears evidence from the state, in this case my department, and from the juvenile and then decides if the juvenile has committed the charged offense."

"What happens after that?" she asked.

"If the judge decides Ryan is guilty, there will be a dispositional hearing for which the court will examine all the evidence leading to the guilty decision. That will help the judge decide Ryan's penalty."

"I hate that Art's blaming Nancy for everything. I hope the judge will see through all his subterfuge."

"I wouldn't worry. The court appointed a guardian ad litem for Ryan. His job is to lay out the whole situation with Ryan's best interests in mind, without Art's interference."

"Do you know who that is?" Rhe asked.

"Yes, and you do, too. Merlin."

"Merlin? Really?"

"Yup." Merlin was the later-in-life husband of our receptionist Ruthie—a motorcycle riding, bandana-wearing, old-time hippy and an all-around good guy.

"That's a surprise! But I don't doubt he'll do a good job. Art won't be able to push his buttons. Is Sawyer still representing Ryan?" Rhe never ceased with her questions. I slouched down in my seat and pulled my hat down over my eyes.

"No, he told me he felt conflicted because he's representing Nancy. With Art's permission, he found another lawyer for Ryan, one with experience in Juvenile Court. I think I'm going to take a little nap."

I closed my eyes.

It seemed like only a few minutes later when Rhe punched my shoulder and said, "We're here, sleepy head. And I need a bathroom." She got out of the car like a shot, heading for the long, single story wooden building that looked like so many other gun range buildings I knew. The bathroom would probably be located in the same spot inside, too.

As I got out of the car, I could hear gun fire and, looking around, I could see roads that led off to the right and left through cleared land. The sound came from both sides, so individual ranges probably sprouted off those roads at intervals. I followed Rhe inside where a smiling, white-haired man greeted me from behind a long counter with display cases below. "That your wife who blew through here?"

"Yup. Long ride, tiny bladder."

"Baby on board, right?" He smiled wider, the wrinkles deepening in his tan face.

"That, too." I smiled back. My greeter was on the short side, thin, and originally had red hair, if his one-day beard had anything to say about it.

"Name's Dave Richardson. I manage the place." He held out his hand. "What can I do for you today?"

I shook it. "Sam Brewster. My wife and I need some practice. She has a 9 mm Glock and I have an M4."

"You've come to the right place. We have ten ranges to accommodate every type of gun."

"I heard from a friend of mine, Kenny Craig, that you have a two thousand yard range."

"Ah, Kenny. He comes here regularly with a bunch of his friends to use that particular range. All of them are long range shooters. We've got the only place in the state for them to practice. He was a sniper in the military, if I recall."

"Yup." At that point, Rhe emerged from the bathroom at the far end of the showroom, adjusting the Rutland tweed shooting jacket I'd given her last Christmas. She had to leave the bottom three buttons open to accommodate her increased girth, but it still looked nice on her. I'd picked the green coat because I knew it would set off her reddish hair. *Husbands can have taste, too.* "Rhe, meet the manager, Mr. Richardson. He says he has ranges suitable for both of us." I turned to the manager. "Let's start with my wife, and I'll stay with her. Just let me know the cost for, say, an hour on two different ranges."

"Thirty bucks. Do you need ammo? Ear protection?"

"We've got our own electronic earmuffs…"

Richardson smiled. "Whatcha got?"

"Howard Leights."

"A bit pricey, but I think they're the best among the electronics. And ammo?"

"Don't need it. We brought our own."

Rhe had been quiet during all this, examining the handguns on display in the case. Straightening up, she asked, "Do you happen to know Elias Morgan, Mr. Richardson? We visited his blueberry farm, and I thought I heard he'd been a sniper."

"Sure," he replied. "Elias has been here pretty regularly, usually with Kenny and a guy named…Patterson, that's right, John Patterson. Do you know him, Mr. Brewster?"

"Hey, call me Sam and nah, I don't recall having met him."

"When you come back, help yourself to some coffee and pastries." He pointed to a small room at the left hand end of the building.

Richardson provided us paper targets, and Rhe and I walked to the nearest range, a short one for her Glock. I could tell Rhe was about to burst—with what, I definitely knew. As soon as we were far enough away from the main building, she grabbed my arm, practically bouncing with excitement, "Sam, all three of the guys we interviewed practice shooting here. Which ones did we ask specifically about whether they kept up their shooting skills?"

"The only one I can remember is Kenny, who said he'd not been here. Why did he do that? He had to know we would come here and discover he'd lied."

"Maybe to draw the focus on him and away from the real shooter?"

I frowned. "Maybe." *And maybe to put us somewhere we could become a target.*

The handgun range was the first one to the right of the building—a short, flat one with a board for targets at the far end. I put Rhe through her paces with the Glock, and once she passed her requirement, we progressed to the rifle range. I scanned the area around the range, which had been dug out into an elongated pit with a high wall of dirt at the far end. The land around the pit had been cleared, but there were woods in the distance, so a shot from the trees there would be easy for any one of the men we interviewed. Out of a sense of precaution, I stopped and scanned the trees. A brief flash of something metallic caught my eye. "Get down, Rhe!" I pushed her to the ground and dropped on top of her, at the same time hearing a whisssshing sound and a thwack in the dirt a few feet away from us. The rifle report occurred at almost the same time. "Stay down and crawl over to the far end of the pit by the targets."

"Sam, what the…?"

"Just do it!"

We elbow-crawled to the pit wall, then sat up with our backs against it.

"Someone shot at us!"

My wife could sometimes be the master of the obvious.

"What do we do now?" Rhe was breathing hard.

"I'm thinking. We were warned—remember the note we found on my Jeep after the meeting in Augusta? I think this is another warning. Those trees aren't that far away. If a skilled shooter wanted to hit us, he would have," I replied. I paused to think for a moment. "If I call local law enforcement, they'll just dismiss it as an errant shot from a hunter or someone on another range. I know how they think. Let me call Bella." I took out my cell phone and punched in her number at the State Bureau of Major Crimes. After explaining the situation, we both agreed it was a warning, and Bella promised to send someone out to talk with us before we left. After I hung up, I said, "Let me call Mr. Richardson. If he'll come out here, I think we can just continue with our target practice as if nothing happened. The message has been delivered, and whoever it is knows someone will soon be out here looking for them." I called the gun range office and as soon as Richardson appeared, I stood up. Rhe grabbed my jacket and tried to pull me back down.

"Sam, you're going to be shot!"

I detached her hands from my jacket and walked over to where Richardson stood with a question mark on his face. "I think someone took a shot at us," I told him. "Probably a stray bullet." Putting on my gloves, I bent down to retrieve the bullet from where it had embedded itself in the dirt. Nothing more happened. I put the bullet in my pocket.

"I can't see how a stray bullet could come from an adjacent range," Richardson said. "It must have come from the woods over there."

"I think so, too," I replied. "I called the state crime bureau to come out and have a look. I don't know about you, but I really don't want to deal with the local authorities. I have a friend at the bureau and she said they'll send someone out. The agent will probably just focus on the woods, but they're going to want the names of your customers who use the longer ranges."

Richardson shook his head, sputtered, and walked back toward the office.

I walked back to Rhe, who still sat against the dirt wall. "Just as I thought, a warning. C'mon. Let me treat you to a bilge water coffee while we wait for the agent to arrive." *And maybe a pastry?*

"You're gonna have to help me up."

❧❧❧❧

That night, after a pizza dinner with Jack and Tyler, who had begged to stay, I sat on the sofa in the family room with Rhe, who nursed a cup of mint tea while I drank some real coffee. It had been a long day of driving, added to by the meeting with the guy Bella sent to interview us. We were both tired, and the missed rifle shot had shaken Rhe.

"So what do we do now, Sam?" Rhe asked yet again.

"Let's see what Bella says on Monday," I replied with a sigh of impatience. "I bet that agent we met found nothing in those woods. Snipers always police their casings and their sites. But maybe the bullet I left with him will have a print. Or maybe the striations will match something in their system. At least we now have evidence that the suspected snipers who swore they weren't shooting anymore were visiting that range."

Our cat Tux, short for Tuxedo because of his black fur with a white chest, chose that moment to leap into my lap, kneading on my pant leg and swiping his tail back and forth under my nose. I stroked him and he hunkered down, purring and still kneading. "Ouch! Buddy boy, it's time to clip your claws. Isn't that Jack's job?"

Rhe took a sip of her tea. "Yeah, but it takes two of us to hold him. We'll get to it. Jack!" Rhe called.

"Yeah, Mom," we heard from upstairs.

"We need to trim Tux's claws tomorrow."

"Okay. Tyler wants to see how we do it," Jack yelled down.

"It's just a ploy for them to get into a giggle fest," whispered Rhe.

As if to punctuate her comment, we heard gales of laughter coming from Jack's room. Just then the doorbell rang. I looked at Rhe and frowned. "At this time on a Saturday night? You stay, I'll go."

I flinched when I opened the door. Nancy Ennis stood there, clothes disheveled, eyes swollen from crying and a huge red area on her right cheek. "Nancy! Good God…come in, come in." I stood back, but a moment passed before she shuddered and stepped inside.

"Who is it, Sam?" Rhe called.

"It's Nancy… Come into the kitchen. There's some coffee still in the pot. Would you like some?"

She nodded, still silent, and followed me to the kitchen where Rhe found us, giving a stifled gasp, then enveloping Nancy in a huge bear hug. "Nancy, what's happened?"

They both sat, Nancy still silent, Rhe holding her hand, while I heated a mug of coffee in the microwave, burning my hand on the handle when I tried to remove it. After a few choice words, I grabbed a kitchen towel to bring the coffee to Nancy and sat down across the table from her.

Rhe got up and retrieved cream and sugar from the counter, adding a liberal amount of each to the coffee. "Lots of cream and sugar, just like you like it."

Nancy gave a half-smile and nodded.

"When you can," Rhe told her, sitting down again and turning her chair towards her.

Nancy took a big gulp of coffee, leaned back in the chair and sighed.

"Who's here, Dad?" Jack called down just then.

"Nothing you need to worry about, Big Ears. And it's time you and Tyler get ready for bed," replied Rhe.

Silence. *Nothing like the threat of bed.*

Nancy shook her head, like trying to settle something in her mind. "I'm so sorry to intrude like this, but I didn't know where else to go. I would have gone to a hotel, but I have no money." After a pause for more coffee, Nancy nervously ran her fingers through her curls and said, "Art has convinced Ryan I'm to blame for his drug habit and if he tells that to the judge, he'll get a more lenient sentence for dealing. Ryan is *still* using and is up and down. When I told him he couldn't show up high for court, he hit me. That's when I knew it wasn't safe for me to stay. You're the only people I felt I could come to. The rest of my family live at least an hour away and, anyway, they've shunned me since my arrest."

I could see her twisting her hands on the table.

"How's Abbie?" Sam asked.

"I told her to lock her door and stay in her room. I didn't want Art coming after both of us."

"Nancy, I'm going to head over to talk to Art and Ryan right now. Perhaps Ryan would be better off in jail, awaiting his trial. Let me assess what's going on." I got up, took my gun belt from the hook next to the back door and buckled up, checking that my radio and

Taser were where they should be. After putting on my shooting jacket, I affixed my badge to the front.

Since domestic disturbances are one of the worst situations for potential violence, I unlocked my gun from our gun vault in the hall closet. Seeing that it was loaded and the safety on, I put it in its holster. Rhe and Nancy sat with their heads together, talking softly, but Nancy's eyes grew wide when she saw the gun. "I doubt I'll need this Nancy, but protocol dictates I have it with me on official business. Rhe, I've got my cell phone, and I should be back in an hour. If I'm not, call the chief of police."

That got a weak smile from Rhe. "I love you, so you be careful. It sounds like Ryan is out of control."

"Love you, too, hon."

On the way to the Ennis's home, I called Phil for backup. Their house sat on a quiet street to the west of Pequod's downtown area. Most of the homes there had been built in the sixties and seventies in an eclectic mix of styles. By contrast, the Ennises lived in an old saltbox, dating from the late 1700's, two stories in the front, but only one in the back because of the steeply sloping rear roof. Flat front, two windows on either side of the central front door, and four above. Nancy and Art had lovingly restored the house in happier days, and I recalled the open house they'd had to celebrate the completion of the restoration. Rhe and I loved that house.

There was no outward sign of the turmoil within. I almost left my gun in the car, thinking if Art or Ryan saw it, the situation might escalate. But I'd been surprised too many times on such calls. After waiting in the car for Phil for several minutes, during which time one of the front curtains twitched, I decided to get on with it. They'd seen my Jeep. I climbed the two steps to the storm door and rang the bell. After some muffled yelling inside, the front door finally opened. Art stood inside the storm door with a look of disgust on his face.

"May I come in?"

"My bitch of a wife sent you, didn't she?

"I'll ask again. May I come in? Backup is on the way, but I'd prefer to discuss what happened calmly before they get here."

Art unlatched the outer door and stood back while I entered. His hair looked like a leaf blower had had at it and his plaid flannel shirt hung half in and half out of his jeans. "Come on into the kitchen," he said, practically spitting out his words.

The kitchen occupied the one story part of the house at the rear. Once we were seated across the kitchen table, I said, "Tell me what happened tonight. I want to hear your side of it."

"It was nothing, really." His voice changed to a persuasive tone. "Nancy made supper, Ryan didn't want to eat and she insisted. He lost his temper when she told him he couldn't be using when he went to court. I acknowledge that he hit her, but not hard, and you have to understand how much on edge he is with these charges against him. I could hardly blame him."

More excuses. "Art, Nancy is afraid to come home. She knows you and Ryan blame her for his drug habit, and she thinks one or the other of you will harm her."

"What a load of crock! Of course we wouldn't hurt her. But she's to blame. She fed his habit with those drugs from the hospital."

There's no reasoning with him. The conversation had gotten to a point too tense to continue, so I asked, "Where's Ryan? I'd like to talk to him."

"Keep Ryan out of this."

"I can't. He hit his mother. That's battery under the law." Art growled and walked down the hall to the bottom of the stairs leading to the second floor. "Ryan, get down here. Now."

I heard footsteps on stairs and Ryan slunk down the hall and into the kitchen, followed by Art. His eyeballs were in constant motion, looking everywhere, his eyes red-rimmed and sunken. The scabs on his neck oozed blood, and I had to assume if he'd received any palliative treatment at the police station, it hadn't lasted. He'd gotten high again and was spiraling down.

"I don't feel so well, Dad."

"I know that, but Chief Brewster needs to talk to you."

"Sit down, son. I need to find out what happened tonight from your point of view."

Ryan apparently didn't hear me because he focused on Art. "You know what I need, *Father*. Why won't you get it for me? I need it now," he said, his voice rising. He began shaking, and his eyes continued to dart around, then settled on me. "And I want this…this pig, out of the house."

"That's not going to happen, Ryan. Now sit down," I replied.

Instead of sitting down, Ryan walked to the kitchen counter, pulled a cleaver from the wooden knife block, whirled around and came at me, knife raised in both hands. "No, I won't, and you can't make me."

What happened next came so quickly I couldn't respond. He pinned my right forearm to the table with a through and through chop of the cleaver. The pain took my breath away. *Where did that strength come from?* I instinctively reached down with my left hand, pulled the Taser out of my belt, flipped the switch and tasered him. Just in time, as he had pulled the cleaver out of my arm, stepped back and then came at me again, this time aiming for my head. Ryan fell back on the floor, twitching. What stomach contents he had, he retched, so I got up, knelt down, and turned him on his left side. Blood from my forearm decorated the table, the floor and now Ryan's shirt. At least it wasn't spurting, so the knife hadn't hit an artery.

"Art! Art. Snap out of it! I need some help here."

Art just sat there, not moving.

I fumbled the radio off my belt and flipped the on switch. "Dispatch, 10-999. I repeat, 10-999, one-five Lincoln Terrace. 5150, send paramedics."

Art still sat, observing everything like a spectator at a football game. I wondered when he'd start to cheer. Just then Phil burst into the kitchen, quickly registering the scene. "Sam!" He kicked the knife out of the way and then strode to the oven, where an array of dishtowels hung on the handle. After wrapping one of the towels around my arm as tightly as possible and using another to clamp down on the wound site, he pulled me up and into a chair. I sat down with a thud, feeling woozy from the sight of my blood. Only my pride kept me from toppling over.

Art finally moved. He got up in slow motion and went over to Ryan, who showed signs of recovery. Phil put his hand on his Taser, but Art said, "Let me do this. It's time." He bent down, rolled his son on his stomach, and pulled Ryan's arms behind him. Phil let go of the pressure on my arm long enough to handcuff him.

Chapter 16

RHE

When I didn't hear from Sam in nearly two hours, I called him, but my call went to voicemail. My anxiety finally topped the billboard when I called twice more with no response. After corralling the boys into the bathroom to wash up and brush their teeth, I got Nancy set up in the guest bedroom down the hall. I didn't say anything about not reaching Sam, for fear of upsetting her more, and anyway, she was dead on her feet. I gave her one of my nightgowns and turned down her bed while she changed. She dropped onto the bed with an exhausted sigh, turned on her side, and was asleep before I covered her and left the room. I could hear the boys in Jack's bedroom, so I opened the door and promised them chocolate chip pancakes for breakfast if they would keep the noise down. Not that I thought Nancy would hear them.

Just then my cell phone vibrated in my pocket. *Sam, finally.*

"Hi, hon," I heard Sam say.

"Thank God. I've been calling and calling. Where are you? What happened?"

"Um… the ER at Sturdevant. It's nothing, really. I'll be out of here in an hour or so."

"Nothing? What's nothing?" I rocked back and forth on my feet. "I'm coming there right now!"

"No, Rhe, honest. It's not a major injury, and you can't leave Nancy and the boys."

"I'll call Paulette." I hung up.

☙ ☙

Fifteen minutes later I entered the ER, a place so familiar to me, but now strange as I looked at it from the outside, my husband a patient. I approached the main desk and cleared my throat to get the attention of the nurse sitting there, one I didn't really know. When she looked up, I asked, "Can you tell me where I can find the Chief of Police?"

She was young, with huge, artificially blue eyes that lasered me as she replied, "Ma'am, you can't be in here. Please go to the waiting room, and I'll call you when you can come in."

"You probably don't recognize me, but I'm Rhe Brewster and I work here in this emergency room. The Chief of Police is my husband. Now, would you please tell me where I can find him?" Her eyes widened, "Oh, I'm so sorry I didn't recognize you. He's in cubicle six."

Beating a path down the hallway, I called over my shoulder, "That's okay." I pulled back the curtain blocking off Sam's cubicle to find one of our neurosurgeons, Dr. Kramer, standing inside. A vascular surgeon I'd met before sat by the bed doing something I couldn't see. I pushed my way to the other side of the bed. Sam wore a hospital gown and lay propped up by two pillows, watching as the surgeon finished up a neat row of stitches, with a latex drain at one end, on his forearm. "Sam! This is *not* nothing! What happened to you?"

After the last stitch was in place, he raised it to show me a similar row on the other side, giving me a lopsided grin.

"Nothing serious," said the vascular surgeon. "Just a through and through knife wound that could have been a lot worse. No major nerves or arteries severed, just some small ones, and a little muscle damage. Once the arm is healed up, he'll need some physical therapy, but I think he'll be right as rain in a couple of months." He gauze-wrapped the arm, covering the stitches but leaving the drain free.

I took a deep breath, then lurched back, off balance. Dr. Kramer came up behind me and dragged a chair under me. "You look like you need more support than he does."

"Thank you, I'm okay. Just tired. So really no permanent damage?" I squinted at the man who'd done the stitching, whose name I'd forgotten. With his longish black hair and large glasses, he looked no older than a med student, and the sweatpants and a tee shirt under his white coat told me he'd been called in.

"No, Dr. Kramer and I don't think so. I'm Dr. Mirzah, Mrs. Brewster. I've seen you here but I've never had a chance to talk to you." A smile hovered and became real. "You're always too busy."

"Well, I'll make time the next time you're here." I smiled back. "Sam, are you going to tell me how you got stabbed?"

Dr. Mirzah stood, pushing the suture kit on the tray table out of the way. "I think this is where we leave you," he said, nodding at Dr. Kramer. "Mrs. Brewster, please check the wound tomorrow for drainage and infection and change the dressing…but I don't really have to tell you that, do I?" Another smile. "I have a couple of prescriptions for Chief Brewster, one for pain and one for an antibiotic. Where would you like them called in?"

I told him and then thanked them both for taking care of Sam. Once they'd left, I pulled my chair closer to Sam's bed. "Okay, spill." I took Sam's good hand in mine, close to tears. At my continued urging, Sam told me everything, and then the tears came. "You could have been killed."

"No, Phil got there in time. And I wasn't killed because I've been trained for just this sort of thing," he replied, reaching over and cupping my face using his good arm and hand, and his thumb to brush away my tears.

"So where's Ryan now?"

"Since his bail is revoked, in the county jail until his court date." He frowned. "I'm really sorry to have worried you, Rhe. I know this isn't good for either you or the baby."

I almost smiled. "Nor for you either."

Just then one of the nurses came in and said we were free to leave, so I helped my one-armed husband into his clothes and shoes. After a stop at our all-night pharmacy, we finally arrived home around one a.m. Paulette lay on the family room sofa, snoring quietly, so I covered her with a blanket before we headed upstairs to bed. My nerves still jangled and I thought I'd never get to sleep, but Sam dropped off immediately, and his soft snoring and comforting bulk next to me soon had me in dreamland.

ೞ   ೞ

"Mom! Mom, Mom, Mom. Wake up! It's time for breakfast, and you promised us chocolate chip pancakes. Tyler's Mom doesn't believe it."

I rolled over and regarded my son through bleary eyes. "What time is it?"

"It's six-thirty. School day. Time to get up." Jack wore his Avengers pajamas and an indignant expression. His hair looked like he'd slept in a wind tunnel.

I groaned and rolled back to find Sam still sleeping soundly. I raised my finger to my lips with a "Shhhh," and slowly got up from the bed so as not to wake him. Jack ran out of the bedroom yelling, "She's coming to make pancakes," while I found my bathrobe and regarded my appearance in the dresser mirror. *Death warmed over, but what can I do?* The household was up, apparently.

I found Paulette and Nancy, already dressed, in the kitchen, coffee made and steaming in mugs in front of them at the table. They leaned toward each other, talking quietly.

"Good morning, not-so-sleepy head. When did you get in last night?" asked Paulette as soon as she saw me.

"Some time after one. I hope you don't mind that I didn't wake you. You slept so peacefully, I decided just to cover you up and let you snooze on."

Paulette got up and poured me some coffee. "Sit. You look… wasted. What happened with Sam?"

Nancy remained silent but I could tell she wanted my answer. I pondered how to frame it when Tyler and Jack thundered into the kitchen. "Chocolate chip pancakes, chocolate chip pancakes."

I started to get up again, but Paulette redirected them to the family room. "Your mother is tired, Jack, but she will make you pancakes. Just cool your jets and get dressed for school." She turned to me, bringing the coffee as I sat down again. "You did promise them, right? This is not a figment of their imaginations?"

I nodded and pointed at the coffee mug. "Is this the real stuff?"

"Oops, sorry, I can make decaf."

"Don't bother. I'm going to make an executive decision that one cup of caffeine is not going to hurt the baby, and after last night, I deserve it. Come sit while I enjoy this." I inhaled the wondrous steam from the miraculous brew, added cream and sugar, and took a big sip, sighing in contentment.

Nancy had remained quiet during this whole exchange, but her tightly clenched hands revealed her anxiety. "Did you tell Paulette why you spent the night here?" I asked her.

"Some of it."

"You both know Sam went over to talk to Art and Ryan. He called Phil for backup on the way, in case you're about to scold him. After you and the boys were in bed, Sam finally called me from the ER. That's why I asked you to stay, Paulette. I had to be vague on the details because I didn't want to upset anyone."

"Something bad happened, didn't it?" Nancy finally voiced her fear.

"Well…" I then gave them a pared down version of events, but I couldn't make Sam being attacked any less traumatic. Nancy let out a soft moan when I got to that part, so I reached over and took her hand. "It's going to be okay. The police took Ryan into custody and he'll be kept at the county jail until trial because he violated the terms of his parole. He'll detox there with medical supervision. Art is fine, home taking care of Abbie, and a couple of surgeons patched Sam up. The prognosis is good—no long term damage."

Nancy looked at me with tears in her eyes. "Really?"

"Yes, really. I think you can go home this morning."

Nancy sobbed softly into her hands, and I handed her a napkin. "What about Art?" she asked as she blotted her tears. "He blames me for Ryan. The tension between us is horrible."

"Don't worry about Art. He ended up being a help to Sam, and Sam's pretty sure your husband may have finally come to his senses. And Abbie needs you. Her world's been turned upside down…"

Nancy began sobbing again. "My fault. Did she see what happened?"

"She slept through the whole thing, thank heavens, until the lights and sirens woke her."

Paulette drained her coffee and stood up. "Why don't I take Nancy home while you make those pancakes?"

"Maybe I can make pancakes for Abbie," Nancy said with a small smile.

"Sounds like a plan. By the time you're back, Paulette, I'll have the boys fed and some for you, too." I gave Nancy a hug before they left, then sighed. She had such a hard road ahead.

I think I made a thousand pancakes that morning, working on automatic pilot until Sam appeared in the kitchen in his bathrobe, which he'd managed to tie, and took my spatula away. "How many of those do you think the boys will eat?" he asked, wrapping his good arm around me and kissing my neck.

"Twenty, if we let them. Paulette will be back after taking Nancy home, and I expect you're hungry."

"I am, but let's serve the boys first."

The boys, who now sat at the table sword-fighting with their forks while I flipped the pancakes, yelled, "Yeah, we want five! No, ten!"

"You get five and then you go upstairs, brush your teeth and pick up your stuff for school."

⚃ ⚃

My shift at Sturdevant the next day was 4 p.m. to midnight, so I prepared a penne pasta casserole with Portobello mushrooms and spinach for Sam and Jack and left it in the refrigerator. Then I penned them a large note in block letters, leaving it in the middle of the kitchen table so they couldn't claim they didn't see it.

THERE'S A CASSEROLE IN THE FRIDGE. BAKE IT AT 350° FOR 45 MINUTES. NO PIZZA. REPEAT, NO PIZZA.

 CR   CR

To my surprise, when I arrived in the ER, I found a message stating I'd be charge nurse for the shift. I wondered what the Pecker would think. *Who had made that decision?* No matter.

We were always busy, but this shift ran on overdrive. Two car wrecks, a couple of drug overdoses from the university, a stroke, a heart attack, and the latest, what looked like another rape victim. I did my best to make sure all the patients were covered, and no one took a break. Around eleven, by which time everyone looked frazzled, things began to slow down. I finally had time to do a rape kit on the young woman who lay on the bed in her cubicle in a fetal position, facing the wall. When I came in, she rolled over to face me.

"Hello, Annie. I'm Mrs. Brewster. I'm your nurse. I'm so sorry it's taken such a long time for me to get to you. Can you tell me what happened?"

From the look on her face, I could tell that Annie, unlike Naomi, had progressed to being angry almost immediately. "I wanna get this guy!" Her eyes sparkled with anger.

"We all do. How about starting with telling me about yourself and how it happened. Then we'll do a rape kit."

Like Naomi, Annie Purcell was a Pequod student. She frequented the same bar where Naomi had been picked up, the Dirty Gull. Her story mirrored Naomi's, except that she hadn't seen the man before. "Do you remember anything at all between drinking at the bar and when EMS brought you here?"

"Nothing, I'm sorry. I barely remember the EMTs. Where did they find me?"

"Lakeshore Park."

She shook her head. "Why on earth would I be there?" she asked herself.

"How about what this guy looked like?"

"I'm pretty sure I'd recognize him again."

"Then I'd like you to visit the police department tomorrow and work with a sketch artist there." I wrote down Deputy Birch's name and phone number for her so she could set up a time for the sketch. I also gave her the Rape Crisis Center's number and strongly suggested she make an appointment. Her anger kept her going through the initial trauma, but I bet dollars to doughnuts she'd experience a different reaction soon.

When I'd completed the rape kit, she called her roommate to pick her up and bring her some clothes. After she left, I called Sam. "Another rape victim came in this evening, hon. The last thing the victim remembered is being at the Dirty Gull."

"Sounds like we've either got a serial rapist visiting that bar or it's a haven for rapists. Give me her name again? I'll dig up the incident report from the officer who found her, but you'll still have to come in tomorrow and fill out paperwork."

I sighed. I had come to realize how much of police work involved filling out forms and writing up incident reports. "How's your arm, hon?"

"Starting to annoy me. I'll tell Birch to expect a call or visit from Annie Purcell. We're certainly keeping our resident Rembrandt busy."

"By the way, how's your presentation to the city council coming along? I thought you were going to work on it tonight."

"It isn't."

"Oh dear. Well, maybe I can help you tomorrow. I won't be home until around one, so don't stay up."

☙   ❧

Sam let me sleep in the next morning. Jack told me later that he'd helped Sam dress, buttoning the buttons on his uniform shirt and tying his shoes.

I woke up to a quiet house around nine-thirty and found a note on the kitchen table, clearly written by Jack. I guessed this was how we communicated now.

THERE'S BREAKFAST FOR YOU IN THE OVEN, MOM. THE CASSEROLE WAS GOOD. WE WILL BRING DINNER HOME TONIGHT. IT WILL BE HEALTHY.

I found the plate of semi-dried out scrambled eggs and three pieces of bacon keeping warm in the oven, made myself some decaf coffee, and sat down at the table, eating while I thought about everything I should do that day. See Kit Moncton about Naomi's rape kit and check to make sure he had Annie Purcell's. Talk to Sam, get our ducks in a row with everything we had on our plate. Stop and see Nancy. And based on what I hadn't found in the fridge, do some shopping. And laundry. I heard a plaintive *meow* coming from the floor beside me and reached down to pet Tux. I gave him some of my bacon, which reminded me we needed cat food.

I decided to make my first stop a sit down with Sam.

α   α

Sam sat at his desk, frowning at his computer. I gave him my biggest smile and set a cooler box with a salad for his lunch to one side. "Thanks for not waking me this morning. I think the baby needed some extra sleep." Talk of the baby never failed to lighten his mood. But not today, as I soon discovered.

"What's that?" he asked.

Definitely in a grumpy mood. "Salad for your lunch."

"Ugh."

"Not to worry. I put in some chunks of ham, a little cheese, avocado, things that you like." I didn't mention the bean sprouts. "What's got you so irritated?"

"Trying to do this presentation for the City Council. It doesn't help that this arm is hurting like the rear end of the devil. Typing seems to make it worse."

"Of course it does. Some of the muscles in your forearm flex and extend your fingers." I pulled his 'guest's' chair, which also served as a place to store files, over to the desk and sat down next to him, on top of the files. "Time to change your dressing. Then we can figure out how to get the presentation done and go over where we are with all these cases. Sound okay?"

He finally looked up at me and nodded. "Okay, honey bunch. And the salad doesn't sound too bad. Does it have croutons?"

"A few. Let's look at the arm." Sam pulled up his sleeve, and I pulled a dressing kit out of my large and overweight bag, put on latex gloves, and used the scissors to cut away the bandage. There was some leakage from the drain, which I cleaned and left in place. The arm looked red and felt hot to the touch. "Did you take your antibiotics this morning?"

Sam looked sheepish. "I forgot."

I finished replacing the bandages. "Then it's a good thing I brought them along. Do you have aspirin?" He opened a drawer and pulled out a bottle. "I'm going to get you some water, so you can take your pills and a couple of aspirin for the inflammation. Do you need a pain killer?"

He shook his head. "Gotta keep my head clear."

When I went to the break area for a bottle of water, I stopped by Phil's office.

When I walked in, he asked, "How's Sam doing?" Then he stiffened and looked down, his half-smile replaced by a look of remorse. "It's my fault he's hurt and we're both lucky it wasn't worse. I didn't tell him I was in bed when he called, and it took longer than I thought to get there."

"Phil, no one is blaming you." I put my hand on his shoulder. "Sam should have waited for you to show up. He can be impetuous, and this time it cost him. Thank heavens you got there in time." I paused, waiting for him to relax. "But today, between the wound and the presentation for City Council, he's a bear. I have a favor to ask. Sam knows what the points are that he needs to make to the council, but I'm certain he's going to need visuals."

"He's on top of it, believe it or not. We already talked about doing just that. As soon as I get his version, I can send Birch out to take photos and will organize the whole thing in a Power Point. I know he's hasn't a clue how to create one."

"Yeah, digitally impaired."

We both laughed.

"Thanks a bunch, Phil. I'm really glad Sam has your help with this. He needs to convince our tight wad city council how much we need a new police station… Do you think I'm being a helicopter wife?"

"Maybe a little." Phil was incapable of lying, which is why I trusted him as much as I did.

I frowned. "What happened last night made me realize how vulnerable we all are, so I'm probably over-compensating. But Sam needs time to heal up, and there'll be less on his plate when this presentation is done."

"Don't worry, Rhe. We've got this."

After I returned with the water and Sam had dutifully swallowed his pills, I moved him to the guest chair and sat at his computer to see what he'd done. He'd written everything that needed to be covered, but it needed some organizing. "Why don't you tell me the most important points you want to make, and I'll rearrange what you've written to focus on those."

After thirty minutes of back and forth, he had a presentation to work with, and I emailed it to Phil. "There, done. Now let's talk about all the other stuff going on."

"Can we switch chairs first, Chief?" He smiled, his first of the day, I'd bet.

When he'd comfortably re-seated himself in his worn-down chair, I pulled out a notebook from my bag and read from the list I'd made. "First has to be the attempted assassination of the governor. We're right back where we started. Where do we go now?

"Well, I got an email back from the lieutenant governor. He's talked with Agent Bongiovanni and the people at the state bureau, and they all agreed we need to get more information on Elias Morgan, John Patterson, and Kenneth Craig. What we had before we interviewed them was pretty bare bones, so we need to start digging—especially now that we know they lied about keeping their skills up. I know Bella will see to some shoveling, but do you think maybe Rutherford Harrington can help us?"

"I'll ask him." I made a note and checked off item number one. "So that's one down. Where are we with the Dirty Gull rapist? The latest victim should stop in today to provide a description to Deputy Birch."

"Kit called me this morning to confirm the analysis of the second rape kit had begun, so maybe you could check with him later."

"And that ties into our stalker. Has Bongiovanni told you whether his digital elves managed to track the source of that demand?" Item number three.

"Yes and no." Sam mouth tightened. I knew mentioning the stalker plucked his irritation like a guitar string. "Yes, he got back to me, this morning actually, and no, they haven't managed to track that, that…."

"Sam, just tell me what he said. I know how you feel." I got up and put my arms around him, gently because of his arm.

"The email pinged from about a dozen servers all over the world, including this department's, before landing here. There's no way of knowing where it originated."

"Damn." I felt like Wiley Coyote in the Road Runner cartoons, with a huge iron anvil hanging over my head. *What's he going to do next?*

Chapter 17

RHE

When I left Sam, after admonishing him to take his pills and rest his injured arm, I still felt awash in all the events swirling around us. Having some direction helped…except where it concerned our stalker.

Beginning my walk from the police department to the forensics lab, I remembered this late fall day was chilly and turned up the collar of my wool coat to cover my neck. In my rush to get on with my list of chores, I'd forgotten a scarf. To warm up, I walked at a brisk pace the length of Hamlin Street, named after Lincoln's first vice-president, Hannibal Hamlin, a Mainer.

The large brick warehouses lining the street had been refurbished in the eighties, subdivided into shops and offices, and they were showing their age. Since the forensics lab occupied the ground floor of the largest old warehouse, the town desperately needed newer, larger, and more sanitary digs. I knew Kip Moncton would provide compelling information to support this request to the city council. I just hope they listened.

When I walked into the main lab at the back of the ground floor, I had to admire the work Kip had done in a struggle to make the lab as modern as possible. He'd painted the walls white and installed a tile floor, with bright overhead lighting, and new, metal lab benches. Kip hunched over a microscope on one of them, moving a glass slide around on the microscope stage, clearly looking for something. He glanced up when he sensed me standing next to him. "Rhe! You're here about the rape kit, right?"

"You got it, but finish what you're doing. I can wait."

"These slides aren't going anywhere, come on into my office." He led me to his glass-walled room with a view of the lab. "All the glass? I need to monitor what's going on in the lab and be available to answer the million daily questions. My techs," and here he gestured to the two people working at different lab benches, "are on a steep learning curve." He smiled and wrinkles appeared at the sides of his warm brown eyes. "Well, maybe only a hundred questions."

"We were lucky to get you, Kip. I know Sam's very impressed with your work and the efficiency of the lab."

"Sam and I just need to convince the city council that Pequod needs a modern lab in a new building. The ventilation system in this building is practically non-functional, there's no air conditioning, and the electrical system can't handle the equipment we need. I think I can make a good case to help Sam's presentation."

Not at a loss for confidence! I wish Sam felt the same.

Still standing, he went through some papers on his desk, pulling out one and glancing at it. "The latest rape victim had no semen residue on or in her. The guy apparently used a condom. The spermicidal jelly is the same as we found with Naomi Parkins' kit, but as that is a pretty common spermicidal compound, it doesn't help us much. You got lucky with Annie Purcell. We found skin under her fingernails. Even if we can get some DNA from the skin cells, next week is the earliest we'll have the DNA sequenced. The state lab has to do it, and they're backlogged. All the more reason for us to be able to do that here. Too bad this isn't one of the NCIS TV shows where the analysis takes only an hour or two." He smiled again.

"That's okay. Sam and I need to review the status of the various investigations we're involved in, and these rapes are just one part. Let us know as soon as you have anything."

"Will do."

℃ ℃

I next stopped to see Nancy. As I approached her house, I saw that the pain and drama inside the house had spilled outside. Clearly

Art had not mowed the grass in the front yard, which reached well above my ankles and was full of weeds. The screen on the storm door, still there in November, hung by a corner, and rolled newspapers in their plastic bags littered the yard. As unloved as the house looked, I hoped the family would be able to keep their home.

I pushed the doorbell. After a few long moments, Nancy opened the front door, remaining inside the screen. She wore a faded stained bathrobe, her hair disheveled, but she gave me a smile. "Come on in, Rhe. We're having a late breakfast, or maybe brunch."

"I can't stay, Nancy. I just wanted to check and see how you all are doing."

"Not even for a cup of coffee?"

"Not even. So how are things going?"

"Art has had a real change in his attitude and is defending me to our annoying relatives. Honestly, they just like to put their noses in where they don't belong. Believe it or not, I think having our son held in jail has removed a weight he—and I—have been carrying around for a long time. He's promised me he'll take care of Abbie while I'm in prison."

Those last words hit me right in the heart. "When's your court date?"

"Next week, and I'm prepared. Did you know someone at the hospital started a Go Fund Me page to help pay our mortgage while I'm gone? Art's salary alone isn't enough."

I smiled. "You have a lot of friends in the ER, kiddo."

Nancy's eyes teared up. "Tell them thank you for me, will you?"

"I think you can tell them yourself at your sentencing. I hear there's going to be quite a crowd. Take care of yourself."

She smiled again. "I will. Can you believe it? Art's going to mow the front yard today. I think it's overdue."

My heart hurt for her. She was so happy, but her future pained me to think about.

ଓଃ   ଓଃ

On my way home, my phone rang, and I pulled Miss Daisy to the side of the road to answer. "Rhe?" I heard Sam's voice. "You need to come back to the PD. Birch made a sketch of Annie Purcell's rapist. You need to see it. I'll explain when you get here."

"On my way."

I parked haphazardly in the department's crumbling parking lot, waved at Feather on the way in, and went directly to Sam's office. He had two sketches lying on his desk and stood up when I came in. "Take a look at the newest."

I came around the desk, looking first at the sketch he pointed to and then the other one. They were amazingly similar. *Something about the eyes, maybe the nose.* I stared at the new sketch for a minute, thinking. Sam stood behind me, twitching. Then it hit me. "He looks a little like Bitsy Wellington! Could they be related?"

Bitsy Wellington, a friend in my youth who had become an enemy, had escaped from the Maine State Prison. She kidnapped me and tried to kill me but had died in a fall from a ledge on Mount Katahdin the previous year. And this person resembled her. *That's what's been niggling at me!* "Sam, can you pull up a mug shot of Bitsy?"

I moved aside and Sam pulled his computer toward him and sat down. Bitsy had been convicted of murdering the original editor of the *Post and Sentinel,* a close friend of mine. When her mug shot appeared, I drew a quick breath. *Yes, a resemblance.* "Do you think we have a lead?"

Sam nodded, picked up the phone, and punched two numbers. "Phil? I need you to do some digging for me. See what you can find out about any living relatives Bitsy Wellington might have. Yeah, that Bitsy Wellington. And see if there's a DNA sample of hers somewhere. Thanks." He turned to me. "Had lunch?"

He looked hopeful, and I could read his mind. *Meat and potatoes, not my company.* "Let's go to the *Pie and Pickle* again. They have a nice tuna fish salad."

CB   CB

After lunch, I stopped at Hannaford's to replenish our refrigerator and bought some fresh flounder filets for dinner. I'd told Sam no takeout. I figured I could make the low fat mac and cheese the boys loved to mitigate the fish.

Once home, groceries put away, I pulled out my laptop and sought out my favorite comfortable chair in the family room. Time to do some investigation on our three lying snipers. I found quite a bit of information about Kenneth Craig, from his military service, to the Chrysler Jeep dealership, and his eventual promotion to management. I even discovered a short news article on his rather messy divorce, but nothing that would link him to the governor. So why did he lie about visiting the Katahdin rifle range?

Less information existed about Army Lieutenant John Patterson. He'd committed some petty crimes when he returned from Afghanistan, but the local DA had dropped the charges, with a requirement for PTSD treatment. I recalled Sam saying he'd check in with the head of the program Patterson attended, and I made a note to ask him if he had. I wondered what beef Patterson could have had with the governor. Was he angry about the war? For what reason would he blame the governor? I thought about his PTSD treatment and wondered if it had anything to do with his health insurance. The Governor had instituted a state health insurance plan with a requirement that everyone enroll unless they were rich enough to pay for private insurance. Even ex-military who had continuing coverage from TRICARE. Many doctors now worked for the state. This had created an enormous backlash from the many Mainers who wanted to keep the insurance and the doctors they had. I needed to contact Mildred Burger at HHS, whom I'd met at the early meeting of the lieutenant governor's task force, to see if they had any record of interaction with Patterson.

I added this to my list of questions, but doubted this line of inquiry would lead anywhere. Certainly the military's TRICARE insurance or the state insurance paid for Patterson's treatment.

Just then the baby kicked. I stopped, leaned back and enjoyed the moment, nearly falling asleep.

Forcing myself awake, I went to the last name on my list, Chief Petty Officer First Class Elias Morgan. I smiled, recalling our visit. We'd been enjoying the blueberry jam on our toast for several weeks, and we'd practically licked the jar clean. I found a lot of information online about Morgan's blueberry farm and its products, together with background on the owner: his military service, his family, two children and six grandchildren. The last bit about the grandchildren gave me a mental twitch. I thought Mrs. Morgan told me they had five. Had one of them died? Insurance came to mind again. Was it somehow involved in the child's death? I knew small, local newspapers with online sites had obituaries, but I didn't know where to begin to look. I pulled out my phone and called Rutherford Harrington.

An hour later, I had a lead. Morgan's granddaughter had died a year ago of cancer, and there was a notice in a weekly county newsletter. No details were given except for the funeral date and time and that her family grieved. I then did a brief search for news of the funeral but didn't find one. *But…* funeral homes and churches often had an obituary of the deceased, along with a place for people to leave expressions of sympathy. I looked up the funeral home, checked the obituaries for the past year and found the one for Elizabeth Anne Morgan. Elias' granddaughter had died of neuroblastoma, a deadly childhood cancer. There'd recently been a report on an experimental immunotherapy treatment with very promising results, one which used cells with a cytotoxic function on tumor cells. I wondered if the Morgans had tried to get her enrolled in that program, or a program for another treatment. Would the state insurance plan or TRICARE pay for it? Another question for Mildred Burger. I emailed her my questions, hoping she could help.

Then I closed my computer and sat there, thinking. *Lots of things on our plate…patience is a virtue. Now to make the low fat mac and cheese.*

ڃ   ڃ

I worked the next night, again as charge nurse, through an exhausting shift with a series of real emergencies. *Why do people wait until the middle of the night to seek medical help?*

It began when a young woman walked through the doors, supporting her father. "Someone help me!" she yelled.

I brought her a wheelchair. "What seems to be the problem?" I asked.

"It's my dad. He's been dizzy and confused for the last hour. And he's having difficulty speaking."

I took him immediately to a cubicle and then called for the attending neurologist to come to the ER as soon as possible. Fear emanated from the poor man's eyes and he tried to talk. He knew he'd had a stroke. As soon as our ER physician, Dr. Gupta, did a preliminary examination, he had me set up an IV to give the patient an injection of tissue plasminogen activator or tPA, commonly called a 'clot buster.' Luckily he'd arrived within three hours after the stroke, so he'd be more likely to recover with less disability.

The next 'biggie' of the night was a burn victim, a teenager who had been challenged by his friends to spray some gas on himself and then light it on fire, to see how long he could stand the fire before putting it out. *Will this boy survive to become an adult, given his stupidity?* The boy presented as calm and responsive, even bragging, and in no extreme pain because third degree burns kill skin innervation. The real pain would come later.

With Dr. Gupta's instructions, I attempted to start an IV and administer antibiotics, but the boy's mother got in the way, alternately cursing her son for his stupidity and screaming he would die if someone didn't do something. Finally Dr. Gupta led her from the cubicle, firmly telling her she was interfering with her son's care and that the extent of the boy's injuries would likely require treatment at the only burn unit in the state, the Maine Medical Center in Portland.

And then came the totally unexpected patient, Naomi Parkins. But this time, she didn't walk in. She came in on a gurney, and I gasped when I saw her. One of my favorite EMT's, Mick, a short, wiry guy who had been an EMT since I started working at Sturdevant, told me, "We got called to a house on Primrose, that street where all the students rent. We found her lying on the front porch, no one at home. I think someone worked her over and I'm pretty sure her lung is punctured. She's been on oxygen since we found her and I got a line in."

While he told me this, we maneuvered her into a cubicle and lifted her onto the bed. Mick left and I called for Dr. Gupta, telling him to bring a chest tube kit. I also summoned the thoracic surgeon on call. I had immediately noted Naomi's shallow breathing. Her skin had a bluish tinge from lack of oxygen, and the pulse oximeter registered only fifty-five percent. Her heart rate was very rapid, and something needed to be done soon or Naomi would die. Just then she coughed and blood dribbled from the corner of her mouth. When I unbuttoned her blouse, I noted several bruising patches over the ribs I knew were already broken. This time bruising extended over her abdomen as well. Naomi became alert for a moment and grabbed my hand, fear contorting her beaten face. Rage filled me. *How could someone, presumably her father, do this to her?*

"My father…I didn't follow your advice. Am I going to die?" I could barely hear her.

"I'm not going to let that happen, Naomi. Keep holding my hand if it helps."

Dr. Gupta arrived with the chest tube kit and put on gloves while I told him about her previously broken ribs. He then made an incision in a space between her ribs and inserted a large caliber chest tube to reinflate her lung. Her oxygen stats improved but I worried about the abdominal bruising.

"I think she might have some internal abdominal injuries, Dr. Gupta. What do you think of doing an MRI right now?"

"Agreed, Mrs. Brewster."

Just then the thoracic surgeon arrived. After briefly speaking with Dr. Gupta, he called for a patient care assistant to take her to Radiology.

After Naomi left, I sat down in the chair in the cubicle to gather my wits. *I should have swabbed Naomi for DNA.* Then I called Sam.

Chapter 18

My beeping cell phone dragged me from a sound sleep, and I had to rub my bleary eyes to see the caller. *Rhe…must be something important.* What I heard was, "Naomi beaten again… could be fatal…you need to get here."

Almost midnight. And I was clearly in a pickle. I couldn't leave Jack alone in the house yet needed to get to the hospital. So I did what any chief of police would do: I got dressed and left for the hospital, but not before leaving a note for Jack on the kitchen table and stationing one of my night patrol cars on the street outside our house.

Once at Sturdevant, I located Rhe in the ER, her face taut with emotion. I knew that look—she had herself under tight control.

"Oh, Sam, they've taken her up to Radiology. It's bad. She may not make it." She leaned into my chest for a moment and I caught a whiff of ER perfume, a combination of hand santizer, alcohol, and disinfectant. "I'm the charge nurse and can't leave. Can you go up and find out what's going on? I'm not sure if she's alert enough to tell you anything, but she whispered 'father' when I spoke to her.

"Leave this with me, hon. More stress won't do you or the baby any good. What floor is she on?"

"Either radiology on three or surgery in the surgical suite wing. Can you find your way there?"

Only been there a hundred times.

È   È

As it turned out, I only needed to go to Radiology. I found a night nurse, introduced myself, and stated my business. She directed me to where I could find Naomi. Turned out she'd been taken directly to the

MRI facility. An older man with tight gray hair and smooth dark skin stood to one side of the door as I entered, viewing something on a computer screen behind a half wall with a plexiglass shield above it. A person I assumed was Naomi lay half in and half out of the MRI machine.

Noticing my presence, the man shook his head. "You can't be here."

Even though I had on my uniform, I pulled out my badge. "Sam Brewster, Chief of Police. And you are?"

"Dr. Edward Thomas. I'm head of radiology."

"Nice to meet you. Wish the circumstances were better. I've been told someone beat this young woman, so this is now police business. I need to talk to her."

"You can't. She's unconscious and I'm in the process of figuring out why." He glanced up at me and immediately back down to the screen, focusing his attention on what looked to be an image of Naomi's head.

After a minute and a deep sigh, he said, "You were awful quick to get here."

"I have a mole who works in the emergency room, my wife. She's treated Naomi several times. The last beating broke some of her ribs. My wife warned her to be careful."

"Well, her warning apparently fell on deaf ears." Thomas turned and picked up the phone on the wall and punched in a number. "Is Dr. Kramer on call tonight? He's here? Great." We waited quietly for a minute or so. "Bob? Ed Thomas. I need you to do a decompressive craniectomy…Yes, stat…on a patient we have up here in Radiology. I'm sending her over to the surgical suites…Right, fine, be there in five." He turned back to me. "Sorry, Chief, but you're going to have to wait."

An aide helped Dr. Thomas to move her, now fully ejected from the MRI machine, onto a gurney. She showed no awareness of her surroundings, even as Dr. Thomas and the aide quickly pushed her out of the room and down the hall to the elevator. As we walked at a half-trot, Thomas told me, "We had to reinflate one of her lungs because a broken rib punctured it. The brain scan I just did showed a more serious problem. I can't tell you more because of privacy issues, but I will tell you that we did an EEG. Do you know what that is?"

I nodded.

"The results were not encouraging and the MRI showed me why."

At the elevator, I waited until they'd left, then walked down the stairs to the ER and found Rhe sitting at the nurses' station, the ER quiet for the time being.

"How's Naomi?" Rhe leaned back to look up at me.

"Not good, I think. Just after I got there, the physician, Dr. Thomas, called down for a craniectomy—is that what it's called? Dr. Kramer, that neuro guy who checked out my arm, is going to do the surgery."

"Probably a decompressive craniectomy," Rhe explained. "They're going to remove a piece of her skull to decompress the swelling of her brain. I assume that's what Dr. Thomas saw on the MRI. And they're most likely going to put her in an induced coma until the swelling goes down. She won't be able to tell you anything for quite a while, assuming she survives." Rhe slumped in her chair. "You can question her brother and her father, but I'm sure they'll lie."

"It has to be done regardless. I'm going to head out and see the father first."

"When? Now? It's the middle of the night!"

"The late hour might shake him up a bit, catch him unaware and maybe result in some more information about what happened."

"Wish I could go with you." Rhe gave me a hopeful look.

"When is your shift over?"

"Another hour. Can you wait? You might need backup." She gave me a wink.

"Later might be even better. Okay, I'll head down to the cafeteria— it's open, right?—and fortify myself with some coffee."

She nodded. "Sounds good. Stay away from the carbs."

ଓଃ ଓଃ

An hour later, with my kidneys floating from two cups of coffee but my body fortified with a blueberry muffin, we took my Jeep and headed north to Naomi's father's small kingdom. At nearly one in the morning, I expected the farm to be dark, but light seeped out around the barn's double doors. As we dismounted from the Jeep, I heard muted chanting coming from inside the barn. Rhe looked at me with raised eyebrows. I pointed to the doors, and we walked as quietly as possible to the barn. As I got closer, the chanted words became clear, a passage from the Bible:

> *My son, do not reject the discipline of the Lord*
> *Or loathe His reproof,*
> *For whom the Lord loves He reproves,*
> *Even as a father corrects the son in whom he delights.*

Rhe acted just as I knew she would. She swung one door open and stepped inside. I followed her and saw about ten people on their knees on the barn floor, some of them slumped forward from apparent exhaustion, repeating the words over and over. One of them was Naomi's brother, Luke. Looking over the penitents like a malevolent buddha, the rotund, unshaven Abel Parkins perched on a hay bale in front of the congregation. When he saw us, he got up and spoke to his son, who stood up and continued the chant, facing us. I noticed a rifle leaning on a nearby post.

Parkins strode toward us, directly through the people kneeling, forcing them to move aside or be bowled over. "What do you want? We're having a religious service here. You need to leave." The chanting continued, quieter now as some of the penitents turned their heads, trying to hear what we were saying.

"And a good evening to you, Reverend Parkins. Pardon me, but this looks more like a form of torture than a religious service." As if to punctuate my comment, one of the young women keeled over in an apparent faint.

"Nonsense. Sometimes a young congregation needs to be taught a lesson."

"That's your prerogative. I'm here to arrest you for the beating of your daughter. She is currently in intensive care at Sturdevant Hospital with a possible fatal brain bleed. Turn around and put your hands behind your back."

He looked surprised, paused for a moment, and then looked back at Luke. He finally said, "A father is allowed to discipline his children."

"Not like that, you can't." I grabbed his arm and turned him, removing my cuffs from my belt as I did so.

"Sam, gun!"

I looked up to see Luke aiming the rifle directly at us. "Young man, I would strongly urge you to put down the gun. There's no need to escalate this further."

"You're not taking my father anywhere. Now let him go." Anger suffused his face.

I could see the glare Parkins gave his son. "Luke, that is not the way to handle this. Do as the chief requested and put the rifle down. Everyone can go to bed. You call my lawyer and tell him to meet me at the police department," he said in an even tone. He turned around, presenting his wrists to be cuffed.

The Reverend's the calmest person in the barn. Why?

I had pulled out my cuffs and Rhe stepped forward to snap them on, while I kept an eye on Luke. He reluctantly set the rifle back against the post, then shooed the penitents out a side door. He stopped beside the girl who had fainted but had managed to sit up. When Rhe started toward her to lend aid, Luke's ferocious look and a vigorous shake of his head stopped her. After yanking the girl to her feet, he shoved her ahead of him through the door.

"You have the right to remain silent. Anything you say can be used against you in court. You have the right to talk to a lawyer for advice before we ask you any questions. You have the right to have a lawyer with you during questioning. If you cannot afford a lawyer, one will be appointed for you before any questioning, if you wish. If you decide to answer questions now without a lawyer present, you have the right to stop answering at any time." I knew the thirty-seven-year old Miranda warning by heart.

Parkins sat quietly in the back of the Jeep on the way to the station, looking out the window at the darkness surrounding us. Once we got there, I took him to an interview room. "Can I get you something to drink? Water? Coffee?"

He finally spoke. "Might I have some water, please? And can you undo these handcuffs?"

Rhe, who had followed us in, squinted at me. I knew what she was thinking. *How can a man who's nearly beaten his daughter to death be so polite and calm?*

Just then came a knock on the door frame, and one of the night-shift deputies stuck his head in. "Chief, there's a lawyer here to speak with you, and there's a call on the line from the hospital."

I answered as I unlocked Parkins' handcuffs. "Detective Brewster will take the call. Would you, hon? You can take it in my office. I'll meet the lawyer."

Rhe went off down the the corridor and I walked to the reception area, locking the interview room door behind me. A lanky man, whom I vaguely recognized from my appearances in court, rocked back and forth on his heels by Ruthie's—no, Feather's—desk. He looked disheveled, as if he had just thrown on whatever shirt and pants were at hand, but he appeared alert enough.

"Chief Brewster, Charles Renwick." He held out his hand.

I shook it. "Right, Mr. Renwick. I've seen you in the courthouse. Sorry you had to be called out at this time of of night."

"I'm used to it," he replied with a half-smile. "Can you tell me what's happened with my client?" His bushy gray eyebrows rose into the wrinkles on his forehead as he asked.

I briefly explained why I'd arrested Abel Parkins.

"How is his daughter?"

Just then, Rhe came down the hall from my office. The tears on her cheeks implied the news wasn't good.

"Has she died?" I asked, knowing the answer.

"Technically, twenty minutes ago. She never regained consciousness, but they've been monitoring her carefully. The brain bleed was so massive, they couldn't even do the decompressive craniectomy before her systems started shutting down. They're keeping her on life support, in case her father would like to donate her organs. They'll shut the machines down if they don't get permission."

I looked at Renwick. "Well, the charge is now either third degree murder or voluntary manslaughter. I'll leave it to the district attorney and the court to sort that out."

Renwick's shoulder's sagged and he shook his head. "I'm so sorry to hear this. Naomi was a lovely young woman. I can't understand why Reverend Parkins would have done such a thing. He is ordinarily a fairly calm individual. I don't believe I've ever seen him angry. Although I know he can be harsh with his followers and also with strangers who show up unannounced at his farm. But I've never seen him physically abusive."

"That surprises me, Mr. Renwick, given that his daughter named him before she died. If you'll follow me, I'll take you to see Parkins. You can break the news to him, and, if you would, ask him about donating his daughter's organs, so we can let the hospital know."

Rhe brushed away her tears and said quietly, "I'll meet you back in your office," and returned the way she'd come.

I took Renwick to the interrogation room and stayed while he told Parkins his daughter had died.

؃ ؃

I joined Rhe in my office after leaving Parkins with his lawyer.

"So what did Parkins have to say when he learned his daughter had died?" she asked as I came in.

"That's the funny thing, Rhe. He broke down crying. If we thought he was a harsh and punishing father figure, he sure didn't look like it."

"Maybe he just cried for himself, feeling bad he's being charged with a serious crime."

"No, I don't think so, hon. He kept saying, 'Oh, my poor girl, my poor lovely Naomi.' Something is fishy, hon, especially since Naomi implied her father did it."

"What if someone told her to say that?" Rhe asked.

"Mmm…maybe her fear of the person who beat her. In any event, Parkins said he would sign any papers brought to him about donating her organs. He wanted others to share in her life." I sighed saying that.

Rhe replied, "Do you think she had more to tell me and she didn't have the chance? No, I have to believe Parkins is putting on an act. How can we find out if he isn't?"

"Depends on what we learn from the lawyer, if he's able to tell us anything. After I left the interview room, I looked in on them through the glass in the room next door, and they were arguing about something."

While we waited for Renwick to finish with his client, Rhe put her head down on my desk and fell asleep. I quietly left the office and went to the interview room. They were finished for the time being, Renwick sitting rigidly at the table. I called the deputy to book Parkins and put him in one of our cells.

After he'd been taken away, I sat down across from Renwick. If anything, he looked worse than Rhe had when she'd heard the news. "Is there anything you can tell me?"

He gave a deep sigh. "Not really. He understands the charges and knows he'll be arraigned in the morning. I asked him if he needed anything and he said no, just to inform his son. He's devastated."

"But how can that be? He's now beaten her twice, the second time fatally."

"I can't tell you anything more, except that he's sorry beyond belief for what happened."

I fixed a look at Renwick. "This doesn't sound like a murderer unless he's one terrific actor."

Fenwich shrugged, and that shrug told me I had more investigating to do.

CB   CB

The next day, Parkins signed the papers for the organ donation and Renwick took them to the hospital. Telling me *someone* should be there with Naomi, Rhe called the hospital to ask them to wait to take Naomi to surgery for the organ harvest. She wanted to say goodbye. Because of the respect the senior surgeons had for her, they granted her request. I've never seen my wife so flattened by the death of a patient, so I drove her to the hospital and went to the ICU with her to give her moral support and to note the time of death.

No medical personnel were in Naomi's room when Rhe and I entered. The only sounds came from the beeping of the monitors and the whooshing and clicking sound of the respirator. Naomi was nearly as white as the sheets she lay on, in the deep sleep of the almost dead.

Rhe went to the bed and took her hand. She looked at me, asking, "Where's her brother? He heard us telling her father about her condition last night. Has the hospital notified him that she's brain dead? Why isn't he here?"

"He was notified, hon. Maybe he came earlier or maybe he just couldn't face it."

She turned to Naomi and leaned over, whispering in her ear words neither I nor Naomi could hear, but which Rhe clearly felt needed to be said. She gently smoothed Naomi's hair, kissed her forehead and the palm of her hand. "You can tell them they can take her now. She's ready."

Chapter 19

RHE

After Naomi's death, the days melted one into the other. Working, helping Jack with schoolwork, and gathering information on the snipers consumed me. Fall's panorama of vibrant colors had faded to the grays and browns of early winter without my noticing. My mood matched the landscape, and even the first flurries of snow dusting the ground, which I had welcomed in the past, failed to lift my spirits.

Mildred Burger at DHHS had still not responded to my email request for information on John Patterson, Elias Morgan and their families with regard to their health insurance. Nor had the Lieutenant Governor replied, when I emailed asking him about threats to the governor concerning his health insurance plan. I still hoped Chief Petty Officer Morgan wouldn't turn out to be the sniper, but at this point, I'd follow any lead.

On my next off day, I went back to visit Kip Moncton, since he'd left a voicemail with Sam saying he had results for us. He ushered me into his office and I sat facing him across his desk, taut with anticipation. "Okay, Kip, what did you find?"

"As you and Sam suspected, the rapist appears to be the same one for both girls. The spermicide was identical, but the skin cells you obtained from under Annie Purcell's finger nails didn't belong to her, according to the DNA. So if you catch the rapist, we can probably nail him with the DNA results." He paused, then said in his soft and measured voice, "I'm very sorry to hear about Naomi Parkins. I know her death must have affected you."

"More than you know." I appreciated his concern.

ʘα   αʘ

I left the forensics lab and walked back up the street to the police station to tell Sam the news. I must have looked startled when I saw Ruthie back at the front desk.

"Hi, Rhe. Surprised? It's good to see you. How're you feeling?" She got down from her tall stool and came around the reception desk to hug me around the middle, about as far up as she could reach.

I hugged her back around her shoulders, looking down on the top of her head and her bright red hair. "I'm feeling fine, morning nausea's gone and my energy is back."

"Baby moving around?" Ruthie stepped back and placed a proprietorial hand on my belly.

"A lot, and at the most inappropriate times." I smiled at her. "So, what are you doing back at the desk?"

"Sam didn't tell you? Feather quit."

"She quit? Why? I got the impression she was doing a pretty good job."

Ruthie smiled. "She told me she couldn't take the pressure. Imagine that."

"So are you here just until they find someone else?"

"Hell, no. I'm in for the long haul. While I love Merlin, being home with him all the time drove both of us nuts."

I felt sorry for Merlin's loss but also a glow of pleasure that Ruthie again sat behind the reception desk. "Well, welcome back. I know Sam must be pleased. I am."

I gave her another squeeze and headed back to Sam's office. He had a 'cat that swallowed a canary' grin on his face when I entered. "You aren't at all happy about Ruthie being back, are you?"

"Nope, not at all. Have a seat." He dramatically gestured to the pile of folders on his visitor's chair. "Whatcha got for me?"

"I just saw Kip. Guess what? Not only did the same man apparently rape Naomi and Annie, but he got a DNA profile from Annie's rape kit. He's mailing you the report."

"That's great news, Rhe. Now if we just could find and catch the sucker."

"Didn't we ask Phil if he could find anything out about Bitsy's living relatives?"

"Sorry, hon, I forgot to follow up. Why don't I see if he's in his office." Sam pressed a button on his phone and I heard Ruthie say, "Yes, Chief?" His face lit up with a silly smile when he heard her voice. "Is Phil in his office?"

"He just came in."

"Thanks, Ruthie."

Phil's printer spat out some paper as we entered his office. "Ruthie told me you were coming, and I do have some info for you," he told us.

"Anything relevant?" I asked.

"I think so. As you know, Bitsy had no siblings, but her mother's sister had two boys rather late in her marriage, Aaron and Morris Wrightnour. So Bitsy has nephews. They should be about twenty-six now."

"Twins?"

"Same birth date. I'm printing out their DMV photos now. I checked on Twitter, Facebook, and Instagram thinking to find background information, but they only used Facebook when they were in their teens. Other than that, they're both silent on social media. I'm trying to uncover their work histories."

I grabbed the sheet from the printer and stared at the faces. They looked nearly identical and both bore a distinct resemblance to Deputy Birch's drawings of the rapist and our stalker. *Oh crap.* "So first we think we have one suspect and now we have two that are identical, Sam." I sighed deeply. "Guess it's time to show Annie and Paulette the photos. See if they can identify one or both of them as the rapist and our stalker. I only wish Naomi had lived to identify him." The pain of her loss reared up, so I forced a smile and patted Phil on the shoulder. "Thanks for this, Phil."

"Are you sure there's no wants, no warrants, or records for either of them?" Sam asked.

"If they have any, I couldn't find them. But I'll keep looking."

Sam and I turned to leave. *Lightbulb!* I turned back. "Phil, could you see if there is a DNA profile somewhere in Bitsy's records? We could compare it to the one Kit has for the rapist and see if there are familial similarities. We need more evidence than the drawings."

Phil gave me his crooked smile. "Good thought, Rhe."

After we returned to Sam's office, I called and left a message for Annie to come in to see the photos. No way would I send this information out on email, not with our stalker out there in the ether. I made a copy to take to Paulette. The big question was how to trap the rapist? Or the stalker? Or both?

When I voiced this to Sam, he replied, "I have an idea. What if we placed an attractive young woman undercover in the bar on Friday and Saturday nights?"

"A deputy? Your deputies are known in Pequod."

"Let's put our heads together tonight."

I gave him an enticing smile. "I like the sound of that."

The DNA was clearly the key, but the fact that the twins would have identical DNA tempered my excitement. Input from my bestie would help, so I called Paulette and invited myself to lunch. She and I had shared some exciting adventures in the past, the last one nearly costing Paulette her life. She enjoyed my sleuthing maybe even more than I do, she made the perfect person to bounce ideas off. Not to mention her cooking, which would definitely lift my mood.

"Come on in," she greeted me, when I opened the back door into her kitchen.

"What's that delicious smell?"

"I'm baking moussaka. We'll have some for lunch and you can take one of the pans home for dinner. And there's garlic toast in the bottom oven to go with it. I know how much you like garlic anything," she added with a wink.

Paulette had a country style kitchen—lots of counter space, wooden cabinets, a terra cotta floor, and a big, wooden plank table. No gleaming white and stainless steel for my friend. I immediately delved into her silverware drawer and cabinets to set the kitchen table.

When the moussaka had finished baking, and generous portions of it along with garlic bread occupied our plates, we both sat down with a contented sigh. I took a huge bite of the bread and entered garlic paradise.

Even before she took her first bite, Paulette hit me with questions. "So, are you any closer to nabbing your stalker? Has he done anything else lately? And what about that rapist?"

I held my hand up, laughing. "Let's eat and I'll try to bring you up to speed between bites."

"Okay, if you say so."

I took a heavenly mouthful of delicious layers of minced lamb in a fresh tomato sauce, fried eggplant slices, and then potatoes, all covered in a creamy béchamel sauce. "Did you add wine to the tomato sauce?" I asked.

"Yes, I did, and that's your one question. Now you have to answer one of mine."

"Well," I mumbled with my mouthful, "I thought I saw something in the sketches drawn by Deputy Birch that reminded me of Bitsy Wellington. We looked for any living relatives and came up DMV photos for two nephews, who happen to look like the men in the drawings."

"What?" Paulette dropped her fork on her plate.

"The confounding issue is that they're twins, so rapist and the stalker could be either one or both of them." I paused to grab another slice of garlic bread.

"Do you have a plan to catch him?"

"Not finalized, but Sam and I think the easiest way would be to set a trap at the bar with someone undercover. We're still thinking about who that could be."

"What do these guys look like?"

"Hold on a minute." I got up, went to where I had dropped my bag, pulled out the sheet with the DMV photos and handed them to Paulette. *Please say you recognize them.*

She stared at the photos, looked up with a quizzical expression, looked at the photos again, and said, "This is the guy who tried to sell your house. I'm sure of it."

I sat back down with a relieved thump. "So either one or the other or both of these guys has been stalking us and is a serial rapist. I gotta call Sam to tell him you've confirmed the ID."

By the time I had finished relaying the news to him and discussing where we might go with this information, Paulette had rewarmed our now-cold moussaka, and we both sat down to finish lunch. I ate my third piece of garlic toast as dessert and leaned back with a small burp. "That was *so* good. You've outdone yourself, Martha Stewart."

Paulette beamed. "Okay, so what are you and Sam thinking about with regard to catching the rapist?"

"Sam thought Deputy Birch could play decoy. She's really pretty and looks young enough. Of all Sam's female personnel, she's the least well known around town."

My best friend face's morphed into her 'I'm thinking' look.

I added, "She's new to the force and is mainly assigned as the community liaison officer to local schools."

"Any other way she has met with people in the community?"

"Well, yes, as part of our Community Watch program."

"There you go. Too dangerous."

"Sam and I considered that."

"How about me? He's never seen me. I may be a little older than the usual barflies at the Dirty Gull, but you know I can play young." Paulette opened her eyes wide in expectation and gave me a coy smile.

Sam and I had indeed enlisted her to play the role of a college student looking for a job on a cruise ship a few years earlier, a job we'd hoped would lead us to an escort service employing university undergrads. And run by none other than Bitsy Wellington. "Not on your life, kiddo. This is way too dangerous. We're lucky you're still with us after that last stunt you pulled, actually drinking poisoned tea."

"But I survived, didn't I? And didn't you nail the poisoner? Besides, who else can you get? Sam would have to pull in someone from out of town, and the decoy has to be a believable townie or Pequod student."

"Absolutely not." *Unfortunately, she has a point.*

Ϙ ʘ

Both Jack and Sam devoured the moussaka and a green salad, and Sam looked longingly at what remained in the casserole dish until I told him there was just enough for the next night. While Jack stayed at the kitchen table to do homework, Sam and I had our after-dinner coffee, or facsimile thereof, in the family room. Although we tried to talk in low whispers, I figured Big Ears could still hear us.

"You don't have to whisper, Mom. I'll put in my ear buds and listen to music."

"Okay, but no rap and not so loud we can hear it, too." Jack had just started listening to music but as yet had no favorite genre.

Grumble, grumble, then silence.

"So," I said, still in a low voice and watching for signs of Jack listening, "Paulette made some good points today about the choice of a decoy to trap our perp." *I love cop talk.* "Your female deputies are fairly well known and I can't do it for the same reason. Paulette volunteered."

Sam came close to spewing a mouthful of coffee. "No! Never! Why would she—you—even think of that?"

"Because whoever it is will have to know this town really well. Any female students I know would be too vulnerable, and an agent or a deputy from out of town would require a lot of prepping. We don't have the time. And you know Paulette is very attractive and looks far younger than she really is."

Sam wiped his mouth and set down his coffee mug. "It's too damned dangerous, Rhe."

"Why? We don't have to catch the guy in the middle of a rape. We have his DNA. All Paulette has to do is get him in a position where we can arrest him."

"A position? What position are you thinking of?"

I swatted him on the arm. "Not that! Just get him to pick her up at the bar, maybe buy her a drink. Then we get his DNA on his drink glass, she gets him to make a move, and we grab him. Easy peasy."

"How are we going to know when she has him 'in position'?"

"I plan to be there, sitting at a table or booth in the back, with a couple of my Pequod student friends, so I can text you what's happening. And I'll wear a disguise."

"And just how are you going to disguise yourself?"

"Maybe as a biker chick?"

Sam didn't smile but picked up his mug and took another gulp of coffee. I could see his mental gears turning. "It might work, but I will need to deputize Paulette. That way the PD can cover any untoward expenses."

"Like what?"

"Like if he tries something nasty with her."

"Oh."

β   β

I welcomed the normality of the next day, with a busy, 8 a.m. to 4 p.m. shift. Midway through the morning, I received a call from Mildred Burger. Unfortunately, the call came in just as a full-term pregnant woman presented in the ER with preeclampsia and her hyperventilating husband. I didn't have a chance to talk to her until my shift ended.

The noise of the ER made any private conversation difficult. Since I needed to get back to her before 5 p.m., I quickly gathered up my things at the end of the shift, took the elevator to the basement, and headed out to my car. I got Miss Daisy started and the heater on before I called the number Mildred had left. It rang once, and a harsh voice answered, "Yes, what do you want?"

"Mildred, this is Rhe Brewster. I'm sorry I couldn't answer your call earlier. The ER resembled a zoo right around the time you called."

"I'm so sorry, Rhe. I thought you were the woman who has been harassing me for the last week or so about her health benefits. I can't seem to explain to her that I'm not the one she should be talking to… Right, you needed to know about John Patterson and Elias Morgan. You know I can't tell you anything protected by HIPAA, but I can talk to you about my personal interactions with them."

"No problem, Mildred. I can imagine you're being hassled by phone on a regular basis."

"You have no idea. You know, I think it would be better if we talked face to face. Do you have any time tomorrow?"

Chapter 20

SAM

We'd been shot at during our last road trip, so I insisted on going with Rhe to meet with Mildred Burger. I drove, Rhe acknowledging my Jeep rode more comfortably in her present condition. During the one hour ride to Augusta, we had a serious talk about our sting operation. "So you're sure Paulette's down with this?"

"Absolutely," Rhe replied. "Telling her you'd deputize her sent her over the moon."

"What about Ted? Has she told him yet?"

"She told him last night. I didn't hear an explosion across the street, so maybe he's okay with it. Let me text her."

I watched while Rhe rapidly thumbed her phone. As a one finger texter, I could never figure out how to use two thumbs or two fingers, so it took me ages to key in a text. Better for me to just call. "Have you and Paulette talked about what night you might do this?" I asked, while we waited for a reply.

"Well, the two rapes occurred on different days but both near the end of the week. So I think we'll do it this Friday and if he doesn't show, we'll repeat on Saturday."

Her phone buzzed. She read the text from Paulette.

"Definitely not happy, but I told him about my safety net. He said it was better than my drinking poison, but not much. He insists on being there."

"That's definitely a no-go. We can't take that risk. I'll have to talk to him. Who's going to be in the bar with you watching Paulette?"

"I've gotten two graduate students to join me. You already know them—Tanya Davis and promise you won't cringe—Zoey Harris."

"Zoey? You've got to be kidding!" I exclaimed.

"I know, I know, but since Will died, she's been in contact with me fairly regularly. She's really grown up in the last few years, Sam."

Zoey had been the undergraduate with whom Rhe's husband, who was also my brother Will, had had an affair. He moved out to be with her. Rhe had hated her with every cell in her body. With time she'd come to realize, as I had, that Will was at least half, or even more, to blame.

"Zoey truly loved him. So we've made peace. If it hadn't happened, I wouldn't be married to you, don't forget." She leaned over and put an arm around my shoulders.

I snuck a quick kiss on her cheek and put my eyes back on the road, even though I would have preferred to keep on kissing her. "What's Zoey doing now?"

"Getting a Ph.D. of all things. And in history. It seems Will had awakened some buried interest of hers."

"And Tanya? Hasn't she graduated?" Tanya had become the center of Rhe's first amateur investigation when an athlete at what was then Pequod College assaulted her. She and Rhe had remained close.

"Almost. She'll complete her doctorate in physics this year. She's more than ready to get out in the real world."

I knew Tanya, a very tall and fit young woman, would take care of Rhe, no matter what. I had learned from Rhe she was the first black Ph.D. candidate, male or female, in any field at Pequod University. I didn't know what Zoey could offer, other than another body around Rhe. "Do they know you're pregnant?"

"Yup, told them both."

"How're you going to look like a biker chick?" I asked.

"I thought I'd wear a long black wig, tank top, leather jacket, jeans and boots. And sunglasses. Tanya and Zoey said they could find some sort of outfit that would fit in."

"Right, sunglasses in a dive bar…"

"Takes all types," she replied with a smile. "Plus we'll have Merlin, in full biker mode."

Merlin's normal garb consisted of a leather jacket that had seen better days, jeans with holes and a do-rag bandana. He also sported a pony tail, although graying now, and was a bandy little man, who walked with a swagger. He would definitely augment Rhe's little gang.

We went over the backup for the operation—Deputies Birch and a newbie to the force, Deputy Dowdy, called Rowdy Dowdy for his off-hour antics, would be outside. Their instructions were to pretend to flirt, mimicking a pick up.

By the time we had gone over all the details and Rhe took a nap, we had arrived at the new office complex that housed DHHS on Capitol Street in Augusta. After parking the Jeep, I nudged my wife awake.

"Where are we?" She startled up, looking around.

"We've arrived, hon. Have a nice nap?"

She stretched, smiled, and after gathering up her bag, opened her door.

∛ ∛

Mildred Burger occupied a spacious office in the new building, with big windows overlooking the street. She stood up to greet us as we entered.

Despite her tiny build, Mildred looked every inch the former Army officer, wearing a fitted gray suit. "Please have a seat." She indicated the two upholstered chairs facing her desk. We all sat, and she moved some folders aside on her desktop. "Can I offer you coffee or water?"

I quickly nodded yes, since the drive had left me needing a caffeine fix. Rhe shook her head no.

"Right over there on the credenza. Help yourself." Mildred pointed at the coffee pot.

I helped myself to a large paper cup, poured myself some coffee, and after loading it up with sugar and cream, sat down again.

"Mildred, as you know, the sniper case has stalled. Sam and I are both pretty sure that one of the snipers we're investigating might be the one, and I believe the state health plan might be the link," Rhe said.

Mildred selected two of the files and looked up at both of us. "As I told Rhe, I can't get into any of their actual health information because of HIPAA. However, I can tell you about my personal interactions with each of these men." She cleared her throat. "One of the hazards of this job is the discontented insured. Normally they are screened and one of my assistants hears their complaints and attempts a resolution. If they remain unsatisfied, they come to me.

"John Patterson had experienced a delay in financial coverage for the program treating his PTSD. Both he and his brother came here personally to complain and refused to leave until I saw them. They were in the outer office for a whole day refusing to believe I was in the field. Security had to remove them, but I did meet with them the following day. I managed to straighten out their situation fairly quickly, and I haven't heard from either of them since.

"Elias Morgan is a different ball of wax. His whole family is doubly insured, by both TRICARE and our health plan. I'm not revealing anything covered by HIPAA by telling you his granddaughter developed a rare form of brain cancer. I know you must have seen it in her obituary. What was not in the news is that both TRICARE and our health plan denied coverage for an experimental treatment."

"I suspected that," Rhe said. "I read she died of a neuroblastoma, and I'll bet the Morgan family asked for the NKT cell treatment."

"You did not hear that from me," Mildred replied in a grim tone. "Unfortunately, neither health plan funds that treatment."

"So what happened when Morgan received the rejection?" I asked.

"Where do I begin?" Mildred slumped back in her giant chair. "I like Elias Morgan. He's basically a good man. But watching his granddaughter sicken seemed to push him over the edge. He came directly here after receiving the first letter rejecting his request for the treatment. He was very aggressive and angry and demanded to see me.

I did meet with him, calmed him down, and told him we'd re-review his request. A rejection letter automatically results in a re-review, but the decision remained unchanged. The second rejection letter ended with his removal from my office and the building by the state police. I didn't press charges because I *did* understand his desperation."

"Was there absolutely nothing you could do?" Rhe asked.

"Nothing. The treatment is hugely expensive and there are many hoops to go through to get accepted. His granddaughter's cancer had progressed too far for her to have it anyway."

I'd taken off my hat when I entered the building and now began to turn it in my hand, as the feeling of Morgan's desperation affected me. *How would I feel if Jack needed this treatment and we couldn't afford it?* I looked at Rhe, whose face reflected my inner anguish. "Did Morgan at any time threaten you or the governor physically?"

Mildred paused for a moment and then replied, "No. But he did say that God would punish us. Whatever he meant by that."

I could see how upset this conversation made Mildred and figured we should wrap it up. "Thanks for being honest about this, Madam Secretary. I appreciate your candor, and we'll take it from here. But I would caution you to be very careful in your public life and vary your route to and from your office. If Morgan is the sniper, he's not finished yet."

"Oh, I'm being careful. We've beefed up security here and I've hired private security for home. What a way to have to live, huh?"

؃ ؒ

I had hardly started up the Jeep when Rhe asked me, "So what's the plan at this point, Sherlock? How do we approach Morgan? Have him arrested under suspicion? We have no evidence."

"I'll make calls to Agent Bongiovanni and Bella when we get back. I'm sure they'll know how to proceed. I think it's their case at this point."

We drove back the way we came, on Route 27 south from Augusta, a picturesque two lane road. We'd barely left Augusta and gotten up to speed when the steering wheel started shaking in my hands. Then the whole car began to shimmy violently.

"Sam, what's wrong with the car?" Rhe's voice rose an octave.

"Something with one of the wheels." I downshifted and tried to pull off the road. At that moment the right rear of the Jeep collapsed. In the rearview mirror, I saw the wheel rolling off into a ditch. I knew if I applied the brakes, only the left side would be affected, pulling us into oncoming traffic. I had to accept we were in an uncontrollable skid. "Grab hold, Rhe!"

I clung to the steering wheel, time passing in agonizing motion as we veered across the oncoming lane anyway, barely missing a car that raced past. The Jeep flew over a ditch, the trunk of a large pine tree dead ahead. All I could think was oh shit, shit, shit…

We came to an abrupt stop when the front end of the car hit the tree. My head slammed into the steering wheel as I heard Rhe's air bag explode. Everything went dark.

Chapter 21

RHE

I'd raised my arms just before we hit the tree, so they took the impact of the airbag. How much time had passed before sounds filtered into my consciousness? I heard cars whizzing by, some squealing to a stop, and then the door on my side opening.

"Are you okay, lady?" The voice sounded far away.

"I think so." The airbag and my arms muffled my voice. *Nothing felt particularly painful. The baby!* I mentally searched my lower back and abdomen for anything, any pain, any cramping. *None.*

"I'm going to deflate the airbag."

I heard the flick of a knife being opened. "No, please don't. Not until I'm checked for neck injuries. I'm a nurse." I tried to look to my left without moving my neck. "Sam? *Sam!*"

The door on his side opened at the same time. From the corner of my eye, I saw Sam's partially deflated airbag and his head resting on the steering wheel. Blood came from his nose and dripped onto his pants. I could see his chest rising and falling, but he didn't move in response to my call. "Don't touch him," I yelled. At least, I think I yelled. "He could have a neck injury, too."

The man who'd opened Sam's door stood back.

"We've called 911, ma'am," said the voice on my side.

Why did I feel so tired? "Thank you. Could you just stay here with us until EMS arrives? Make sure no one moves us?"

"Of course."

I heard the voice shout something about putting out flares, but my mind couldn't focus. I tried to relax my head onto my arms and the airbag. *Was it just for a moment?* I heard an ambulance siren, its wailing coming closer. *They got here fast. Or did they?* Then more talking, very professional and assertive. I felt a cervical collar fitted around my neck, and, after some puncture sounds, the release of pressure on my face and arms. Strong arms lifted me out of my seat and laid me flat on the ground.

"How's my husband? How's my husband?" *Could they hear me?* "Please, take care of my husband first. He hit the steering wheel." Then the sound of an ambulance pierced my ears, gradually fading in the distance.

"We've already taken care of him, ma'am. He's on his way to the hospital," said a woman.

"How is he? Is he conscious?"

"Yup, he was awake but not making much sense. Said something about lug nuts."

A penlight flashed in my eyes. "I'm pregnant," I said, as a pressure cuff squeezed my arm, then slowly released.

"How far along?" the soprano voice asked.

"Just five months." Hands palpated my head and started moving down one arm.

"Do you have any pelvic pain? Any cramping?"

"None so far." Hands moved to my torso. I winced a little as they passed over my ribs.

A male voice at my feet responded, "You're not bleeding. That's a good thing." Hands finished palpating my legs. "Bruised ribs, maybe, otherwise no breaks."

From the corner of my right eye, I could see a young woman, sitting back in a squat by my side. "Can I sit up now? I'm feeling better."

"Thanks, Chris." The female EMT then resumed talking to me. "Before we sit you up, I need to ask you some questions."

"I know, I know. I'm an emergency room nurse. My name is Rhe Brewster and I was traveling from Augusta to Pequod with my husband Sam Brewster, Chief of Pequod Police.

"Today is Wednesday, November tenth, not sure of the time, but I do know that the Jeep in which we were riding lost its rear right wheel."

"AO times four," she called to the Chris person I couldn't see. "She's okay to transport."

Deep brown eyes in an upside down, concerned face hovered over me. Then someone propped me up in a sitting position. I swayed for a moment but took a deep breath and things settled into place.

"How do you feel?" A tenor voice came from behind me.

"Sore, alert and oriented. Thank you…Chris?"

"Brown, Chris Brown, paramedic. This is my partner, Angela."

"Chris," Angela said, "she's pregnant, so lights and sirens."

They're so professional. "Thank you, Chris, Angela."

They carefully stood me up and carried me more than walked me across the ditch to a gurney by the side of the ambulance. With their help, I lay down on it, and they started an IV. I noticed a highway patrol officer standing off to one side. "May I talk with him before I leave? It's very important."

"Make it quick," replied Chris, and motioned to the patrolman to come over.

"Officer Crabtree. What can I do for you ma'am?"

"The right rear wheel of our Jeep came off just before we crashed. My husband's vehicle is serviced on a regular basis, so this should never have happened. Can you find the wheel and the lug nuts?"

"Yes, ma'am. We can do that, already found the tire."

"If you find the lug nuts, can you bag them for evidence and check them for prints?"

The officer smiled, crinkling the skin on either side of his mouth. Ubiquitous state trooper sunglasses hid his eyes. "I thought you were a nurse."

"I'm a multitasker." I smiled up at him. "I also work as a part-time investigator with the Pequod Police."

"Busy lady. So you think this wasn't an accident?"

"No, I'm pretty sure it wasn't. Promise you'll do a thorough investigation?"

"You have my word on it, ma'am. Who should I contact about the accident?"

"Deputy Chief Philip Pearce at the Pequod PD. And my neighbor, Paulette McGillivray, so she can take care of our son after school. Tell her not to worry." I gave him her number.

"Time to go, officer," said Chris, moving to get me in the ambulance.

"Can you get me my purse from the front seat floor?" I yelled as they lifted me into the vehicle.

⚃ ⚂

It certainly felt odd to be the person on the uncomfortable ER bed behind a blue curtain, I thought as I waited for an MD to examine me. The nurse had repeated the trauma assessment and after a brief obstetrical exam, apparently concluding I was non-emergent. *So this is Maine General. What a great way to see it.* I begged her repeatedly to check on Sam's condition. She said she would, but she didn't return. *I'm not a good patient.* Beep, beep, beep. *The machines attached to me are annoying. And I hear them every day.* I tried to lie still, consumed with worry about Sam and the fear I could lose the baby. *I need to do something. But what can I do? Grrrr.* I clenched my fists in frustration.

Finally, the curtain whisked aside and a masked, white-coated individual entered my cubicle. He looked about eighteen years old. *Good grief.*

"Hello, Mrs. Brewster, I'm Dr. Chen. I won't ask how you're doing. You've had a terrible afternoon."

I had to smile, but then frowned as I asked, "Do you know anything about my husband? Is he going to be okay?"

"Yes, Nurse Clay told me you were very insistent and I did check a few minutes ago. We've admitted him and sent him to X-ray. More than that I don't know, I'm sorry. Let's check you over. I understand you're an ER nurse, so you know the routine. Are you at Sturdevant?" His voice sounded calm, well-modulated, and he exuded professional competence. *So much for first impressions.*

"Yes, for the past ten years." I waited patiently while he did his exam, chatting about this and that, while looking in my eyes and ears and checking my heart rate, rhythm, and oxygen levels on the infernal beeping machines. *He's very good at distracting the patient.*

"Pain anywhere?"

"A little in my neck."

"Headache, nausea?"

"No."

"Let me have the ultrasound technician come in and check on the baby. Is the baby moving? Yes? I want to check anyway. And it may give you some peace of mind. And, just to be on the safe side, before we remove that collar I'm sending you up to X-ray to check on your neck. If they give me the all clear, I can release you. But if I do release you, your neck and other body parts are going to be very sore tomorrow. I'll give you a prescription for some pain meds."

"Thanks, Dr. Chen. I appreciate it. By the way, just how old are you?"

His dark eyes wrinkled with his smile. "Twenty-nine."

"Could have fooled me."

℣   ™

The ultrasound check demonstrated Little It was just fine and kicking my bladder to prove it, and the X-rays and MRI showed nothing wrong with my head and neck. I returned to the ER in a wheelchair, as per hospital protocol, having received a clean bill of health. As soon as he saw me enter, Dr. Chen came over, gave me my purse, and removed my collar. He handed me a written prescription. "I forgot to ask where your pharmacy is," he said apologetically.

"No problem, this works. Thanks again. If you ever want to move to a smaller hospital…"

"I'll think about it."

At that moment, I heard a familiar voice. *Phil!* He stood talking to the nurse at the admittance desk, asking for me. I waved. He saw me and walked over to my wheelchair.

"Am I glad to see you!"

"I got here as fast as I could. There are a lot of people in Pequod wanting to know if you and Sam are okay. How's the baby? Ruthie is beside herself." His voice resonated heavily with concern. "Don't get up—you look like you've been through the wringer." He wheeled me over to an empty waiting room chair, where he sat down. "Are you sure you're okay?"

'Which question should I answer first?" I smiled at him. "I'm actually fine, just a little sore. The baby is also unharmed, but I don't know about Sam."

"He's going to be okay, Rhe, more than okay. I've already seen him. They couldn't locate you when I arrived, so I went looking for Sam."

"How did you manage that?"

"I used my badge and superior social skills to get to the inpatient floor and extract his room number. I have to admit, he looks like an MMA athlete after a bout, but his nurse said he should make a good recovery."

"What's wrong with him?"

"That, they wouldn't tell me. I'm not family. And he was asleep when I went in to visit him. You can find out when you see him."

"Then let's go!" I stood up quickly and wobbled.

"Let's take the wheelchair, Rhe."

CB   CB

Sam did indeed look like he'd been in one of those MMA fight cages. A splint covered his nose, held in place with tape, both eyes were shut, dark purple and blue and swollen. A cast covered one wrist. He snored, so I knew he was sleeping, not comatose.

Phil pushed my wheelchair next to the bed, on the side of his good arm. "I'll wait outside. I'll be there if you need me."

I sat, drowsing, waiting for him to wake up. Finally, after one particular loud snort, his eyes opened and he looked around, spotting me.

"Rhe, honey, you're okay? The baby's okay?"

I took his hand and kissed it. "We both are, and I met an ER doc I would love to see at Sturdevant." This last comment accompanied a smile.

"Made a boyfriend, did you? Should I be jealous?" Because his nose had swelled shut, his voice sounded tinny and nasal.

"Not on your life," I replied, tears beginning to form even as I continued smiling. "Did they tell you what happened to you?"

"Broken nose—you can see that—and a slight concussion. They're keeping me overnight. And a broken wrist, dammit, same arm as the knife wound." He held up his other arm. "Oh, and two bruised ribs. Just don't make me laugh."

"It could have been a lot worse, Sam. Your airbag only partially inflated." By now the tears dripped from my chin.

"Aw, hon." He reached over and wiped my chin. "We're lucky, aren't we?" He just stared into my eyes while I nodded, listening to the damned beepings of the infernal machines. Finally he said, "Losing the lug nuts makes it clear someone tampered with the Jeep. Someone wants us dead. The highway patrol and a policeman stopped by earlier..." He closed his eyes and drifted off.

I sat there, holding his hand and thinking furiously. *Are we too close to discovering the person who shot the governor? Did the sniper want to silence us?* Somehow I doubted it. The shot fired at us at the gun range had been deliberately off target. But what about the person stalking us? Had he upped the ante? We needed to get any CCTV video from the area where we had parked in Augusta. I needed to know who led the investigation. I needed...to talk to Phil. I got up from the wheelchair and lurched toward the door.

Holding the door frame for balance, I looked to the left and found Phil sitting just outside, head in hands. He looked up, raising his eyebrows.

"Sam and I spoke briefly, but he's gone back to sleep and I think that's the best medicine for him right now. He's got a concussion along with a broken wrist and nose and sore ribs."

His look lightened in relief. "It could have been so much worse. What do you want to do?"

"Stay here with Sam." I swayed and Phil lowered me into the chair next to him.

"In my professional opinion, Rhe, I think that's a bad idea. I think I should get you home for the night. We can drive back up here tomorrow, after you get a good meal and a night's sleep."

Phil, our caretaker. My stomach rumbled. I hadn't eaten since breakfast. "Okay, I guess there's not much I can do here."

"And Paulette's called me several times. Jack is frantic."

"I can call Jack from here," I said, looking around for my bag, which held the phone somewhere in its recesses, and deciding what to do. "Mmm…perhaps you're right. Sam will probably sleep for several hours. Let me leave my number with the nurse, in case anything changes, and I can call Jack from the car."

戈 戈

On the way back to Pequod, after calling Jack and assuring him both Sam and I would be fine, I fell asleep. The police cruiser felt so much more comfortable than Sam's Jeep, not that I'd ever tell him. I faintly heard Phil talking to someone at one point but didn't truly wake until he pulled into Paulette's driveway. "I can get Jack, if you're okay with taking us home," I said, rubbing my eyes and face.

"Well, that's not the plan. You're staying here tonight so Paulette and Ted can keep an eye on you and the baby. There's a hot meal waiting for you."

"What time is it?" I asked, looking around in the dark.

"Nine. Time to call it a day."

"But you haven't eaten either."

"Paulette made me a plate to go. I have to get back to the station and follow up with the state troopers and the local LEOs." He got out of the cruiser and came around and opened my door. I held onto both sides as I got out.

Just then, Jack burst through Paulette's back door and rocketed down the stairs, flinging himself at me. "Mom, Mom, are you sure you're okay?"

Paulette stood right behind him, saying with a smile, "I'm not sure he believed you. Phil, this is for you." She handed him a tin foil-covered plate. "And let's get you into the house, my friend."

Phil raised the plate to his nose and inhaled with a big smile. "I'll call you in the morning, Paulette, to see how Rhe's doing. If she's doing well, we can go back up to Augusta to check on Sam."

 C୪   C୪

During my superb meal of lobster stew, I made a careful explanation to Jack about what had happened. Paulette had warned me he'd been extremely anxious, and after I'd eaten, I had to gently peel him off me in order to get to bed. Jack had already experienced one serious loss in his life, and anything threatening me and Sam threatened him, too. I gave him multiple hugs and kisses to reassure him, then said, "I can't wait to brush my teeth and get to bed. What about you?"

Paulette had thoughtfully brought over my toiletries and a change of clothes for both us, so we climbed the stairs to our respective bedrooms. Tyler was hot on our heels, saying "Just like my Mom. All those kisses, ee-uww."

The following morning, I awoke to assorted aches and pains, but nothing I couldn't manage with a hot shower. I'd called Phil to let him know I felt good enough for the trip back to Augusta and then oversaw Jack's preparations for school. We all had a good breakfast of Belgian waffles, with a blueberry topping. I took an over-the-counter analgesic for my aches with my coffee, after deciding not to use the stronger medicine Dr. Chen had prescribed.

Jack hugged me fiercely before he left. "Tell Dad he needs to get well really fast, so we can go to a football game. When will he be home?"

"Aaah, watch my ribs, kiddo. I'm pretty sore."

"Are your ribs broken?"

"No, just bruised. You'll see Dad later this afternoon. And watch his ribs, too." I tousled his hair, kissed him on the forehead, eliciting an "Aw, Mom," and watched with concern as he went out the back door. Ted was the school driver today. Paulette and I remained sitting at the table, having real coffee. I had poured myself a full mug, figuring I deserved it and hoping the baby wouldn't object. "I've been thinking that whoever tampered with Sam's car will target Jack next."

"Oh, Rhe, certainly not." She reached over and covered one of my hands with hers. "I can't imagine anyone targeting a child. I thought the sniper did this."

"No, and I think Sam will agree. If we were targeted by the sniper, he could have killed us at the firing range. It has to be one of Bitsy's nephews. This is pure evil, and he's escalating. Just like his aunt…I'm going to talk to Phil about assigning a deputy to keep an eye on both boys after school." I took another sip of my coffee. "Are we still on for Friday, assuming my husband is up and around?"

Paulette brightened. "It's a go as far as I'm concerned, assuming you're both up to it. Would you like to see my outfit?"

Just then there we heard a knock on the back door, and I could see the outline of a man's head through the frosted glass. "It's Phil. Want to give him some coffee while I pack up? Can you wait to show me your outfit until tonight?"

Paulette faked a look of disappointment, then nodded.

Before we left for Augusta, I dropped off my clothes from the accident at the house. *Maybe I should burn them?* Seeing Sam this morning would be just what I needed to calm my continuing dread of what might happen next. I'd feel better, knowing we would face it together. And I needed to talk to Phil about protection for Jack.

Chapter 22

RHE

On the way north to Augusta, I explained to Phil why I thought Jack needed protection after school let out, and he made some calls to arrange it. Sam had dressed by the time we arrived at the hospital but the lengthy discharge process kept us from getting back on the road until well after noon. Sam rode in the back seat of the cruiser at Phil's insistence, so he could stretch out and rest his head on a pillow.

For some reason, my concern for Sam had overridden my normal thought processes. When Sam asked Phil about covering his absence at the police department, my mind finally emerged from the fog of the accident. "Phil, what have you learned from the state troopers about the accident?"

"Actually, they've been very efficient. They're forwarding some CCTV footage from a camera trained on the street near where you parked. No fingerprints on the lug nuts, though."

"So he wore gloves…" I replied.

"He wouldn't need to wear gloves to remove the lug nut, Rhe. You just use a wrench with the appropriately sized socket. He only loosened them," replied Sam. With his nose in a splint and properly swollen, he sounded like Bart Simpson's sister, Lisa. "And some wrenches fold, so he could have put it in his pocket."

"Did they find a wrench?" *Too much to ask.*

"Nope, but they're looking. Oh, and the governor called this morning to check on Sam."

"Nice of him," Sam said. "Probably worried it had something to do with the sniper investigation."

Which it doesn't," I replied. "I'm convinced of that."

Phil took us to the police station rather than home, because Sam wanted to look at the CCTV footage from Augusta. When we walked in the door, Ruthie jumped down from her stool and ran to Sam, almost knocking him over as she hugged him around his waist. Her eyes teared up as she stood back and looked at the both of us. "You could have been killed. And just look at your face, Sam! We really need to catch that son-of-a-bitch. Everyone here is hopping mad."

Wow, I thought. *I've never heard Ruthie swear before!*

"Don't worry, Ruthie. We'll get the guy. Has everyone besides me and Rhe looked at the footage from Augusta?"

"Pretty much. I've matched his face to the DMV photos of the twins. But we can't tell which one," replied Deputy Birch, who had just entered the reception area.

"Time for me to take a look. Phil, can you project to the screen in the conference room? And put up the DMV photos. Birch, join us, please."

Ruthie scuttled away as we headed down the hall to the conference room, coming back breathless just after we'd all settled around the table. She had two coffees and from the wonderful aroma, a box of fresh pastries from *Pie and Pickle*. "Now don't bug him about the calories, Rhe," she said, setting everything down in front of us. "You both deserve some coddling."

I had to smile. Deputy Birch and Phil sat across the table and Phil plugged his laptop into the TV. I shoved the pastry box to them as soon as Sam and I had helped ourselves. "Have some."

Birch grabbed an apple fritter, which left a couple of ordinary powdered doughnuts. Phil gave us a grin, as he placed one of them on a napkin in front of him. Ruthie knew he liked plain doughnuts.

With a few keystrokes Phil brought up the footage. It clearly showed the front of Sam's Jeep from the sidewalk side and a man bending down with a wrench, working on the back right wheel. He didn't take any precautions to hide his face, and I wondered if he knew about the camera or just didn't care. "Where was the camera located, Phil?" I asked.

"Hidden in the fold of the retracted awning of a café, about two doors down. A local LEO sent me a picture of the storefront and awning, and I had to look hard to spot it. I doubt the suspect saw it."

"Then we caught a break," said Sam, between mouthfuls of his chocolate croissant.

"Wait a minute," said Birch. "Can you bring up the DMV photos side by side?"

Phil tapped some more keys and the two visuals popped up.

She stared at the DMV photos for a long moment, then said, "Look carefully at these photos. You can already see these are twins, but I think these men are mirror twins." Sam and I must have looked puzzled because she immediately added, "Mirror twins are twins whose features appear asymmetrically—that is, on opposite sides. When these twins face each other, it's as if they're looking in a mirror."

"What are you seeing that we don't?" I asked.

"Look at their hair. They have different cowlicks – a tuft of hair growing in a different direction from the rest of their hair. One is tufted to the right, the other to the left."

'Well I'll be damned," said Sam. "Good job, Birch. Too bad we can't see this jerk's hair under the baseball cap. Or get a good view of his eyes."

"But we can see his hair," she relied. "There's one shot where he pushes his cap back to get a better look at the wheel. Can you find it, Deputy Chief Pearce?"

The video backed up and then jumped forward until we could see under the front part of the cap. The cowlick tufted to the right. We looked again at the Rightnour DMV photos. Morris's cowlick bent to the right, Aaron's to the left.

"So it's Morris," Sam said. "Gotcha! I know it's a long shot, Phil, but can we get a BOLO out on this character? Coordinate with the state troopers and the police departments in this region, and put it out on Sunday."

"Why Sunday?" he asked.

"Because we don't want to spook them. We're counting on one twin showing up at the bar tomorrow night."

CB   CB

On Friday night, I sat in a booth in a corner of the Dirty Gull, at the right end of the bar. With me were Merlin, in his usual attire. Zoey sat next to me wearing dangling earrings and more than filling out her tank top, and Tanya, dressed in athletic gear adorned with the Pequod U logo, sat on my other side. I wore a long, wavy, black wig, sunglasses, and a tee shirt with an eagle on the chest and flags on the sleeves. With the outfits, dim lighting, and the fog of smoke from illegal smoking, I doubted we'd be noticed.

Paulette sat on a stool at the bar, legs crossed and nursing a ginger ale. She had teased her normally curly hair into spikes and she had on a short imitation leather skirt and a tight sweater. Ankle boots with heels completed the ensemble, along with a stack of bracelets and outstanding makeup, applied by her daughter Sarah. She looked ten years younger—not cheap but definitely sassy. As a result, she drew the attention of a number of men in the bar. They would approach and offer to buy her a drink, and she would politely blow them off, all without a fuss. We heard every word because she had a microphone hidden in her cleavage.

Previously coerced by Sam's threat of losing the bar's liquor license, the bartender had some flutes of ginger ale underneath the bar to serve her from time to time. It passed as champagne in the cloudy glasses.

Finally at about 10:30, I nudged Merlin, sitting to my right. "There he is," I whispered. One of the twins had strode through the door, letting in a blast of cool air that temporarily blew away the smoke inside so we could see him clearly. He stood looking around. Paulette noticed him and caught his eye. She gave him an enticing smile and turned back to her drink. He sauntered up to the end of the bar farthest from her and started talking to another woman, keeping an eye on Paulette at the same time. He had on a ball cap, unfortunately, so I couldn't identify which twin he was.

After some time, he worked his way down the bar and sat down next to Paulette when a hairy biker, bursting out of his tight leather pants, vacated the seat next to her. Our twin was definitely more attractive that the previous occupant of the stool—thin, shaven, and wearing pressed jeans and a red plaid shirt with a dark blue padded vest.

Raucous noise filled the bar, and we watched as he leaned over close to her ear to speak. "What's a gorgeous woman like you doing here? You're certainly a class above the ones I usually see here."

"Thanks for the compliment...I think. To answer your question, I'm waiting for a friend," Paulette replied.

"Male or female?"

"Male."

"Can I keep you company until he arrives?" He placed his hand on her thigh.

She delicately lifted his arm by pinching his sleeve with two fingers, removing the offending appendage. "I guess so." She added a shy smile, looking at him from under her longer than normal eyelashes.

Atta girl, string him along. Get him on a leash, and let's see what happens.

"Can I buy you a drink?"

She nodded.

"What are you having?"

"Champagne, I love it."

"Champagne? Here? Okay...more champagne for the lady," the twin said to the hovering bartender. "And I'll have a Maker's Mark, a double." His eyes scanned the bar as he made the order. At that moment, as planned, Zoe and Merlin leaned into each other, faking some laughs. Tanya called out, "Bartender, we need another round of beers here!" From behind my shades I watched as our twin took a brief look at our group, then turned away to focus on the rest of the room. The bartender reached below the counter and came up with a flute of ginger ale, which he placed in front of Paulette. When the twin focused back on her, we collectively let out a breath.

"Be right with you," the bartender called back to us. He reached for a bottle of bourbon from the shelf behind the bar, opened it and poured a generous amount into a glass. "Here you are," he said, turning back to the bar and placing the bourbon next to Paulette's 'champagne.' "Shall I keep a tab?"

The twin nodded, and Paulette drained the drink she already had and picked up the second.

"You must be addicted to that stuff," the twin said. "Too sweet for me."

Paulette gave a small burp. *Great touch.*

Remembering what we'd first ordered, the bartender moved to the handles of the beers on tap and filled four glasses, then placed them on a tray, which a server brought to the table. She looked askance at the half-full glasses on the table, then shrugged and walked away.

For the next forty-five minutes, we listened to the patter between Paulette and our suspect while they continued drinking. As we'd expected, he asked a number of questions about Pequod, why she had moved here, where she lived, what she liked about the town. Her family, sports, recreation, favorite restaurants. He deflected Paulette's questions or answered with what we knew were outright lies. When Paulette excused herself to use the ladies room, we watched the twin look around again before dropping something into her drink.

Paulette returned and took what appeared to be a good sip of her drink, then said, "Hey, look at that. My champagne has lost its fizz. Can I get a fresh one?"

The bartender took her glass and placed it under the counter, where he had all the glasses we'd asked him keep for evidence, including the twin's.

"Coming up in a minute," he replied, waiting for a distraction to replace Paulette's drink. He didn't need it.

"Looks like your friend's not coming."

Paulette shook her head, burped again. "Guess not." She wobbled a little on the bar stool.

"What say we go somewhere else without the noise and smoke? You up for that?" I could hear the vibrato of anticipation in his voice.

"Sounds like a plan." She smiled at him.

He stood, called for the bill, paid it and then steered a slightly staggering Paulette out the door. *Brilliant performance. Now if the people outside will do their jobs.*

I retrieved my radio from my bag. "Sam, are you there? They're coming out. Do you have them?"

Sam had parked in an unmarked car at the far end of the street in a spot not lit by a street lamp. "They're talking just outside the door. Don't come out yet." Then, "They're moving down the street, toward the waterfront. Birch and Dowdy are following. He has to make a move before we can take him, and I'm hoping if he's going to the park like the last time, it's out in the open."

Merlin got up so I could squeeze out of the booth, "You guys stay here. Do NOT move. You've been great." I threw some bills on the table. "Have another beer on the department." Then I ran for the door, fumbling with the radio. "Sam, where's Phil?"

"I'm sending him to the park."

Outside, I hoofed it in the direction of the park, trying to keep at a reasonable distance behind them, traveling in and out of the pools of light dropped by the street lamps. I worried about Paulette but also about being seen by the twin. Having a baby on board did not improve my speed, and I was puffing hard before I got to the end of the street. I took a left on Main, heading toward the darkness of the park, facing the aptly named Waterfront Street. I could smell the reek of the bar coming from my clothes, and I wondered for a moment whether the owner should be required to provide chemical masks. I turned left on Waterfront, with the park on my right between the street and the harbor. A few street lights dimly illuminated the park.

When I reached its edge, I saw two figures struggling at the harbor's edge. *Paulette!* Two other figures quickly approached them from my direction. Another ran from the north end of the park.

I bent over, hands on hips, trying to take in more air, head up, watching. One of the figures went down. The other stood there.

I jumped when someone came up behind me and took my elbow. Sam.

"What in hell do you think you're doing, running like some water-crazed camel?"

"Really? Is that all you can say?"

I noticed Sam also gasped from the effort of running because of his swollen nose, and he held his broken arm to his chest. Despite his injuries, he half-tugged, half-supported me, as we both approached what I could see had become a group. Phil and Deputy Birch held flashlights on Officer Dowdy, who was in the process of handcuffing the man on the ground.

Paulette, her clothes a bit askew and minus one earring, stood panting but smiling. "I guess I surprised him when I turned out not to be drugged. He never saw my upper cut coming."

I hugged her. "What did you do?"

"I kneed him in the groin and as he bent over, took the heel of my hand and rammed it up under his nose. Then I clocked him one on the side of his head. Did I break his nose? I hope so!" She bounced up and down on her toes, like a prize fighter, juiced with adrenalin. "That police training on how to handle a mugger sure paid off."

Dowdy and Birch lifted the dazed twin to his feet. Blood ran freely from a shattered nose. He tried to bend over. "That bitch, she attacked me! She's broken my effing nose and uuuuuugh…my balls."

We could now see his cowlick bent to the left.

"Which one is it?" asked Sam.

"Aaron Rightnour," replied Deputy Birch.

So where's Morris?

"Do the honors, Deputy," said Sam. "This is your arrest."

"Aaron Wrightnour, you are being arrested for rape and attempted rape. You have the right to remain silent…" her voice trailed off as she and Dowdy headed out of the park with their prisoner.

૎   ૎

Three hours later, after Paulette had given her statement, Sam and I invited ourselves to her kitchen—ostensibly for a late night snack and some hot cocoa, but really to make sure she was okay. As we all sat at the table, Paulette told her husband what had happened.

"We had the situation in hand," Sam said reassuringly. "We would have gotten to them before he could do anything. Your wife just decided to do it her way."

Ted just shook his head. "I guess we can do without the home alarm system, then. I have a wife who can neutralize any threat." He took one of her hands in his and leaned over to kiss her cheek. "You are one amazing woman, hon, but you scare the hell out of me. I suppose it's useless to tell you not to do that again?"

Paulette winked at me.

Chapter 23

SAM

What Mr. Renwick had told me about Parkins' loving relationship with his daughter and his pacific nature nagged at me during the next week. Parkins had been held over without bail because of the severity of the charge against him, and thus far I'd had no communication from his lawyer. I decided to check with Dan Katayama, our county public prosecutor, to see if he had anything new on the case, but he told me he'd also heard nothing. Then, on Friday, Mr. Renwick called me.

"Good morning, Chief. I was wondering if you and I might meet with the county prosecutor about Reverend Parkins. His trial is scheduled for next month, and there have been some developments."

"Sure, just tell me when and where."

"How about 2 p.m. this afternoon, my office?"

"I'll see you there."

Renwick's practice was housed in one of the pseudo-New England salt boxes built during the last several years to house two to four office suites. Because of its proximity, I took advantage of the crisp winter day and walked. *Rhe will be proud of me.*

I climbed the stairs to the second floor of the office building, where a receptionist greeted me when I entered. The small front room of Renwick's office was modestly decorated with thin carpeting, a few framed photographs of Pequod and some wooden chairs. A door in the rear of the room presumably led to his office.

"Chief Brewster? Go right in. Mr. Renwick is expecting you." The receptionist gave me a brilliant, white-toothed smile and indicated the door.

Renwick and Dan Katayama sat across from each other at conference table in the office. After we all shook hands, I took off my coat and sat down opposite Renwick, alongside Dan. "So what are these developments you mentioned?"

"I think you know I had some reservations from the start about Abel's guilt."

"Doesn't every defense attorney feel that way?" I asked.

"True, but even Mr. Katayama has his doubts."

"I do, Sam," said Dan. "When I interviewed Reverend Parkins, Mr. Renwick present, I first asked him about the fall that sent Naomi to the hospital a few days after the rape. He claimed he had nothing to do with it, since it happened at the house where Naomi and her brother lived. Then I asked him to describe where and when he fatally beat his daughter. According to Parkins, she'd come to him to beg his forgiveness, and he'd lost control of his temper. This scenario doesn't fit with what Mr. Renwick said he'd observed about his client over the years—that while Reverend Parkins has a temper, he is not physically abusive. There's clearly more to this situation."

"You know," I replied, "Rhe and I had serious doubts whether Naomi had incurred the injuries from falling down the stairs at her house. The house is single story and has no basement. Only two stairs lead up to the porch."

"If her injuries didn't result from falling down stairs, what did happen?" Dan asked.

"I believe her brother beat her. Something was off when we met him at the hospital and he has a real temper based on his response to his father being arrested," I replied.

"So Luke may have beaten his sister the first time, but with regard to the fatal beating, we have no evidence, other than Reverend Parkins' word, that he is the one who did it." Dan shook his head.

"But I think we do now," replied Renwick. "Two of Abel's congregation came to see me yesterday. They confirmed Luke has an easily triggered temper and added that he's physically assaulted at least two their members. They insisted the reverend has never resorted to brutality and would not have harmed his daughter."

"But that's hearsay at best, right Dan?" I asked.

"True, but there's more," Renwick answered, clearing his throat. "One of them overheard Luke talking to his father about Naomi's rape. Luke was insistent that his sister be punished severely and told his father that he would 'do it,' whatever that meant. Abel told his son not to intervene, that he would handle it. I believe Luke didn't listen."

"Isn't this still hearsay?" I asked.

"Maybe, but I think this can serve as evidence," Renwick replied, "because it raises reasonable doubt. But we still need to get the truth from either the reverend or Luke."

"Got any ideas?" I squinted at both of them.

Dan smiled grimly. "I think we need to get the two of them in the same room and apply some pressure."

ങ   ങ

The next day, Abel Parkins, his son Luke, Dan Katayama, Charles Renwick, and I met in an interrogation room at the police station. Renwick sat next to his client, and Dan and I sat across the table from them. Luke sat by himself at one end.

"I don't understand the purpose of this meeting, Charles," said Parkins.

Luke glowered at us, "Yeah, why am I here? I thought you indicted my father for killing Naomi."

"It turns out some new information has come to light, which we think you ought to consider before we go to court," Renwick explained.

"And that is?" asked Luke.

Renwick then told tell Parkins and his son everything he had learned from the congregation members. When I told them what Rhe and I had discovered, Luke's face paled, then reddened.

"There are a few things both you and your son need to understand," Dan said, looking at them in turn. "First, although there is no death penalty in Maine, Naomi's death was particularly brutal, and thus if you are found guilty, Reverend, you will be sentenced to life in the state prison. To be honest, the inmates there do not take kindly to child killers."

"I'm a man of God. I hardly think they will…"

"I'm afraid God won't help you," I replied. "You'll be a dead man walking from the time you enter the prison. And the real killer will be free to kill again. How would you feel if that happened?"

"Don't say anything, Dad," said Luke, standing up, his face now the color of a beet. "Don't you dare say another word." He glared at his father, his pupils dilated in fear and anger.

"Is that a threat, son?"

"You're damned right it is. I'll kill you, I swear it, if you open your mouth."

I stood and went over to Luke, pushing him back down in his chair. "Your father can say what he likes, Luke, and you will *not* make any more threats or I will arrest you, understand?"

Reverend Parkins was silent for a good minute, head down, seeming deep in thought.

When he looked up, he took a deep breath and exhaled with a groan. "Luke has always had a short fuse, and over the years, he's become harsh and judgmental, despite God's teachings of forgiveness and love. Perhaps he learned that from me. I've had to stop him from physically punishing members of my congregation on several occasions, and I know there were instances when I didn't catch him." He paused, taking another deep breath. "He became unhinged when Naomi told us she'd been raped. I didn't help things by telling her in front of everyone that she was a harlot, had shamed us and then threw her out of my congregation. I did *not* beat her, not then and not ever. I know Luke wanted to, but I tried mightily to dissuade him. When she came to visit me after her hospitalization for the first beating, she cowered in his presence. He later bragged to me he had put the fear of the Lord in her. Clearly. I didn't stop Luke from punishing Naomi."

"And I'll arrest him for that beating," I said to Parkins.

"There's more, unfortunately. When you came to tell me she had died, I knew immediately Luke was responsible. He didn't have to tell me. I could see it in his lack of surprise. At the time, I truly believed I should assume the guilt for what had happened to my daughter because I hadn't stopped him. But with the Lord's guidance and much prayer, I've come to realize that taking the blame for Luke will only embolden him. You are right. He might kill someone else in his righteous zealotry."

Luke struggled to stand under the pressure of my hands on his shoulder. "You're a liar, old man. *You* killed her! Stop telling them these lies! The harlot deserved what she got!"

Removing my handcuffs from my belt, I let Luke stand. He lurched to go around the table toward his father, but I jerked one arm back and cuffed it. Renwick, who was between Luke and his father, got up and blocked his way so that I could grab Luke's other arm and apply the other cuff. "Luke Parkins, you are under arrest for the murder of your sister, Naomi Parkins. You have the right…"

As I recited the Miranda warning, Reverend Parkins bent his head forward and lifted his voice in prayer, tears running down his cheeks. "For God says, 'If my people, which are called by my name, shall humble themselves, and pray, and seek my face, and turn from their wicked ways; then will I hear from heaven, and will forgive their sin, and will heal their land.' I will pray for God's forgiveness of you, my son."

Luke spat at his father as he left the room.

Renwick and Parkins stood as if to leave.

"Not so fast, Mr. Renwick. Your client still has to answer for his daughter's death, even if he himself didn't kill her. He incited his son. Reverend Parkins, I am arresting you for aiding and abetting in the death of Naomi Parkins."

He hung his head in resignation while I recited his Miranda rights again.

Chapter 24

SAM

The Saturday morning after the resolution of the Parkins' case, I rolled out of bed before even Jack stirred. Eight-thirty found me in an interrogation room at the police station, across the table from Aaron Wrightnour and his lawyer, who apparently would work at any hour and thought I should, too. He had called me late the night before, asking to meet as soon as possible. We'd settled on eight-thirty. I'd met Wilmer Bixby before when he cross-examined me in a previous court case, trying to destroy my reputation and that of the department in an effort to save his client. He hadn't succeeded then, and I wouldn't let him do so now. I knew he would love to tell the court that the police department and its chief had been uncooperative. His small black eyes, so dark the irises blended with the pupils, reminded me of a rodent. His overbite and tobacco-stained teeth only reinforced this unfortunate impression.

"Aaron Wrightnour, do you understand the charges against you?" I asked, after I'd turned on the recorder in the interview room and stated the names of those present.

Bixby whispered in his ear. Then Wrightnour replied, "That woman tricked me last night. I'm innocent." His voice was high-pitched, not what I had expected from the size of him. "Do you understand that last night aside, you are charged with the rape of two young women and the death of one of them?"

"It was *not* me! It was my twin brother Morris, and you can't tell it was me from the DNA."

Bixby had clearly explained this to him, but no way would I let him know that could stop us. "Then why were you the twin at the Dirty

Gull last night? And why did you pick up Ms. McGillivray, put a drug her drink and assault her in the park, if that's your brother's MO?"

"I might a done it, you know, last night, but I didn't do no rapes. I'm not saying Morris did it, but you can't prove it was me and not him that raped them women."

"We do have enough evidence to compel a DNA sample, and I will have a warrant for that tomorrow."

Bixby started to object, then stopped.

He knew very well we'd find the DNA would be the same as Morris's when we got a sample from that brother. So he saw no reason to block the warrant. "And where might we find your brother?"

The lawyer whispered in his ear again. Aaron leaned back and made a zipping motion over his lips. "It seems you have a problem there," Bixby said in his oily voice. He leaned forward and gave me a yellow smile. "You and I both know the only charges you can hold him on are those from last night. I intend to ask for a bail hearing first thing Monday morning. Have him ready for release at that time. There's no way a judge will deny him bail. Your DNA evidence from the one rape is worthless, since it can't prove without a doubt my client did it. I'm going to push to get him released ROR."

Released on his own recognizance? In a pigs' eye. But I would really need some help to get him bound over for trial without bail. Time to consult with Kip Moncton. I took a deep breath. "We'll see." I'd had a deputy standing just outside the door to the interrogation room. Now I stood, opened the door, and told him to come in and take the prisoner back to his cell.

Bixby got up and left with Wrightnour, giving me a smirk as he passed. "You got nothing."

Once back in my office, I called Kip, while I rested my casted arm on my desk. The pain had abated to a dull, nagging ache, but I wouldn't take any pain medication in case it impaired my thinking. "Sorry to interrupt your Saturday, Kip, but I really need your help. I've got a tough situation here." And I explained where we were with our mirror twins. "What can we do?" I heard a deep sigh at the other end of the line.

"Sam, there are two ways we can document differences. One inexpensive, and you don't want to know the price of the other one. "

"Okay, tell me inexpensive first."

"That would be fingerprint analysis."

"Don't twins have identical fingerprints?" I asked.

"Nope. No two people, even twins, have the exact same fingerprints. Twin prints will be very similar, but not identical. Which is why we will need to print all ten fingers from each twin, in order to find the differences."

"I know we usually need ten or more points for an absolute fingerprint ID. Would you get less than ten with twins?"

"Actually *twelve* matching points are irrefutable evidence in most legal cases. If we get less than twelve, let's say only eight, and we declare that the prints are different, the twins' lawyer will probably argue this degree of difference is not statistically significant. Hence the need for the other analysis."

"Okay, what is it? And spare no expense." I heard a chuckle at the other end of the line.

"That would be a relatively new technique to analyze DNA from twins, called sequence mutation analysis."

"Uh, English please?"

"Okay, I'll try. If you remember your college biology, you know DNA is made up of a sequence of base pairs. The environment can cause DNA mutations in this sequence, for example, sunlight, cigarette smoke, and radiation. These are random and can happen anywhere in the DNA sequence. Sometimes the mutation can lead to serious effects like skin cancer and lung cancer. Are you with me so far?"

"Yes, but these guys don't have cancer."

"Right, but sometimes a mutation doesn't change the protein encoded in the sequence and it stays the same. So there's no overt effect. But think about it, Sam, these sequence mutations are totally random. It's incredibly unlikely they'd be the same in both twins. And the discrepancies between the twins' DNA sequences can be used to identify which twin did the rapes."

"Okay, what do you need?"

"A DNA sample from each twin."

"You've already got sample from one of the rapes. With the consent of his lawyer, Aaron agreed to give his DNA because he thinks it'll be the same as his brother's. He's claiming his brother did the rapes. Can you compare what he gives us with the DNA from the rape?"

"Yup. If the samples have the same sequence mutations, we've got him for the rapes. But what if they're different? How do you plan to get a sample from the other twin?"

"Gotta catch him first. Assuming we can find the other twin, how long would the DNA work take?"

"One to two weeks. But it's going to cost, because we aren't set up to do sequence analysis here. I'll have to send the DNA out to a specialized lab."

"Bottom line?"

"A thousand dollars and time."

I took a deep breath in. That would take a huge chunk of the department's budget. *I'll find it somehow. I'd love to nail both these creeps.* "It's a deal. I'll send the other twin's DNA along when we catch him." Now to convince a judge not to release the twin we already had.

I looked up the court schedule for Monday and found Judge Jeffries would preside. Not good news. Jeffries had been rounded up in a raid my department had made on a high-class brothel with college student 'escorts' a number of years ago. Not one, but two, pricey lawyers plus friends in high places had managed to get him released with no charges and quashed any publicity. He'd stayed on the bench, and he and I had not been on the best of terms since then. On the other hand, knowing what I knew put him at a disadvantage. I needed him to ensure we could keep the one twin in jail while we looked for the other one.

As the county prosecutor, Dan Katayama would be representing the people that day. Dan was a combination of bloodhound and border terrier, and I couldn't recall the last time he'd lost a case, so I knew we'd be in good hands.

One other thing to follow up on: the information we'd gathered from Mildred Burger about the possible sniper, based on their health insurance grievances. Last night I'd finally texted Agent Bongiovanni and Bella Dundzic with the information and asked for their thoughts. They texted back they would do a conference call, about fifteen minutes from now. This left me just time enough to run to the *Pie and Pickle* for some take-out breakfast. I thought food might help with the headache that had developed behind my eyes during the phone call with Kip.

Before my phone rang, I gobbled down a Western omelet with a side of hash browns and bacon. *At least I can still eat with one arm.* The call was short: they'd take the lead at this point, and I was more than happy to have them do that. By the time we hung up, the headache had reached almost unbearable on the pain scale. So I closed up shop and headed home, where I could take the pain meds the docs had given me and then a long nap.

ڃ   ڃ

On Monday morning, Rhe and I went to court to be there for Nancy Ennis at her sentencing. Every member of the ER staff not working filled most of the seats in the courtroom. Sawyer Smith sat next to Nancy as her lawyer, and Dan Katayama presented the case to Judge Jeffries. He did a fair job of it, avoiding embellishment and hyperbole, and then Jeffries asked if Nancy would stipulate to the charges. I could hear Rhe, sitting beside me, draw a sudden breath.

Nancy, her face almost as pale as her white blouse, stood unsteadily, with shaking hands. Her husband sat behind her. Art leaned forward and whispered in her ear. Without turning to him, she replied with a watery half smile. "Yes, your honor, I will."

I could see her shoulders rise as she inhaled deeply and then told her story in a soft but steady voice. She made no excuses and gave only the facts. At one point, I heard a "harrumph" coming from the row of seats behind the prosecutor and spotted Manning. The judge glared in his direction, and Manning retreated into his seat.

Nancy concluded, "I willingly accept whatever punishment is due me, your honor. I deserve it."

Jeffries then asked, "Do either of you lawyers have anything more to say?"

"I do, your honor."

My head jerked up in surprise. The prosecutor had spoken.

Judge Jeffries acknowledged Katayama with a tilt of his head.

"Your honor, it has been my privilege to speak with many of Nurse Ennis's colleagues over the past week or so. Clearly, she's a skilled nurse, valued by her colleagues, and to a person, they told me her family had bullied and threatened her to steal the drugs."

I looked over at Art, whose head hung so low I couldn't see his face.

"While her colleagues didn't excuse what she did, they understood and forgave her. Ms. Ennis has no prior record and did not steal the drugs for distribution or sale. In addition, no patients were affected by the thefts. For these reasons, I ask that you apply the minimum sentence."

Manning exploded to his feet, waving his arms. "I object, your honor! This woman committed fraud and stole from my hospital." He extended his arm, pointing at Nancy, who shrunk back. "She's a disgrace to her profession and should be punished to the full extent of the law."

Jeffries looked down his nose at Manning. "Dr. Manning, you have no standing to comment at this sentencing. Any comments you need to make should have been made to the prosecutor before this morning. Sit down, or I will have you removed from the court."

Manning remained standing for a moment, then slowly dropped back into his seat.

"Ms. Ennis, the court finds you guilty of the charges as stated and accepts your allocution. These charges bring a normal sentence of five to seven years. However, based on the recommendation of the prosecutor, I sentence you to two years. With time off for good behavior, you should be released at the end of the first year. I wish you all the best in rebuilding your life."

Manning jumped back to his feet. "I object! These court proceedings are a joke. I'll get you removed from the bench, Jeffries. I know things about you. You'll regret this."

The sharp, repeated sound of the gavel shocked everyone in the courtroom. "I would be very careful what you say, Dr. Manning. Bailiff, remove this man from the court."

Despite Manning's continued loud objections, the bailiff half-dragged him from the courtroom, sporting a big smile while he did it.

Everyone gathered at the railing behind Nancy. She hugged Art and yelled "I love you all," and put her hands behind her to be cuffed.

Rhe turned into my chest, tears flowing, dampening the front of my uniform.

"It's okay, Rhe. She'll be sent to a minimum-security facility. Dan will see to it. And she'll be home in a year."

"But to what? No one can hire her as a nurse with her record."

"Something will work out. Think positive." I gently removed her to a few inches away. "I need to talk to Dan. Next up is the bail hearing for Aaron Wrightnour. Have a seat. I'll be right back."

I moved through the gate to the front of the courtroom. Dan looked up from his paperwork. "Thanks for the heads up this weekend, Sam. Wrightnour is a nasty piece of work. I'm going to do my best to see he stays in jail. Any luck locating the brother?"

"Not yet. Do you think Jeffries will be open to persuasion?"

"You never know with him. I was a little surprised he listened to me this morning."

"Maybe he's found religion?"

Dan chuckled, his eyes turning into upside-down smiles, a feature Rhe thought endearing.

ڃ ڑ

At eleven, Wrightnour entered the courtroom in the usual orange jumpsuit with PPD stenciled on the back. He wore handcuffs in front but no chains, as per the insistence of his lawyer. Rhe and I were the only other people still there, sitting three rows back on the prosecutor's side. Spotting us, he gave us his best smirk and waved with his cuffs, then walked to the table where Wilmer Bixby sat. The bailiff then removed his cuffs.

"The prisoner will sit down," the judge ordered.

Bixby jerked on Wrightnour's arm, pulling him down into his chair.

"Is everyone present and accounted for?" Jeffries asked.

"Yes, your honor," came back the chorus.

"If so, then you may proceed, Mr. Katayama."

Dan then succinctly summarized the charges and asked for remand of the prisoner. As he did so, Kip Moncton slipped in the rear doors of the room and walked up the aisle to sit beside me. "I got a message from the prosecutor I might be needed."

I nodded.

Jeffries asked, "How do you plead, Mr. Wrightnour?"

Bixby and his client stood. "Not guilty!" Wrightnour's voice could probably be heard in Aroostook County.

"Remind your client I'm not deaf, Mr. Bixby. As to the question of bail…"

Bixby interrupted, "Your honor, with regard to the charges stemming from last night, the situation was a total misunderstanding. And as for the rapes…"

"Yes, I know, I know. Your client claims his twin did them. However, I understand there now exists a way to identify one twin's DNA from another's. Given that the court doesn't yet know which of the twins committed the rapes, I am loathe to release this man. He could very well be a danger to the public. Remand!"

"But your honor…"

"Save it for the trial, Bixby. Let me take a look at the court calendar." Here Jeffries paused and consulted a schedule on his bench. "Since we don't want to abrogate his right to a speedy trial, how does three weeks from today look, counselors?"

Bixby nodded, but Dan shook his head.

"Problem, Counselor?"

"Yes, your honor. There's no way of predicting if Chief Brewster can find the other brother in three weeks."

"I'm afraid he'll have to. I won't let this drag on forever."

Dan's head dropped. "Yes, your honor. Three weeks."

Bixby positively beamed and gave a murine smile to his client. He whispered in Wrightnour's ear just before the bailiff replaced his cuffs and led him away.

"Sam!" Rhe clutched my arm. "Three weeks is not enough! It might be impossible."

Kip added, "Don't forget we also need time to do the analysis."

I smiled at both of them. "I've got a plan, but I'll need your help, Rhe."

Chapter 25

RHE

We returned home from the court session to have a lupper—a combination of a late lunch and an early supper. This worked out well, because Jack stayed at Tyler's and I had a shift in the ER that began at four. I decided to wait to ask Sam about his 'plan' until we were eating, since we'd bought an everything-on-it pizza, his favorite food, on the way.

As soon as we were in the door, I set the pizza box on the kitchen table, hung up my coat by the door and got out two plates. "Don't think we're going to make a habit of this." I gestured to the pizza which still emanated its mouth-watering smell that'd driven me crazy on the way home. "It's just that after this morning, Little It told me she needed some comfort food." I sat down.

"*He* needs some comfort food. Like father, like son." Having shed his coat, Sam gave me a wicked grin as he sat down at the table and lifted the box cover. Two pieces immediately traveled to his plate. I also grabbed two pieces, cramming the end of one into my mouth. I was so incredibly hungry. While chewing the pizza, I mumbled, "So what's this plan of yours?"

"Mmm, talking with your mouth full. What would Jack think?"

My husband could be so irritating. I snatched the pizza box away as he went for another slice.

I swallowed before I replied, "Spill if you want more."

"Okay, okay." He grabbed the box back. "I've been thinking that identical twins can have a deep, unexplained, connection. If Morris discovers his brother is in big trouble, he'll probably show up thinking he can exonerate him by proving their DNA is identical. The prosecutor wouldn't know which one to charge. I hope he doesn't know about this latest sequencing technique." He slid another two slices on this plate, and I held up my hand to stop him from taking any more.

"But won't this be in the newspaper? I saw a court reporter back in the corner this morning, scribbling furiously." I finished my second slice and took the last one.

"I had a little talk with our friendly neighborhood editor at the *Post and Sentinel* last night, after you conked out on the couch. Since he gave us some help finding information on the snipers, I asked him for another favor: not to put anything in the paper about the sequencing technique but to play up the seriousness and the lengthy jail time if Aaron were convicted. And also mention that if the twin couldn't be located, the prosecution would proceed with just Aaron's DNA."

"What did you offer him for this favor?"

Sam smiled. "An exclusive, of course."

I reached over and gave him what I hadn't eaten of the last piece. "Sam, you're brilliant!"

"Aw, shucks, all the women say that!"

ڃ ڃ

I left for the hospital before four p.m., with a hole in my heart from the thought of never seeing Nancy's bouncing curls and smiling face there again. I also had an uneasy feeling our beloved CEO would find a way to exact revenge for Nancy's light sentence.

When I arrived, the ER looked to be in disarray. Long lines of people sat in the waiting area, and voices called for assistance. We clearly lacked enough staff to handle the influx, and I asked a nurse rushing by what was going on.

"We're down three nurses," she called over her shoulder.

"Why?"

She turned and walked backward saying, "Don't know. They didn't show up and I haven't had time to call them. By the way, you're listed as the charge nurse. Feel free to jump in!" She smiled and hurried down the corridor.

The Pecker. He's behind this. After I'd thrown down my coat and bag, I called upstairs to the ER department and asked for as many faculty and residents as they could spare to come down. Then I did indeed jump in.

When my shift ended at midnight, I discovered the next shift also lacked three people. This time I sat down and called to find out why. The first nurse I called expressed shock when I told her what had happened.

"But I received a text message around eleven that I wasn't needed," she told me.

"Did you know who sent the message?"

"I wouldn't miss a shift based on an anonymous text," she replied huffily. "I checked the number and it belongs to someone in the CEO's office."

The other two nurses told me the same story. Then I called Sam and told him I had to pull a double shift and explained why.

"Manning clearly wants the ER to be overwhelmed. He named me as charge nurse, something he swore he'd never do. I know what he's thinking—if someone dies as a result, he can lay the blame at my feet. I have a nasty feeling this staff shortage will continue, so I'm going to inform the hospital board as soon as possible. It's time to poke the damn bear."

"Anything I can do to help?"

"Can you take blood pressures?" I replied with a smile. "Right now the only thing I need is a break to feed my growing daughter."

"*Son*, and I'll wait to see you in the morning before leaving. Take care of yourself, hon. My life would be empty without you, dear."

In response, I sang him the first verse of the Supremes' old hit.

☙ ❧

I dragged myself into the house at eight-thirty the next morning and collapsed in a kitchen chair without even taking my coat off. Fatigue had turned my muscles into limp elastics and my feet felt like blocks of cement.

Sam stood at the cooktop, from which came the tempting odor of bacon. I saw some French toast in another frying pan. He came over, kissed my neck, and helped me out of my coat. "Breakfast is ready. After which I will massage your feet and put you into bed."

I moaned with the anticipated pleasure. The foot rub proved even better than the French toast and bacon I'd gobbled down. Sometime during the rub, I fell asleep. I awoke to the sound of my phone ringing and tried to ignore it, but whoever called persisted. Finally I threw back the blanket Sam had covered me with, groaned as I stood up, and stumbled into the kitchen to retrieve the phone from my bag. I didn't recognize the number.

"Ms. Brewster?" The very young voice tried to sound officious.

"This had better be good, whoever you are. I just pulled a double shift and you woke me up from a very pleasant dream. And you are?"

"Lila Young. I work in Dr. Manning's office."

"And?"

"I'm calling to tell you that you missed your morning shift in the ER. One more and you will be dismissed."

"My morning shift? Did you not hear me? I had the four to midnight shift last night and stayed to work the next shift because some ER staff didn't show up for work. I only work three days a week. How can I be scheduled for another shift today?"

"I'm only telling you what the note said."

"Who wrote it?"

"I really don't know. I found a printed request on my desk, telling me to call you with this directive when I got in this morning."

"Well, whoever wrote that had to be confused. Shift changes are run through the Department of Emergency Medicine the last time I looked. Could you please scan that request and send it to me by email. Now, please."

"Yes, ma'am."

"And send one to Dr. Tony Churchill. He's the chair of Emergency Medicine. Thanks, Lila."

I hung up and decided that even as tired as I felt, this mess needed to be cleared up. I called Tony. The departmental secretary, perhaps hearing the strain in my voice, put me through immediately.

"Tony, this is Rhe Brewster. Something strange is going on with the ER staffing, and I think you need to be aware of it."

"I'm glad you caught me, Rhe. I just heard from some of the faculty that you called them down to the ER to help out last night."

"I did indeed. And it has to do with the shift staffing or rather the lack of it. Someone from the hospital told three nurses not to come in for their shift at four p.m., and another three at midnight. As the charge nurse designated by Manning, I pulled a double shift to make sure everything got covered."

"You must be exhausted. The last time I noticed, you were pregnant."

"Still am."

"Well, I thank you for doing that. I hope you aren't scheduled again for a couple of days."

"That's the thing. I got a call about ten minutes ago from a Lila Young in the CEO's office to tell me I was late for the morning shift, and if that happened again, I'd be fired. What the hell is going on? I thought your department handled the shift schedule."

He took a deep breath and exhaled. "We do. It's Manning. He thinks our department and the ER in particular are inefficient, and he wants to cut costs. He's been threatening me with all sorts of things, cutting my budget—which he already did—and now this."

"Does he have the right to change the shift schedule?"

"Apparently he thinks he does."

"Tony, I've had more than enough of that man's conniving. He has been after me, as you well know, for several years now. It's time to call him out. I plan to ask the hospital board if they'll let me speak at their next meeting."

"You couldn't have chosen a better time, Rhe. I'm already scheduled to meet with them, and I can't think of a better person to take with me."

"Just tell me where and when."

"The board meeting is scheduled for tomorrow. I'll email you the time and place and also ER staff schedule. And believe me, I will make sure everyone scheduled will be there."

Too tired to crawl into bed when the call ended, I fell back on the couch, insensate until Jack came blasting in the door after school.

I heard his coat fall to the floor, followed by his backpack. The refrigerator door opened, then closed, and footsteps came into the family room. "Mom! Are you sleeping?"

Master of the obvious. I opened one eye and looked at him. "I was. Is that an apple you're eating?"

"Mmmm."

"Good man. Come here and tell me about your day." I skootched over on the sofa to give him room to sit next to me.

"You know Ms. Mackril? She comes in once a week for special subjects. Today the Fish…"

"Jack, that's rude."

"No, it's not. She opens and closes her mouth like a fish and her name is Mackril. Everyone calls her that. And I've heard you call someone a woodpecker."

"Then you and I both need to be more civil. How would you like it if someone called you Jack the Sack or Jack the Smack?"

"Mom, you're rhyming."

Hah— a diversion, as usual when Jack doesn't want to talk about something. "So what did Ms. Mackril talk about today?"

"She said we are going to get a new student next week, and he has cerebral palsy. She wanted to tell us about it and asked us to be helpful to him."

"So what do you think?"

"I think it's a hard thing for that boy, and I'm happy the class agreed to be helpful."

I smiled and tousled his hair. "Anything else today?"

"Well, when Tyler and me got out of school…"

"Tyler and I."

"Yeah, okay, Tyler and I. We came out of school to wait for Paulette, we noticed a car parked at the way far end of the pick-up lane. It just sat there and didn't move forward. The cars behind it started honking and then had to drive around it."

"And what happened?"

"It followed us home."

I knew it. The twin had returned, just as Sam predicted. "Can you tell me more about the car and the driver?"

Jack looked thoughtful for a moment. "It was gray and had four doors. It looked like someone had sanded it in places, you know, very light in big spots. And old, like something you'd see in a movie on TV. The driver was a guy, I'm pretty sure, but when I turned around to look at him, he pulled his cap down so I couldn't see his face. Sort of a baseball cap."

"What happened when Paulette dropped you off?"

"The car went around us and went down the street pretty fast."

Shit.

"Is something wrong, Mom?"

"Probably nothing, Jack, but you are one eagle-eyed kid."

He beamed. "Got it from you and Dad, right?"

I smiled at that. "I think I'll still check with your dad. If you see the car again, let me know. How about some hot chocolate while you do your homework?"

"Can I go over to Tyler's when I'm done?"

"Sure. And I'll walk you over."

While Jack worked, I went into the family room and called Sam. When I told him about the gray sedan, he checked with Phil to see if the detail supposedly keeping an eye on Jack had actually been at the school. Turns out a jewelry store robbery had been called in and the deputy figured he should be there. I wouldn't want to be in that deputy's shoes this afternoon.

 C&3   C&3

The next morning I took the kids to school, dropping Sarah off first, then heading to South Pequod Elementary. Both boys were surprised when I parked and walked them in, running my eyes up and down the tree-lined street looking for a gray sedan.

"Why are you coming in, Mom?"

"I need to talk to the secretary in the principal's office about a safety program." I crossed my fingers inside my coat pocket.

The boys ran off, chattering and calling out to friends and heading down the corridor to the right, while I turned left and entered the principal's office. The principal stood behind the desk where Ms. Wilson, the receptionist, usually sat.

"Hi, Ms. Hernandez!"

"Hello, Ms. Brewster. What can I do for you today?" she asked with a warm smile.

"I have a concern I'd like you to convey to Jack's teachers and the office staff."

"Sure thing. What's the problem?" Mrs. Hernandez, a lovely lady who wore colorful dresses even in winter and had the patience of a saint, frowned slightly.

"Can we go somewhere we can talk in private?"

Her frown deepened. "Sure, come on into my office."

Once inside, I closed the door but remained standing. "Someone followed Tyler and Jack home last night. A man in an old, sanded down gray sedan. I know you think I'm being overly protective, but there have been some threats made to Sam and me lately. I'm worried that guy might try to get to us through Jack."

Ms. Hernandez sat down in the desk chair with a thud. "Oh, dear. What can we do to help?"

"Just be alert. And please make double sure someone accompanies the kids out to the car for their pickup in the afternoon and that the driver is someone you know. Don't let anyone other than us or the McGillivrays pick the kids up or take them out of school. Can you relay this to the office staff and especially Ms. Wilson?"

"Don't you worry, Ms. Brewster. We won't let anything happen to the boys. I'll make sure of it."

I gave her a reassuring smile. "I know you will."

☍ ☍

After leaving the school, I headed to the hospital for the board meeting, set to convene in a very comfortable and sumptuously appointed fifth floor conference room. I found Tony Churchill sitting in a chair outside the room with a pile of papers in his lap. "They'll call us when Emergency Medicine comes up on the agenda. Have a seat." He gestured to the upholstered chair next to him.

"Been waiting long?"

"Not really, but I'm not on the board so I didn't get the agenda— so who knows how long we'll be cooling our heels."

"Are those handouts for the board?"

"Yeah, they tend to fall asleep when the lights dim for a PowerPoint presentation."

An hour and a half later, the door to the conference room opened, and an older woman in a secretarial suit beckoned us into the room. Bored faces greeted us. Coffee cups and crumpled paper napkins littered the table and a large empty platter covered in crumbs, sat on the sideboard. *I bet we're last on the agenda.*

The chairman of the board, Dr. Fisker, whom I'd met at a hospital fund-raising event, motioned us to sit down in the two empty seats at the opposite end of the table from him. "Dr. Churchill, we've heard Dr. Manning's opinion about the Emergency Medicine Department," he began, tilting his head towards Manning, who sat beside him. "Now we'd like to hear yours."

"If these could be handed out, I think we'll have a basis for discussion. But I'm wondering why I couldn't listen to what Dr. Manning had to say."

Fisker had the decency to fluster. "Well, er, Jim requested you not be here."

Papers began to rustle as the board members got Tony's handouts. He then gave a succinct ten-minute presentation, using data he'd collected to back up his assertion: the department's and the emergency room's finances were in the black and the members of his department were academically active. He listed the number of patients treated on average on each day of the week, the referrals, and then went into the faculty's and residents' publications. I thought the presentation a winner.

When Tony had finished, Fisker turned to Manning. "You told us the department was five million dollars in debt. Where did you get your figures, Jim?"

"Well, I have them."

"It would appear that your numbers might be incorrect. Can you lay your hands on them right now, so we can compare?"

"Well, no, I'd have to dig around in my office, but I have them somewhere." By this time, Manning's face had deeply flushed. He clearly hadn't been expecting Tony to make the detailed presentation.

"Do you have anything else you want to convey to the board, Dr. Churchill?" Fisker asked.

"Yes, I do. In my opinion, Dr. Manning is trying to subvert my leadership and either eliminate the department and the ER or remake it in his own image. Ms. Brewster here will relate what happened this past weekend with regard to our ER shift schedule"

I took a deep breath and gave them a report of my experience and the meddling in the shift schedule by the CEO's office.

Fisker's forehead rose in disbelief. "Why would he do that, Mrs. Brewster? Couldn't that have just been some mischief played by one of the office secretaries?"

"It is my personal opinion Dr. Manning did that to set the stage for something serious to happen to one of our patients. Something that would discredit the ER department and also me, as charge nurse. I can't imagine what motive a secretary would have to change the staff schedule."

Manning rose to his feet and pointed at me. "You, you…" he caught himself. "Need I remind the board that a drug-addled nurse stole drugs from the ER. A fine example of the department's personnel. She should have been sentenced to a long prison term for what she did. But they gave her only two years! I wouldn't be surprised if *you…*" and here he shook his pointed finger at me, "… were opening the drug cabinet to give her the drugs!"

I took a deep breath. "As revealed in court on Monday, a session which you attended, Dr. Manning, Nurse Ennis stole the drugs without any assistance. The video evidence came from a camera *I* had placed to monitor the drug cabinet. Her husband and son bullied and psychologically beat her into doing what she did. She did not use the drugs herself, nor did she endanger patient care with the amounts she stole. The court took that into consideration in sentencing her."

Manning's tightly controlled demeanor suddenly devolved in front of everyone. "You bitch. You've been out to get me since you first started working here. Your lawsuit was total bullshit. You, you…" He pushed back his chair, rose, and ran around the table toward me, now totally unhinged in his anger.

The board members sat transfixed. When he reached Tony, who sat beside me, Manning raised his arm to take a huge swing at my head. Tony stood and reached out to block Manning's arm. I flinched and covered my head with my arms. A crack of bone could be heard in the room. Manning tried to hit me again, but Tony, holding his clearly broken arm at his side, lunged at Manning. Both landed on the floor. The board suddenly woke up—one of them pulled Tony to his feet, while another pinned Manning down. I heard a voice saying, "Get me the police." Manning struggled mightily and threw off the person holding him, but two others replaced him.

I remained sitting through all this, stunned at the attack, until Tony, now very pale, slumped down in his chair, cradling his arm. Voices filtered in. "What's going on with Manning?" "I think he's having a psychotic breakdown!" "Has someone called the police?" "Get Security up here. We need some stronger bodies."

Dr. Fisker appeared in my view, taking my arm and asking if I were all right. I focused on his face and replied in a shaky voice, "I'm fine, I'm fine. Dr. Churchill isn't." After taking a deep breath, I pulled my chair over to Tony and gently palpated his forearm. Giving him a grim smile, I said, "I don't need to tell you that your radius is broken. Why don't we head downstairs and get an X-ray? Feeling up to taking a walk?"

"Sure."

We both stood. "Gentlemen and lady of the board," I announced loudly over the ongoing fracas, "I'm going to take Dr. Churchill to get an X-ray. The police can find us in Radiology."

The air suddenly rushed back into the room, the board members stopped talking, and everyone nodded.

On the way down in the elevator, I thanked Tony profusely. "You got between me and Manning and saved me from a serious injury… at a heavy cost to you."

"Not a problem. We need you to work in the ER, not be a patient there. I'm going to make sure Manning's charged with assault and battery. But I don't think we've seen the last of him."

"Why not?"

"Because the old boy network generally doesn't fire faculty unless there's a mismanagement of money. They'll find a way to explain what happened, and he'll get off with a slap on the wrist, even from the law. I predict the board will force him to take an anger management course under the threat of being fired, and he'll be back making our lives even more difficult in a few weeks."

"Then we should file a lawsuit."

"Will that work?"

Maybe. "I filed one, and the hospital did settle with me. Do you remember when I was attacked and beaten in the ER? Nothing happened to Manning, even though he'd been the one to call off security. His secretary got fired instead. But I have something Dr. Fisker will want to hear that could see Manning out the door."

"And that is…?"

I shook my head. The doors to the elevator opened, and as we stepped out, my phone rang. *Sam.* "What's up, hon?"

"There's no easy way to tell you. It's Jack." His voice wavered. "When Paulette went to pick up the boys at school, Tyler was there but not Jack. The receptionist told her a deputy had picked up Jack earlier in the afternoon."

"But if he was picked up by a deputy he should be safe, right?" A wave of dread rolled over me.

"None of our deputies were at the school at that time."

Chapter 26

RHE

My knees wobbled and I clung to the elevator door frame with one hand, staring at the phone in the other.

The door opening onto the Radiology floor started to close, and Tony asked, "Are you all right?" He hooked his unbroken arm around my waist for support and gently pulled me out of the elevator door.

I held up one finger. "Where are you?" I asked Sam.

"The school."

"I'll be right there. Tony, I've got to go. It appears my son has been kidnapped." I straightened up, deposited the phone in my bag, and took a deep breath. "I'm going to leave you here, if that's okay."

"Good Lord, Rhe, just go. Except for the arm, everything else is working. I can get an X-ray on my own."

There were two police cars at the school, lights flashing, plus Sam's Jeep and Paulette's car. All empty. I figured everyone had to be inside, and I climbed the broad cement stairs to the school entrance. I pushed the buzzer, announced myself on the intercom, and went in when the door opened. Paulette and Sam immediately enveloped me in a hug.

To one side stood Ms. Hernandez, shaking her head back and forth, tears coursing down her cheeks. "It's my fault, Ms. Brewster. I told everyone but Jane Linden, our office volunteer in the afternoon. I'm so sorry." She started to sob.

I pulled away from the arms around me and went over to her, putting my hand on her shoulder. "It's going to be okay. We'll find him," I said with a conviction I didn't have. "Sam, what happened?"

He led me to the worn wooden bench outside the principal's office where we sat. "Someone dressed as a deputy came to the front office and asked for Jack. He told the volunteer he'd been sent to take Jack home. He showed her his badge and she never thought to question him. This deputy continued to be very friendly and calm even when Jack said he didn't know him. He told Jack he knew us and mentioned a bunch of things about you and me. So Jack relaxed and left with him."

"Did you show Jane a picture of the twins?"

"I did, and she confirmed it was one of them."

"Our stalker. And it's Morris because Aaron is sitting in a jail cell."

"Where's Jane now?" I asked him, looking around.

"She had a full-blown anxiety attack, with difficulty breathing, so I called EMS. She's okay but they made her go home."

"What do we do now?"

"Wait. You know he's going to contact us."

I knew, like me, Sam felt fear and seethed with anger. But for my sake, he held those feelings at bay with a resolute demeanor that helped me stay calm.

α β

We went back to the McGillivray's, where Paulette had whipped up a late lunch. Not that I felt like eating, but the baby insisted. While we sat at the kitchen table, waiting for the phone call and picking at our ham sandwiches and coffee, I told Sam and Paulette what had happened at the board meeting that morning. Any sense of satisfaction I might have had with the result, other than feeling lucky Manning hadn't clocked me, had evaporated.

"I owe Tony a huge debt," Sam said. Just then his cell phone, which he had placed on the table, buzzed. He looked at the screen. "Unknown number."

"It's got to be Morris. Put it on speaker so we can all hear him." Paulette reached for my hand.

"Is that you, Morris?" Sam asked, after clicking both the speaker and answer icons.

A pause for a second or two, then he replied, "Well, ain't you the smart one. So nice to talk to you both. I assume this is Sam and Rhe?" Underlying venom made the voice guttural.

"Yes. You have our son, Jack?"

"He ain't *your* son, Sam, He's Rhe's. I'm right, ain't I?"

Exasperated at his diversion, I said, "Put him on the phone right now. We need to know he's alive."

"Well now, Rhe, I might just do that. But first I need to know how bad you want him back."

"What do you mean?" Sam's voice wavered.

"Well, now, that's real simple. Rhe for Jack."

A long pause, then I said, "Certainly. When and where?"

Sam's face flushed a nasty shade of pink and he shouted, "No, never, you can't do it! I forbid it!"

I shook my head and placed my hand over the phone. "We need to get our son back, Sam. I'm his mother and Morris wants *me*. Let's talk about this, but not right now." I heard some garbled words coming from the phone, so I took my hand away.

"Lookee here, while you two argue, I'm willing to wait. I'll call back in, say, an hour? Think it over and think about Jack."

Sam shouted into the phone, "No deal if we don't hear Jack in the next second."

We heard some whispering, then Jack said, "Mom, Dad, I'm okay. Can you…" His voice wavered with fright.

"That good enough for you?"

It was definitely Jack. "Okay," I told him. "One hour."

Ψ   Ψ

Sam looked at me, shaking his head. "You can't do this, Rhe. You have another child to think about. You know it won't end well for either of you."

Paulette added, "You can't do it this time, my friend."

"I'll wear a vest and have an invisible escort, right? Either of you gotta better idea?"

"State Major Crimes," Sam replied. "I shoulda called them earlier. I've got Bella on speed dial. She'll come up with something."

Just then, Phil came into the kitchen from the family room. Sam had sent for him when we first arrived, hoping he could trace any call that came in. "Got some news. The idiot stayed on the phone just long enough for us to get a trace. This is no world class criminal."

"So where is he?" Paulette asked.

"You won't believe this, but he's apparently holed up in the old Logan place, the one on the cliff north of town, just before that row of McMansions."

"I know that house," said Paulette. "It's been for sale forever and looks it."

"Have you been inside it, Paulette?" I asked. "Could you tell us what the interior is like?"

"A long time ago, a bunch of my teenage friends and I poked around in there for fun. We didn't wreck anything, just dared each other to go down into the basement or spend a night there. Get me a piece of paper and a pencil, and I'll sketch the layout."

"I'm calling Bella." Sam stood up. "I know there's no time, but maybe she can give us some advice."

Sam retreated to the family room where I could hear snatches of their conversation. "Jack…located the kidnapper…where are you?… Okay, sounds like a plan." He came back into the kitchen, looking slightly relieved. "Bella is actually in town today. She and Marsh had something planned but when she heard about Jack, she said she'd be right over. I hope you don't mind that Marsh is coming with her. I told her we were here with the McGillivrays."

This was beginning to feel like a three-ring circus, but we needed all the help we could get. Paulette went upstairs to reassure Tyler for the umpteenth time that we were doing everything we could to find his best friend, but came back down shaking her head. "Tyler is beside himself. He wants to go look for Jack."

Shortly after, we heard the front door open. "Sam, Rhe?" I heard Marsh call.

"In the kitchen."

Bella and Marsh came in, with a waft of cold air. Bella bent over to give me a hug and Marsh squeezed my shoulder. "Let's get to it, then, shall we?" Bella said. She and Marsh joined Sam and me at the table, and Paulette poured them mugs of coffee.

"Remind me why this man is so determined to kill you, Rhe," said Bella.

"It has to do with his aunt, Bitsy Wellington. It's a long story, but in a nutshell, she escaped from the prison where she served time for the murder of a friend of mine. She believed I was the cause of everything that happened to her, so she kidnapped me and took me to her campsite in the woods on Mt. Katahdin, where she intended to kill me. When I escaped, she pursued me with her hunting rifle. She had me cornered, but she lost her footing, fell over a cliff, and died as a result of the fall. Morris is her nephew, and he apparently believes I killed her. So he's out for revenge. That whole family is warped and evil."

"Got it, and we can be pretty sure of his end game, Rhe. We just need to figure out how to stop him before he gets there."

That's Bella, all six feet of her and all business. Then we decamped to the family room where all of us could sit comfortably, including Phil. I told Bella where Morris had Jack and gave her the sketch Paulette had made of the house interior.

"I take it this place is somewhat derelict?" she asked.

"Yes," replied Sam. "A lot of the windows are broken or gone, and the front porch is caving in." He pulled up a picture, showing the three-story, white Victorian, a peeling decrepit version of its previous glory. A sad house.

"How many entrances?"

"Three," Paulette replied. "One from the front porch that goes into the foyer. One off the back porch, and one from the porte-cochere on the side."

Bella looked puzzled at the last reference.

Paulette explained. "It's basically a covered area where horse-drawn vehicles and later cars could draw up to the house, like a carport."

"How many deputies can you assign to this?" Bella asked Sam.

"I have four, one of them a former sniper."

I gave him the squint eye. He'd never mentioned this before, and no deputy's name appeared on the list the lieutenant governor had sent us.

"Does your department have a SWAT team?"

"No, there's never been a need," Sam said. "And I'd be afraid this guy's response to a SWAT team would end badly. One thing in our favor, though. He doesn't seem very bright." He then gave Bella the kidnapper's name and the fact that he'd been stalking us.

"All right, I think I have the picture now. I've got an agent in the area, so that gives us five pairs of eyes. When he calls back, tell him you'll do it, get a time, ask for proof of life again."

Sam's phone rang just then, seemingly on cue, and he hit the speaker button again. We had a very brief conversation with Morris, who did most of the talking. I was to come alone at ten p.m., enter through the front door of the Logan house, and, oh, bring him a pizza. One with all the toppings. Then Jack said a few words.

We all let out a breath when Sam ended the call.

"Either this guy is as stupid as you believe, or he's wicked smart," Bella said. "I suspect the former. But that makes him very unpredictable. Do you have a thermal imaging camera?"

"Yes," answered Phil. "But we'll need a warrant to use it. Got an idea of which judge, Sam?"

"Judge Jeffries is on the bench for this guy's brother's court case, so try him."

Bella then called her agent and Sam called deputies Birch and Dowdy. Phil got on the warrant. At that point, I started to feel light-headed and my breathing increased, the beginning of a panic attack. I'd never had one but had seen them all too often, when the world overwhelmed my patients and their bodies responded to the stress.

Marsh, noticing my distress, advised me to get my coat and go outside. "Take a walk, breathe deeply, and try to think about something else." *Right.*

But Paulette made me, taking me on a long walk down the street, while we let the little gray cells of four brains formulate a plan, with Bella in charge.

ڃ   ڃ

After a lot of squabbling, those brains finally agreed I had to go. There was no other way. On the way to the Logan mansion, my hands became squishy with sweat on Sam's Jeep's steering wheel, and I took slow, deep breaths to calm my inner jangles. The smell of the pizza on the passenger seat nauseated me. A huge bulk loomed out of the darkness as I came to the end of the driveway—Logan Manor. I parked by the front steps precisely at ten. When my headlights faded, impenetrable darkness surrounded me, except for a dim light in the windows to the right of the front door. I used a flashlight to get out of the car and walk around to the passenger side to retrieve the pizza, then maneuvered my way up the front steps. I walked very tentatively across the porch to the door, carefully avoiding any rotting boards. The unaccustomed weight and bulk of my bulletproof vest, almost the largest the police department owned just to fit around me, made me unsteady on my feet, and I double-checked the knife I'd slipped into my coat pocket. Taking a deep breath, I reached out to knock on the filthy etched glass of the front door. It jerked open. Morris stood facing me.

"Well, well, we meet at last."

When I shined the flashlight directly in his eyes, he batted it out of my hand.

"Gimme that pizza."

I handed it to him. "Let's cut the pleasantries, Morris. Let me see Jack...*now.*" I already knew from thermal imaging that there were only the two of them in the house.

"My, my, aren't you all civil. Tsk, tsk. I just thought a little conversation might be in order."

Swallowing my fear, I scowled at him until he led me from the foyer into a large parlor on the right. The dim light came from a camp lantern sitting on a box, just enough to see my son tied to a wooden chair with a high back, arms behind the chair, legs strapped to the chair legs.

"Mom! You came!" Jack's voice was high-pitched and wavering.

I rushed over to check him out, finding no physical trauma. The mental trauma would come later.

"I told you he's okay. I treated him real well." This came out of Morris's mouth along with some of the pizza he'd jammed into it.

"I'm okay, Mom. Really. He didn't hurt me. But I need to pee like mad and I'm really hungry and thirsty."

I looked at Morris. "You treated him real well, did you?"

Morris gave me a sneer of a smile. He set the pizza box on the floor. "You can untie him now." He still wore his fake deputy uniform, and he pulled the gun from his holster, aiming it at me. "This ain't a fake, in case you're wondering. Untie him. Now!"

I went around behind the chair, where Jack's wrists were tied together with zip ties. "You got a knife to cut these?"

"Nope."

While I hated to do it, I had to bring the knife out of my pocket. Morris hadn't thought to check me when I got here, but he'd inadvertently foiled my plan to stab him.

"Well, lookie here, she came prepared. When you're finished cutting those ties, toss that knife over here." He motioned to the floor beside him with the barrel of the gun.

This guy is just plain lucky. But stupid. I cut through Jack's wrist ties and then the ties binding his legs. He stood up shakily and I pulled him into a hug. "Can you walk?"

"Yes."

"I need you to walk out of here, as fast as possible, run if you can," I whispered.

"I'm not leaving you, Mom."

"You damned well are, boy, but not before you tie your momma to the chair. Just like I did you." Morris pulled out three plastic flex cuffs from his pocket and threw them at us. "Sit down, Rhe. You, boy, do as you told or I'll just shoot her right here and now." He extended his gun arm in my direction.

Jack looked from Morris to me. I sat down on the chair, facing the front windows. "Do it, Jack. You have no choice. And then you *are* going to leave, understand me?"

Jack looked in my eyes and his eyes widened. *He understood.* After lashing me to the chair—not as tightly as Morris demanded—he leaned over, hugged me and kissed my cheek.

"Okay, boy, scram." Morris gestured toward the foyer. "*Get the hell out of here.*"

One last look, and Jack turned and ran, wobbling from the long time sitting in the chair.

When we both heard the front door close, Morris re-holstered his gun and pulled up another chair from where it lurked in the shadows along the back wall. Before he sat down, he went from window to window on the front and side of the room, peering out into the dark.

While he took a tour of the broken floor to ceiling windows, I glanced around the room: high ceilings with ornate cornices; faded busy wallpaper peeling in long moldy strips; plaster revealed in many places; a large, carved fireplace at the far end; a wide board floor scuffed to bare wood and layered with dust; and a crystal chandelier hanging from the ceiling and dripping cobwebs. This old lady of a once-grand house made a depressing setting for our final confrontation. Knowing that Sam and company were outside, I anticipated what would happen next and my breathing hitched up. *Is this the wrong decision? Too late now.*

Morris sat in a chair facing me, after picking up a slice of pizza.

Another stupid move. His back's to the front windows.

He laid the gun in his lap while he ate. "We're going to have some fun, ain't we? But first I want you to tell me how Aunt Bitsy died. And don't lie." He gesticulated with the point of a pizza slice.

I cleared my throat. "We were standing on a rocky outcrop on Mount Katahdin, where she'd cornered me with a rifle. She stood near the edge, backed up and lost her footing. When she landed, she broke her neck. That's the truth, even if you don't want to hear it."

"Nah, not the way it happened. You pushed her."

"You weren't there. How would you know?" Aware that everyone needed time to get into place, I needed to keep him talking. "Do you know why she hated me so much? I don't."

"I know you treated her badly when you were kids and you was out to get her."

"For what? I don't recall treating her badly. I know she envied my popularity, but what could I do about that?"

"You hurt her. She told me."

"Did she ever tell you how I hurt her?"

Just then, we both heard a creaking noise from the back of the house.

Morris's concentration went from the pizza to the hall door. "Did you bring company? I told you to come alone." He rose from his chair, dropping the pizza.

"Morris, this is an old house. It creaks."

"Yeah, right. I don't trust you."

Morris immediately spotted the figure, clad all in black, which had silently appeared in the hall doorway— one of Bella's agents. Morris reacted with a speed I didn't think possible, placing himself behind me, while turning my chair to the right so it faced the intruder. The agent's arm moved as he tried to find a clear shot, but by now, Morris had the barrel of his revolver drilled into the side of my face. I pulled my head as far away as I could from the painful pressure. I could sense more than see his finger on the trigger.

"You don't want to do that, Morris," the figure in black said. "So far you've not killed anyone. That's in your favor."

"If I'd had my way, this bitch'd be lying cold in her grave by now. Seems having the wheel come off that Jeep weren't enough. Go ahead and shoot me, but it won't stop me pulling the trigger and blowing her brains out. If you drop your gun, you might buy Rhe here some more time. I'd enjoy that."

During this exchange, my heart rate soared, along with my adrenaline levels. My heart pounded so loudly, I could hardly hear what they said. I had no doubt the bullet from the gun against my face would do its damage long before Morris himself was hit. A twinkle of movement caught the corner of my eye. I turned my head ever so slightly to the left, toward one of the front windows. Deputy Birch's face appeared in one of the broken windows, then the barrel of her police pistol. She motioned me to duck.

I jerked my head forward and down and a shot rang out. Something wet hit my face. I heard a thump behind me, then silence.

Chapter 27

RHE

As he'd been ordered, a deputy drove us back to Paulette and Ted's after Jack and I were checked out by EMS. We sat in the back seat, Jack enveloped by both Sam and me. The entire McGillivray family waited in the driveway to greet us, Tyler jumping up and down with excitement. Since none of us had eaten before I'd left for my meeting with Morris, Paulette served us all a late comfort meal in the kitchen—fried chicken, macaroni and cheese, and chocolate cake. Laughing and talking over one another, we filled the room with happy noise, a release from the earlier tension. To our never-ending gratitude, Paulette and Ted didn't ask for details about what had happened, although Jack did not shy away from telling everyone about his experience. We gave them a succinct summary about it over coffee, after the children had left the room. Soon enough everyone started yawning, at which point I decided that Sam, Jack and I needed to head home. We walked back to our house with the light of hundreds of stars showing us the way, even Jack admiring the celestial show.

ଓ ଜ

Sam and I sank into the comfort of the couch in our family room, where a crackling fire in the stone fireplace sent red and orange sparks up the chimney and the slight smell of wood burning gave the room a cabin-like feel. Sam had his arm around me, and I sagged into him in exhaustion. Jack had collapsed without a word at the far end of the couch, sound asleep, with a wool blanket tucked around him. "No school for him tomorrow," I whispered, hoping Sam would agree.

"Yup, he'll need time to decompress."

"Paulette's going to keep Tyler home tomorrow, too, so they can be together, hopefully doing boy stuff. I plan to call one of the child psychiatrists at the hospital in the morning to see if they have time to fit Jack in right away."

"I'm not going to argue with you about that. Today's experience has altered his world. I worry he'll never feel safe again. And we're the reason."

I nodded in agreement. "And at some point we need to think about that. But not tonight." I scrunched even closer, if that were possible, and sighed deeply. Then nothing.

03　03

The next day Sam, Taylor, Jack and I shot basketballs at a local playground, ate hotdogs, and went to a movie the boys had begged to see. A day just for fun. We returned in time for another family dinner with the McGillivrays: spaghetti and meatballs, just for the boys, but also for Sam, who'd never met a meatball he didn't love. We found comfort in sitting around the table with our friends and, for once, talking about nothing serious.

The boys were yawning when we sent them into the family room to play a video game. They'd probably fall asleep before long, controllers in hand, but Paulette said to let them be. Sarah offered to help her mother pick up and wash dishes, but Paulette reminded her of her homework. Sam and Ted helped clear the dining room, and when we'd brought everything into the kitchen, Paulette said, "Just leave everything, and I'll make us some coffee. Sit." She gestured at the kitchen table.

Something's up.

When we all had steaming mugs in front of us, Paulette said, "Ted and I have something to tell you."

"Don't tell me…you're pregnant!"

My attempt at humor fell flat. *This is serious.*

Ted rotated his coffee mug in his hands. "I've lost my job."

Sam and I both drew in a sharp breath. "When, how?" Sam asked, gobsmacked by Ted's news.

"Three days ago. We were going to tell you, but with everything happening with Jack…"

"But why, Ted? You've been with your company for ten years. You're a manager. What happened?" Sam was incredulous.

The creases on Ted's forehead deepened. "My firm is merging with another, bigger firm. My position overlaps one of theirs, held by a younger man who earns a lot less than I do. I've been eliminated because of redundancy and cost."

"But your experience!" My outrage spilled over. "You are a superb electrical engineer."

"Only the bottom line is important to the big brass. They've been very generous, though. I have three months' severance pay and can keep my health insurance for a year. And of course my retirement fund remains intact."

Paulette leaned over and took Ted's hands, which had been clasping and unclasping on the table top, in hers. "Basically, if he can't land another job in three months, well, we do have some savings, but we'll have to sell the house. We just needed to let you know."

I sat, stunned. I couldn't imagine having this family, these friends, moving away. I wanted to be a millionaire and tell them I could pay off their mortgage. I wanted…

Sam broke into my thoughts. "Whatever we can do to help, you know we will. You just have to ask."

Ted shook his head. "Thanks, Sam, but I think this is something Paulette and I need to work out. I'll find something, maybe not as good a job as I had, but there'll be something out there for me."

The tone of his voice betrayed his doubt.

Paulette straightened up, leaned back in her chair and took a deep breath. "To change the subject, there's something else that's been bothering me."

"What's that?" I asked.

"From everything you told me, the twins are—were—two grapes short of a fruit salad. So how did they manage to do all that digital magic that led to your house going up for sale, charges on your cards, the illegal sale of your passport, and that untraceable email?"

Sam and I both smiled. "Smart cookie, your wife," I said to Ted. "We've been thinking about that, too."

"There's another spawn of Bitsy out there," added Sam. "And we wonder what he or she is going to do now without her twin puppets."

"I think whoever it is," I continued, "has two options: either give up or regroup. Of course we hope they'll give up. But in any event, regrouping will take time, since he or she no longer has the twins to do the actual dirty work. There's really nothing we can do except try to identify who it is. And be prepared."

Paulette nodded in agreement.

By that time, Sam and I were yawning, so after some hugs and reassurances to Ted, we woke Jack, who was leaning against the softly snoring Tyler, and headed for home. After seeing him to bed, I changed into some pajamas, reminded Sam that Jack had an appointment with one of the psychiatrists at the hospital after school, and he had to be the designated chauffeur because I was working. "I bet he'll be the center of attention at school tomorrow. Everyone will be dying to hear what it was like being kidnapped and how he got rescued. He might end up feeling like a hero. I hope Dr. Bryant will discuss that with him." I stood at the window of our bedroom, looking out into the cold night, the dark sky pinpricked with stars. "Do you think we really have to worry? You know, about the mind behind the twins?"

"I do," Sam replied. "But I think if they are still determined to destroy us, they're going to take their time to get it right the next time. This person plans ahead, is methodical, but above all, doesn't want to get their hands dirty. So maybe they have a job or position they can't afford to risk." Sam wrapped his arms around me from behind and kissed my neck. "Honey pie, would you consider taking a leave of absence from the department for a while? I'm not saying permanently, but for now. Jack needs you more, and I think it's time you realize you're actually pregnant and maybe take the time to enjoy it."

I knew he anticipated some huge objection from me, but his suggestion made sense. With a sudden release of tension that surprised me, I found myself saying, "Good idea. Can I begin my leave tomorrow?"

He hugged me tighter. "You can be so exasperating, wife of mine, but sometimes you just knock my socks off."

"Mmmm… are you too tired for me to knock your socks off again before we sleep?"

β β

Paulette still played the role of comforter-in-chief, telling us the previous night to come over for breakfast. When I got up, I still felt drained and silently blessed her. Sam had left early, before I could force myself out of bed, shower, and get dressed in my scrubs for work. And then I had to rouse Jack. When Jack and I walked into Paulette's kitchen, the smell of a fully functioning café reached our noses. A pile of blueberry muffins sat on the kitchen table, with something else baking in the oven. Coffee brewed, and Ted sat at the table, laptop open, dressed in casual clothes. The sight hurt my heart.

"Relax, help yourself to coffee and a muffin. Sam took a bag of them before he left." Paulette stood at the stove, making pancakes. "For the boys and Sarah, but I can make more." Cooking was one way Paulette relieved tension.

Jack immediately sat down next to Tyler and helped himself to six pancakes. I glared at him and he put two back but drowned the remaining four with syrup.

"Thanks for the offer, but I'll just grab a muffin. I need to get to the hospital before my shift so I can find out what's happening with our CEO. Ted, are you taking the kids to school today?"

Ted looked up and gave me a rueful half-smile. "Yup. For now I'm a fully functioning child delivery service."

"Jack has an appointment to talk with someone at the hospital this afternoon, so you only have to worry about Tyler and Sarah. Sam will pick up Jack."

"No problem."

Paulette handed me a paper bag into which she'd placed two muffins and put a travel mug with coffee on the table. "I added your usual cream and sugar. The coffee is decaf."

I wish she didn't know me so well.

愓 愒

At the hospital, muffins eaten and coffee consumed in the car, I waved to Lyle Pendergrass as I came in through the loading deck.

"Heard you had a bit of excitement a couple of nights ago. I'm glad everything turned out alright, Mizz Brewster."

"Thank you, Lyle. We are, too."

"Also heard you were in a kerfuffle with the Pecker the other day."

"Right again, Lyle. Where do you have your spies? By the way, thanks for your help with that visiting nurse matter. I sent an email to the board about it. I'll let you know the outcome."

He smiled and blushed.

Once on the fourth floor, I headed straight to the departmental office of Emergency Medicine to check on Tony. I knew he came in early, so early that he beat the departmental receptionist. The door to Tony's office was partially ajar and I heard him talking to someone.

"Right, I've taken care of that. See you this afternoon."

I knocked on his door and opened it further.

"Rhe! I'm glad you came here before your shift. Thank heavens you recovered Jack and no one was hurt, except for that kidnapper. I'm not sure I could be as brave as you." He stood up from behind his desk and motioned to the chair at its side. "Have a seat."

"Thanks for the compliment, Tony, but I think, in this case, a fool ran in. And Sam agrees." I noted that despite the cumbersome cast on his forearm, he had dressed in a starched shirt, sleeve rolled above the cast, and star-spangled blue bow tie.

"I want to hear all the details, Rhe, but right now I need to tell you what's happened since the board meeting. As we had thought, the police arrested Manning and booked him on assault charges. Also as we thought, some of his highly placed colleagues got him out on his own recognizance in no time and he came back to the hospital."

"I was afraid of that and also of what you're going to say next."

"It's not all bad. The board met after his arrest, discussed what had happened and considered the contents of the email you had sent to the chairman about Manning's extracurricular activities in his office. They placed him on leave, with pay of course, until they can look into your claim more fully. They also decided they needed to examine the hospital's finances. The CFO's now on the hot seat. He's a crony of Manning's and isn't happy the board's hired an outside auditor. You and I both know the only thing that would get Manning fired is financial mismanagement. I hope the auditor finds it."

I sighed. "Otherwise, he'll be back here bold as brass in no time. And our lives will be hell."

Tony smiled. "Another personal injury lawsuit won't make things pleasant for him, so as of last night, I talked to a lawyer who'll file the suit on our behalf. I hope that's okay with you."

"Sure, I'll gladly sign on." I started to rise. "Time to get to work."

"One more thing, Rhe. Would you be willing to take on one extra shift a week, for say, the next two weeks…until we can get personnel in the ER straightened out.

I hesitated. I'd just taken a leave from the police department. "Sure, if it's only a couple of weeks. But only one shift, and I choose my hours." *We can use the extra money now.*

୧   ୨

The next few weeks slipped by without any upheavals, although Jack was plagued with nightmares at the beginning. We purchased a new Miss Daisy. She couldn't replace my old Jeep but she had a good heater. Kip Moncton had worked his magic and definitely identified Aaron Wrightnour as the rapist, although his lawyer argued without effect that we had had Morris killed to win the case. Deputy Birch received a citation for her work on the case. Jack engaged in serious talks with the psychiatrist, which alleviated some of his need to know where Sam and I were at all times and his nightmares became less frequent. The psychiatrist suggested both of us join Jack in some family sessions, which we did. I began to wish this productive but calm life could go on forever.

As Tony and I sorted out ER staffing, rumors began to swirl that the outside auditor had found some serious problems in the hospital's finances.

Happenstance had me working a shift in the ER on the day the board fired Manning permanently. He didn't take it well. Two security guards had to escort him from the hospital. Everyone in the ER could hear the shouting and banging coming from the elevator and our curiosity drew us like magnets to the hallway. In the melee, Manning had somehow managed to hit the buttons for every floor, and the elevator opened on the ER floor. There he stood, face flushed a deep red, restrained by two security guards with huge smiles on their faces. I stood among the gathered crowd, and Manning's beady eyes found me immediately.

"You…you…you...you did this to me."

Everyone clapped, and he drew back in surprise.

"No," I shouted over the clapping. "You did this to yourself."

The doors slowly shut. Our last view of our beloved CEO was of the guards pinning him to the back wall of the elevator to keep him away from the buttons. *Lyle is going to love the perp march to the loading dock door.*

ෙ ෙ

Sam and I wondered what was happening with the investigation into the sniper shooting that had begun the madness of the last several months. We finally got word from Bella that the Major Crimes Unit had cleared John Patterson, whose alibi for the time of the shooting had held up. Now they sought Chief Petty Officer Elias Morgan, who'd disappeared.

Sam called me at home around two the afternoon following Manning's ejection from the hospital. His call found me sitting, totally relaxed, reading a book with my feet propped up. *When have I ever had time for this?*

"What's up, hon?"

"Rhe, I'm coming to get you. We need to get to Augusta."

"Why? What's going on?" I sat up straight and swung my feet to the floor.

"Mildred Burger just called me. Elias Morgan is in her office and has locked the door. He says he will only speak with us."

"Dear God. Okay, I'll be ready when you get here. Have you called Bella?"

"I did and she's already on her way there with some of her agents but won't do anything until we get there. You are *not* going into that office unless I decide the situation is safe."

"Fine. I'm okay with that." *This fool is not rushing in again.*

I called Paulette to tell her where we were going and why. Phone on speaker and in one hand, I bundled up in the kitchen for the trip, while she gave me her usual lecture about putting myself in a bad situation. I told her what I'd agreed to with Sam. By then I had on the blue, down-filled puffer coat Sam had bought me to fit my expanding belly, wool-lined snow boots, and a red wool cloche that came down over my ears. I was prepared for the Maine winter.

Sam pulled up in front of the house almost immediately after I walked out the front door, locking it after me.

"You want to take my car? It's newer and warmer," I asked as I got in on the passenger's side.

"Nope, we need to go," he replied as he stepped on the gas and we pulled away. "Jack taken care of?"

"Yes, Ted is picking the kids up after school. Paulette will tell Jack where we are and the rules you've laid down for me. And we can call him when he gets home."

Although we were less than 50 miles from Augusta, we had to take route 27, which meant slow going. Just outside of Pequod, it started to snow. "Great, just great," complained Sam.

I patted his arm. "Relax, Nanook, only snow showers today." I watched as some of the tension fell from his shoulders. "Anything else I need to know? How's Mildred doing?"

"She's very calm under the circumstances, and her military training helps. She told me he didn't have a gun, and I hope that's true. Have I told you that you look like a red and blue penguin?"

Chapter 28

SAM

I did *not* want to take Rhe with me to Augusta and risk dragging her into a dangerous situation, especially if Morgan had a gun and maybe PTSD as well. However, he'd specifically requested both of us be there, and I couldn't risk the circumstances becoming volatile if we didn't follow his demand. On the way to Augusta, I asked Rhe pointblank how she felt about going into Mildred's office and facing Morgan.

"Look, Sam, this situation results from his granddaughter not getting a medical treatment that might have saved her. He loved her deeply. Do you think he would harm a pregnant woman?"

Put that way, I had to agree with her.

On the way there I used flashing lights and if any driver wasn't impressed with that, I leaned on the horn. We made it to Augusta in record time.

γ γ

When we arrived, there was a SWAT unit on the street. An agent from the state's Major Crime Unit took us to the waiting area outside Mildred's office in the HHS building where MCU agents and a representative from the FBI's Augusta office milled about. Bella greeted us and introduced us to everyone, then asked, "Are you both ready to do this? Rhe, you can refuse. I would certainly understand."

"Is he armed?" I asked. "If he is, then Rhe is *not* going in."

"We've only know what Mildred told you—he's not armed and he locked the door. You two are the only people he wants to see."

When we both nodded, she picked up the phone, punched in an extension and announced, "The Brewsters are here. I'm sending them in."

We heard the door unlock and Mildred say, "It's okay to come in."

I opened the door and preceded Rhe into the office to shield her just in case. I stopped just inside to scan the room and glanced out the windows to the street. I saw a flash of light on something metallic on the roof of the building across the street. Bella had a sniper in place.

Seeing Morgan sitting calmly in a chair by Mildred's desk, I moved aside so Rhe could enter, then gently closed the door. Mildred walked back to her desk.

"Hello again, Mr. Morgan. I understand you want to talk with us. May we sit down?" Rhe asked, taking off her coat and hat. I pulled two desk chairs from the table at the side of the room and placed them so they faced Morgan at an angle. His hands, empty, rested in his lap, and he nodded at my request. His face was unexpressive and his eyes sought ours, and from the relaxed way he sat, he seemed resigned. Mildred was, as usual, ramrod straight in her seat, but I saw no expression of tension or fear in her face. She gave us both a grim smile.

Rhe, who sat nearest to Morgan, leaned over and took one of his hands in hers. "I'm sure you've been struggling these past months. How truly awful to lose your beloved granddaughter. I can't imagine the pain you're still feeling."

My wife, a serial nurturer. How does she do it?

Morgan's eyes filled with tears, which slowly overflowed down his cheeks. He nodded. "I was in such a dark place…it was like I was somebody I didn't know…so blinded by rage and hate…all I wanted to do was lash out at the person I held responsible for her death. I can only thank God I didn't kill the governor that day, and I believe He saved me through you."

"So you admit to being the person who shot the governor?" I asked.

"Yes, sir, I do. My wife and I have prayed mightily on what I should do, and I knew I needed to come here and apologize to Ms. Burger. Then I had to apologize to you, since you were in my sight that day and I could have killed you as well.

"If I just surrendered to the FBI, they would have locked me away without giving me a chance to apologize, to make my peace. I'm ready to confess and I'll accept whatever punishment is meted out. I have accepted God's wish that I let go of my anger."

"Mr. Morgan, was that you who shot at us at the gun range on Mt. Katahdin?" Rhe asked.

"No, that was a friend. I didn't know about it until after. He told me he was just trying to warn you, to get you to stop your investigation. Believe me, if he had wanted to kill you, he would have. I don't condone what he did, even though it was out of concern for me."

"Who was it?" I asked.

"*That* is something I will never tell anyone." He shook his head.

"Are you ready to surrender?"

"Yes, I am, Chief." He stood, turned his back and put his hands behind him. "Hook me up."

Before I did, Rhe embraced him, whispered something in his ear, and stood back.

His tears fell more freely. "Thank you, Miz Brewster. You're most kind."

 ≁

Rhe herself wept as we escorted Morgan out of Mildred's office. Mildred followed and gave us both a hug, thanking us for coming so quickly and resolving the situation peacefully. After the ensuing commotion of the formal arrest, the reading of Morgan's rights, and his removal by the FBI agents, we bundled up and headed back to the car.

"What did you say to Mr. Morgan?"

"Nothing important."

Rhe was good at deflecting things she didn't want to answer, just like Jack. "I know what's coming now will be so hard on his family. At least there won't be a trial and perhaps his military record and the situation surrounding his actions will mitigate his sentence."

"I hope so." Just then, my phone rang. It was Ted McGillivray, talking so fast I could barely understand him. "What? Ted…slow down. What's happened? … We're on our way back now." I turned the flashing lights on again and hit the gas.

"Sam, what's wrong? Is Jack okay?" Her voice echoed with fright.

"Everyone's just fine, Rhe. But our house just exploded."

"Exploded? Where was Jack?" Rhe's voice was loud enough to hurt my ears.

"He's fine, with Ted and Paulette."

"Oh, dear God. We must be cursed. What more can happen to us?" She started to cry.

And I began to wonder if this was the act of whoever had been handling the twins.

RHE

On the way back we asked Ted again if Jack was fine and then spoke with him directly. He seemed nonplussed by what had happened, alternately wailing about losing his games and toys and then talking excitedly about all the trucks and commotion on our street.

"Jack, have you seen Tux?" I asked.

"No…no! Where is Tux?" I heard him yelling.

There will definitely be more sessions with the psychiatrist.

Our street was blocked off when we arrived, but one of Sam's deputies stood guard and removed the barrier so we could pass. The scene was chaotic with neighbors and looky-loos crowding the sidewalks, the flashing red and blue lights of the police cars, an EMS bus, and fire trucks. And permeating the air, the smell of what had been our life together, burning.

By the time we reached the remains of our house, a small number of firemen moved through the wet wreckage, stirring up embers and spraying the last remnants of fire and sparks. Where our house once stood was a wasteland of debris, a few heat waves rising into the cold evening air. To access the house, the firemen had dragged my new Jeep into the street. It was miraculously intact, except for a coating of soot and a shattered windshield. None of our neighbors' houses seemed damaged, except for a few broken windows.

*But where will we live? We have a baby coming in a few months…*my thoughts plummeted in despair.

Jack raced up to us, jumping into Sam's arms. I hugged him around his back. Paulette and Ted appeared suddenly, wrapping us both in an embrace when Sam let Jack down.

"I am so, so sorry, Rhe."

The love in Paulette's words unleashed the tears I'd been holding back.

Paulette hugged me tighter. "We could have lost all of you."

Then the totality of it hit me—forget the loss of our house, we *could* all be dead. My knees buckled. Sam quickly grabbed me around the waist.

"You need to sit down. There's an EMS truck over there, and…"

I took a deep breath and wiped the tears from my face with my sleeve. "I'm fine, Sam. Really." Then I thought of what I'd asked Jack. "Tux! What happened to Tux? He was in the house!" I looked around frantically until I saw a fireman approaching us, holding something small, wrapped in a blanket. "Is that our cat? Is he dead?"

"No, ma'am. But this cat just used up eight of his nine lives. We found him under a bush. The blast musta blown him out of the house, and he's a little dazed, but I think he'll be okay. You might oughta have a vet look at him though." He handed me my cat, wrapped like a burrito. He was purring.

I walked back to Paulette, crying again. "He's alive. We're all alive. That's all that matters." I sobbed uncontrollably, and someone placed a blanket over my shoulders.

Sam looked around, then focused on Ted, "Do they know how the explosion happened yet?"

"I asked, but they wouldn't tell me. They're waiting for you."

Sam strode off, looking for the fire chief, and returned a few minutes later to where we all stood, hugging each other. "They think it was a possible gas leak," he told us. "But they won't be sure for a day or so. Their arson investigator needs to probe around in daylight. Until then, there's nothing we can do. Did you guys see anyone near the house before this happened?"

"Sorry, Sam," replied Ted. "We were all inside and only knew something was wrong when we heard and felt the explosion. Look, you two need to get inside. It's freezing out here. You're staying with us as long as you need."

"And no arguments," Paulette added.

We retreated to the warmth of the McGillivray house, where Paulette had already started a dinner. Sam began the long process of recovering our lives by making a call to our insurance agency to arrange for a claims adjuster to come out. While Paulette banged around in the kitchen, Sam and I sat in the family room, looking at each other, numb and speechless. Jack stuck to my side like a limpet. Ted handed us each a glass, into which he poured a good dollop of brandy for Sam and a very, very small one for me. When my shakes had retreated and I'd finally warmed up, I could feel the flush on my cheeks from the brandy. I had one arm around Jack. "I can't believe this happened. The history of our lives was in that house. We have nothing left…"

Everyone was quiet for a long moment, then Paulette emerged from the kitchen, saying, "Except yourselves. Things can be replaced. You can rebuild. The important thing is that you're all alive and you won't stay that way if you don't eat, so don't argue. We're having fish chowder." Only Paulette could make us smile.

We tried to talk about everything but the house during dinner, although the subject was an elephant hiding in the corner. The four adults stayed at the dining room table drinking coffee, after Sarah and the boys had cleared away the dishes. Sam took out his little pad and silently started making a list of things we would have to do in the coming days.

"I wonder if that explosion was truly an accident," said Ted, finally riding the elephant. "Especially after what we talked about the other night. Sam?"

"That's what it'll be called, unless the investigator finds concrete evidence of arson. Still, I've been wondering how Tux ended up under that bush. If he'd been in the house, he would have been killed. I think someone took him outside before it blew."

I nodded, wondering if maybe our cat, who was currently in the family room curled up next to our friends' golden retriever, hadn't really lost any of his lives.

ζ ζ

The next weeks were a blur of activity. So many things to do—buying clothes for Jack, uniforms for Sam and scrubs for me, along with casual clothes, personal essentials, new computers and downloading what we had saved from the cloud. Sam and I both had to work, Jack went to school, and there were more sessions with the psychiatrist. We fell into bed at night totally exhausted and discouraged.

The insurance adjuster came out and gave us the estimate of what her company would pay towards the replacement of the house. It wasn't enough, and we had to straighten out the mortgage situation with the bank. Mortgage payments, even for a house that had burned down, still had to be made, but the bank agreed to suspend payments for six months.

Sam, Jack and I spent any spare time poking at the remains of our house with sticks, hoping to find something salvageable, especially any of my jewelry. I found a mug that Sam had given me, now chipped but still a memory, a blouse that might be wearable after several washings, and two of my necklaces and one earring buried under a pile of sodden paper. Jack screeched with joy when he found his baseball. But essentially nothing remained.

One evening, when Sam and I stood at the edge of our property, looking out over the ocean, he wrapped his arms around me and asked, "Do you really want to rebuild here?"

I considered the question for a long moment, then replied, "Not necessarily. We have so many things to consider. Paulette and Ted may have to move. We'll need to find a place to stay anyway because we can't mooch on them forever. Oh, and the baby will be here soon and I want a nest." I leaned back and sighed. "Building a new house will be an ongoing headache. You did tell Ted we're going to pay them the rent money we get from the insurance company, right?"

"Yup. He refused to consider it at first, but finally relented. I think he's somewhat relieved. It'll give him more time to find a job. You really didn't answer my question."

"I have an idea. Maybe you'll think I'm crazy, but we need to take a drive tomorrow afternoon, with Jack."

 CB　　CB

A few days later, we called a conference for both families after dinner. We gathered in the McGillivray's family room, assorting ourselves on the comfortable leather sofas or, in the case of the boys, sitting cross-legged on the floor.

"Okay," said Paulette. "What's this all about? You two have been very mysterious lately." She jiggled in her seat, clearly wondering what on earth we had to tell them.

"Well," said Sam, "we've decided not to rebuild the house."

That led to a chorus of "What?" "Why?" "What are you going to do?" The only person not surprised was Jack, who had a Cheshire cat smile on his face.

"We've always wanted to buy one of the old Victorian houses here in Pequod—no, *not* the Logan place—and fix it up. A house that will be truly ours." I told them.

Stunned silence. Sam jumped in. "I think we've found one, and the money we've been given to rebuild will cover all that."

"But how will you pay off your current mortgage?" *As always, Paulette the practical.*

"We got an estimate on the value of our land. Remember our house was built in the eighties, when land here was cheap. What it's now worth now is more than enough to pay off our mortgage and make a down payment on another house."

"So you'll be moving away," said Tyler, giving Jack a sober look.

I couldn't help it. I broke into a smile. "Not necessarily. What if you came with us?"

"What do you mean?" asked Ted, squinting at us. Paulette just looked stunned, as if I told her I was having quintuplets.

"Look," replied Sam. "The house we're thinking about is, like most Victorians, enormous, with more than enough room for two families. What if we build a home for you all on the second floor? There's land enough for that garden you always wanted, Paulette, and the boys can have a half basketball court, a soccer goal, whatever. At least consider it, and come with us this weekend to take a look at the place."

The McGillivray family looked at each other, still dumbfounded by our proposal. "We'll have to think about this," said Ted after a long moment, looking at Paulette, for confirmation. She nodded. "It might work, but it's a big change. There are some real advantages to your proposal but also some disadvantages. We'll discuss it and decide what's best for the family. And also, if we decide yes, we'll need to figure out how to afford it."

"Fair enough," Sam replied.

Tyler, Sarah and Jack had already formed a triumvirate in one corner of the room, talking excitedly about the possible move.

Just then, a little foot soccer-kicked my abdominal wall. *Oof! Is that a yes from her?*

Acknowledgments

Getting back into the swing of writing my mysteries took some time after finishing my four-year labor of love and research, *The Last Pilgrim*. The cadence of the speech in that book differs from the more modern, and I had to make a mental adjustment. I thank the members of my critique group for helping me over the hurdle. To the fans of the Rhe Brewster Mystery Series, I apologize for the delay in this new book.

Death at the Asylum was written during the Covid pandemic, which, while eliminating many of the normal distractions, also was the time when we moved from our home of 35 years to something smaller and more manageable. Thus I wrote through an emotional upheaval and an even greater distraction.

My supporting village hasn't changed much during all this time, except for the addition of Realization Press as my publisher. My thanks to its owner, Drew Becker, for putting up with all the changes that took place with *The Last Pilgrim*.

My husband is still the backbone for my writing. He accepts my hours of absence from normal house duties and even social events, and he is the chauffeur for our trips to Maine, including one that took us to what was the Kennebec Arsenal. The site of the arsenal is so beautiful, we've returned several times. It also triggered the idea for this book, becoming the site for the prologue and opening chapter.

The Arsenal has a long history. Developed between 1828 and 1838 because of border disputes with neighboring Canada, it was garrisoned until 1901, after which it was turned over to the State of Maine. Its buildings were then used by the adjacent Maine State Hospital for housing mental health patients. I took the liberty of naming this book *Death at the Asylum*, given the arsenal's former existence as part of a mental hospital. When the hospital closed its doors in 2004, the arsenal property was sold to a developer, with historic preservation restrictions. It sat, untouched, with broken windows, sprayed graffiti and leaking roofs (which is when we first saw it), until 2013 when new roofs installed and windows were boarded up. The developer has confirmed that the Arsenal's eight granite block riverfront buildings will be transformed into a vibrant retail and residential complex with a boutique hotel at the center. Restaurants and cafés will be a part of the complex. No date is set for the work.

So many thanks are due to the members of my Early Birds critique group, I don't know where to start. They are the ones who do the heavy lifting of helping me improve what I write: Denis Dubay, Dawn Ronco, Bob Byrd and Elizabeth Calwell. Since all of us have one or more published books or one on the way, this is truly an outstanding group of people to work with, each of them contributing different talents.

To my editor, Alison Williams, who has endured through all five of the *Rhe Brewster Mysteries*, I send gratitude for her grit and perseverance while I've been developing as a writer. She rocks!

To my beta readers, Joan Lichtman and Marlene Brigida Baldwin: You are the best, picking up on errors and making suggestions. And, finally, thanks to Mary Boutin, my eagle-eyed text editor and high school classmate, who reads each chapter three times, seeking out typos, grammar and spelling errors, and in the case of this book, a missing piece of pizza.

Some of my high school classmates appear as characters in my books, and I hope they enjoy seeing themselves in print.

Other than the visits to the Kennebec Arsenal and Augusta, Maine, the research for this book was largely confined to online searches and my own medical background. The information on sniper rifles came from Bob Byrd, a member of my critique group and a gun aficionado.

My next book in this series is tentatively entitled *Death in an Old Stone Well*. But first I have a book about Daniel Boone to finish. Stay tuned.

N.A. Granger

January 2023